In search of the golden gir

Looking in surprising c⟨...⟩
golden girl, Dirk and H⟨...⟩
few waves. Who can forget the sizzling siblings?

Not the handsome Indian Holy Man, who initiates
Honey in the delights of luxuriously slow sex.

Not the lissome Chinese acrobats, who perform for
Dirk the erotic show of his life.

Not the beautiful young blonde herself, the object of
Dirk's wild passion and Honey's sensual curiosity.

All over the world, beautiful men and women remember
their encounter with Dirk and Honey with a rapturous
sigh. And so will you.

—THE—
EROTIC
QUEST
—OF—
DIRK
AND
HONEY

ROLAND DE FORREST

Futura

A Futura Book

Copyright © 1983 by Warner Books, Inc

First published in the United States of America in 1983 by
Warner Books Inc., New York, USA

This Futura edition published in Great Britain in 1989
Reprinted 1989

ISBN 0 7088 4188 0

Reproduced, printed and bound in Great Britain by
Hazell Watson & Viney Limited
Member of BPCC plc
Aylesbury, Bucks, England

Futura Publications
A Division of
Macdonald & Co (Publishers) Ltd
66–73 Shoe Lane
London EC4P 4AB
A member of Maxwell Pergamon Publishing Corporation plc

—THE—
EROTIC
QUEST
—OF—
DIRK
AND
HONEY

1.

HONEY

"Ricardo," she purred, and pulled free from his fevered clutches. "You're making it extremely hard on me."

His flashing black eyes twinkled with amusement. "*Sí.* And you make *hard-on* for me. See?" Proudly he stepped back, revealing the tented front of his velvet robe. Slowly, like a master unveiling a work of art, he pulled loose the belt and opened the robe, exposing his erect demands. His sleek cock was the color of sandalwood.

Tempted, Honey eyed him for a long moment. Ricardo Prado was about the most appealing hunk of man she had encountered lately. Just over six feet of hardened flesh, tapered waist, slim hips, muscular thighs, with curly black hair and a boyish, devil-may-care charm that had won her over within moments of their meeting in Mexico City at the National Soccer Championships. Hailed as one of the world's greatest players, a natural successor to the sensational Pele, Ricardo was to be the subject of her

7

next exclusive and internationally published article. But ever since their arrival back at her palatial home in Hillsborough, California, his mind had been more on in-depth screwing than on in-depth interviewing.

"Pack it away, lover boy," she sighed in resignation, and gathered her notes from the bedside table. "I've work to do. We'll play later. I promise." She threw him a dazzling smile and, tossing her shoulder-length waves of Titian-colored hair, walked quickly out of her bedroom, her full hips swaying provocatively under the sheer iridescent green of her chiffon caftan.

Like a dutiful puppy, Ricardo followed, the pout evident in his tone as he spoke: "Work, work, work . . . I want to fuck, fuck, fuck."

"*You're* on vacation," she said over her shoulder and headed for the grand staircase leading to the ground floor. "I'm on a deadline. Your interview has to be on the wire by this afternoon. And Honey Wildon *never* misses a deadline."

He caught her arm, swinging her around, pulling her close, crushing her heavy breasts into his bare chest. "You've got time," he growled good-naturedly, and pressed his mouth on hers. As they kissed, she could feel his hardness pushing at her belly like an insistent divining rod. For another moment she wavered, a demanding warmth rushing up from her loins, filling her with an intense desire. Reluctantly she broke away and gave a friendly squeeze to his hard-on. "Ricardo, you *are* insatiable."

He frowned. "What's that mean?"

"The male equivalent of me," she answered with a smirk, and began descending the carpeted stairs, her knees weak from the fires boiling within her groin. "Now don't follow me. The servants will see you."

"Servants," he snorted at the top of the stairs. "I not care about servants."

She laughed gaily and kept descending. "That's because they're not yours. They're mine. In fact, some were even here when my parents were alive." At the bottom she paused, looking back up at him. He stood, feet splayed, frowning down, his robe wide open, one hand stroking determinedly on his hard peter. With his free hand he blew her a kiss. "Honey," he said hoarsely, "you are one hot girl."

"I'm a woman," she said easily, and breezed out of his sight and down the hall into the study, her father's former library. With fierce concentration and firm discipline acquired through her years as a top-flight journalist of international reputation, Honey was soon deeply involved in finishing her article on Ricardo. He had not been a difficult subject to capture on paper. His likes were simple: soccer, hot women, and fast cars, exactly in that order. What intrigued her, and what she had chosen as the slant of the article, was his familial devotion, an almost worshipful allegiance to his mother and his younger siblings. With the fabulous money he was earning as Mexico's top soccer star, Ricardo had lavished the good life on his family while choosing to live by himself in relative austerity—except for his shiny red Porsche Targa.

When she was writing, time passed quickly for Honey, and now she was unaware that Ricardo, clad only in tight Speedo swim trunks, stood quietly in the open doorway, observing her. He had never encountered a hotter woman or a more beautiful conquest. Statuesque—nearly five-nine —her luscious body was a bountiful collection of soft curves and voluptuous endowments. Her smooth, unblemished skin was the color of fresh milk. Her breasts were full, rounded peaks and they strained at the filmy material of her gown. Her exquisite profile bent intently over the typewriter, and her long, dark red tresses gleamed like burnished metal in the morning sun, which streamed in through the French doors leading to the poolside terrace. As he watched her, he could feel himself thickening in his swimsuit. Never before had he had a woman who enjoyed sex as much as he did. The mere thought of her enthusiastic performances in bed caused his cock to blossom into a full-blown weapon. He wanted her desperately right then, right there.

He took a step into the book-lined room. Turning her astonishingly blue eyes on him, she smiled at his bulging swimsuit. "Why the periscope? Going for a swim?"

"*Sí.* In you."

"*Por favor, mi toro.* Later."

He rubbed the persistent throbbing in his nylon swimsuit. "No. *Now,*" he demanded.

"Tough maracas, Ricardo," she murmured. Honey had returned to the typewriter, her fingers raising a steady, electronic clackety-clack.

With studied nonchalance he moved behind her chair, peering over her bare shoulders and down the front of her low-cut caftan. As she breathed, the soft swell of her snow-capped peaks filled him with new urgings. With the same quickness that marked his performance on the soccer field, he shoved a hand down between her warm, soft breasts, relishing their fullness.

"Ricardo," she complained, still typing. "You promised, when I asked you here, that you'd let me work when I had to."

"You work too much," he said softly and cupped one full breast, loving its weight in his sweaty palm. Bending down to nuzzle her long neck, he inhaled her sweet aroma—like a garden of roses on a hot, sunny day. It reminded him of her pussy, and that made his blood simmer.

Still typing, she arched her head back into him. "I love my work. As you do yours."

"But I no work now. I play." With a fingernail he flicked at one of her nipples, pleased to feel it elongating at his touch. He pressed the hard bulge of his swimsuit into the back of her head and demanded, "How long?"

"About seven inches, if I recall correctly," she said crisply, and continued to type.

He jerked his hand free of her breasts and marched around the desk. Standing directly in front of her, he began tracing with his fingertips the long boner compressed painfully in his trunks.

She ceased typing. "Ricardo, why don't you take a swim? Cool off for a spell. Give it a rest."

Instead of replying, he yanked free his hard-on and pulled back the skin from its glistening head. He bobbed it at her, a lustful, sly grin on his darkly handsome features. Honey eyed the end of his pointing dick, noticing a small drop of moisture at the dime-sized slit. It was that mere speck of pearly fluid that crumbled her resolve. With a rustle of chiffon, she bounded out of her chair and, with heavy breasts swaying, flew to the hall door and closed it. She turned, leaning back against the door. "*El Máquina,* take off those trunks."

Willingly he obliged, pushing them off his trim hips and stepping out of them. Proudly, even vainly he stood, letting her drink in his aroused beauty. "Now you," he ordered.

Still standing by the door, she gathered the skirt of her light green caftan and vigorously pulled it over her head, flinging it aside. Her full figure rose like a classical statue from the plush pile rug. Her alabaster skin glowed

11

like polished ivory, her rounded, full breasts heaving, the bright red triangle between her softly rounded thighs beckoning like a warming bonfire. His eyes bulged at her breathtaking beauty, and his prick grew even harder. "Come here," he croaked.

"Show me again," she breathed. "That trick from last night."

Needing no further encouragement to show off his prowess, he fell forward onto his hands, and pressed straight up into a rigid handstand. He walked toward her on his hands, his lean, brown shaft bouncing out behind him like a stiff rooster tail. Straight to her feet he moved and, opening wide his legs, placed one on either side of her, his feet flat against the closed door, well above her shoulders.

With enormous pleasure she looked down at him from that odd angle. She reached between his legs and leaned over his ass, grabbing his stiffness, pulling it toward her mouth as she bent her knees, lowering her fiery bush to his awaiting, upturned head. As his tongue sliced into the already wet lips of her delta of love, she sucked in the plum-sized head of his engorged dick, tracing its hard under-ridges expertly with her exploring tongue. His own tongue was stiff and jabbed at her clit, raising the temperature of her internal furnace. From her mouth, greedy slurping sounds mingled with moans of pleasure. Her knees and his arms buckled at the same time, and both of them collapsed onto the rug.

Rolling her over on her back, he fell between her upraised knees and, with the dexterity of a natural athlete, plunged his pulsing peter deep into her vessel of warmth. With a deep sigh of contentment, she locked her long legs around his trim waist and pressed his firm chest into her soft mounds. "Ahhhh, *excelentísimo* Ricardo Prado," she groaned. "Fuck me, fuck me, fuck me ..."

Ever since she'd first fallen into bed with him in her Mexico City hotel room, she had been amazed at his endurance and stamina. He was a marvelous fuck—not just slow, easy proddings, either, but increasingly energetic, even zestful lunges deep into her most innermost core, raising her to unbelievable heights of ecstasy. He could go at it for hours, and she could testify under oath that only the night before he had kept up his ramming for over two and a half hours straight before her climaxes had ceased and her sore pussy had begun to dry up. And still he had been ready, even eager for more.

Now, once again, he attacked her with youthful exuberance. She could feel his balls bouncing against her perineum, and their lusty rhythm skyrocketed her own. Pools of their perspiration formed on her, adding a slippery external lubricant. The internal walls of her love box were awash in their own drippings, and his driving cock felt like a hot poker, satisfying and exhilarating. Quickly she began to peak, an exquisite anguish rising within her to almost unbearable heights. Like a sudden clap of thunder she came, drenching the heat of his red-hot poker in a shower of viscous fluids. A muted scream of release broke from her.

Still pile-driving his hips, Ricardo raised his head from the hollow of her neck and grinned, panting, "Score one for you, *sí*?"

"*Sí sí*," she groaned.

"I play hard when I'm behind," he growled and, lowering his head, raced to catch up by shifting his hips into even higher gear. He was slamming so hard into her that all she could do was hang on to his taut frame and ride out the match. Reeling in delicious aftershocks, she did not have long to wait. With a satisfied burst of air through his nostrils, he climaxed, shooting a hot goal deep into the wet net of her vanquished cage.

13

They clung to each other, there on the rug, gasping and wheezing. Much to her astonishment, just as ther breathing had begun to normalize, she could feel his cock, still buried to the hilt within her, thickening and growing hard again. Slowly his hips began to move. "Ricky, enough for now," she admonished playfully, and, with a shove, managed to push him off her. Scooting out from under him, she rolled to one hip and weakly scrambled away on her knees.

He followed, also crawling. Like a dog in heat, he sniffed at her, nudging with his nose the loose lips of her inflamed pussy, which hung down like soft moss beneath her pear-shaped ass. Reaching her desk, she pulled herself upright, and for a moment she thought she would keel over from the rush of blood from her head. Dizzily she batted away his face from her rear end and swayed to the French doors, throwing them open.

The Bay Area sunshine bathed her with a soft golden glow, caressing her fair skin with new warmth. The Olympic-sized swimming pool, only steps away, glistened like a bright blue mirage. She glanced back at him. He had sunk back on his haunches, his black eyes locked on her intently, expectantly, his hard member poking up out of his lap like a flagless pole. "You are too much," she sighed in appreciation, and with a flirtatious smile she dashed outside, down the brick stairs of the terrace. On the edge of the tile coping of the pool, she paused briefly, threw her arms over her head, her full breasts pointing skyward, then dove cleanly, gracefully, expertly—a flash of pale white against the sparkling blue—before disappearing into the refreshingly cool water.

Swimming underwater, she tried to reach the far end before her lungs exploded. Triumphantly she touched the tile and, sputtering for breath, broke through the water's surface, shaking her red hair. Sleeking it back from her eyes, she turned to locate Ricardo. At the far end of the pool, the three-story brick mansion rose majestically, dwarfing him in the doorway to her study. With a little-boy pout, he stood forlornly, observing her, his brown peter jutting out in front as if straining to reach her. She smiled encouragingly and waved, calling out, "Come on in. It's divine." He shook his head glumly.

Laughing gaily, she climbed out of the pool, grabbed a large, yellow terry towel from one of the chaise longues and, patting her face dry, moved to him, noting that his cock was drooping as much as his face. "Why didn't you join me?" she asked.

"The servants . . ." he offered lamely.

"Oh, pooh," she said, and rubbed the soft towel over her bounteous curves. "Even my parents swam nude. Can't you swim?"

"Where are they?" he asked evasively. "Your mother and father."

Suddenly pensive, she answered, "They died in a plane wreck in Alaska. When I was twelve." She toweled her thick hair vigorously and brushed past him, reentering her study, aware that she had a pressing deadline to make. From the Persian rug near the hall door she grabbed up her filmy caftan and began pulling it over her head. When she emerged, she saw Ricardo studying the silver-framed photos on the wall opposite her desk. She glided to him, pointing to the largest photograph, which showed a handsome, laughing couple. "That's Mom and Dad at the opening of one of Dad's copper mills in Montana."

"Who is this?" he asked in a jealous tone, waving at another photo, this one of an attractive young man, as lean and lanky as a young Jimmy Stewart.

"My younger brother, Dirk," she replied. "He's a very famous photographer. You'd love his work. Here . . ." She pulled an oversized, expensively bound book from the nearby shelves. "This is his latest collection." She handed him the coffee-table-sized book, hoping it would keep him occupied for a spell, and returned to her desk chair, sinking into it with gritty determination.

"Naked women!" he exclaimed, thumbing through the studio portraits.

She laughed at his surprise. "Female beauty is Dirk's passion. *And* his forte."

"You in here?"

"Not on your life."

"You should be."

She smiled. "*Muchas gracias.* Now please let me finish." Finding where she had left off in her notes, she began typing with renewed vigor. All the energetic screwing and swimming had left her feeling refreshed; her skin tingled with energy, and as she typed, the words seemed to leap onto the pages as if by their own accord. This interview with Ricardo, like all of her exclusive interviews, would run under her own byline, "Honey Wildon Presents," in over ninety newspapers and magazines around the world.

A prolonged sigh from Ricardo broke her concentration, and she glanced up. He had settled onto the love seat, his eyes glued to the open pages of one of Dirk's exquisite photographs, his dick rigid once more. She could not believe her eyes—he was obsessed. He caught her watching him and leaped to his feet, rushing to her. "Let's fuck," he broached in a coarse whisper.

"You're going to wear that poor thing out," she said with a shake of her drying locks, and returned to her typing. "Another half hour, then watch out. I'll screw that thing limp if it kills me. And what a lovely way to die."

Wordlessly he sank to the floor, out of sight on the other side of the large Louis XIV desk. Suddenly she gasped with pleasure. Underneath the desk, he had hiked up her gown and buried his head between his legs. She clamped her thighs tightly around his ears, hoping to cut off his darting explorations. With a concerted effort she attempted to concentrate on the interview. His tongue lapped wickedly at her pussy, instantly inflaming it with an intense heat. The faster he tongued, the faster she typed. Soon her fingers were flying, and she rushed to finish before all thoughts ceased and pure sensation took over.

She was fighting a losing battle when a discreet knock came at the hall door. She was so startled, she rasped, "Come in," before she realized she had done so. The door opened and Caroline, her adorable downstairs maid—a fetching lass in a short black uniform—entered, carrying a yellow envelope on a silver tray. "Excuse me for interrupting, Miss Wildon," Caroline said, glancing at Ricardo's discarded swimsuit on the rug, "but this just arrived."

Too heated to speak, Honey held out a trembling hand, grateful that the desk covered Ricardo's lingual liberties. Shyly, Caroline approached and stood by the side of the desk, raising her knowledgeable eyes from Honey's bountiful breasts. "Are you feeling well, Miss Wildon? You look terribly flushed."

"I'm feeling sensational," Honey managed to get out, and tore open the envelope. It was a telegram, and she extracted it with no small degree of apprehension. Before she could read it, a small groan of desire escaped her lips.

"Bad news?" Caroline asked with obvious concern.

Flustered by her own excitement, Honey glanced at the telegram's message. It was one word. The word was SNATCH. "I pray not," she murmured, and looked up at the lovely girl through glazed eyes. "That will be all for now, Caroline."

"Very well, ma'am," the girl said softly and, with a lingering glance, withdrew and closed the door behind her.

Clutching the disturbing telegram, Honey sank lower in her chair, pushing her flaming cunt deeper onto the eager face of the busy Ricardo. He had locked onto her love button with such urgency that she felt ready to dissolve in a conflagration of lust. "Oh, Ricky," she gasped, and promptly flooded his face with joy juice. Paroxysms of pleasure wracked her torso and, eyes closed, she collapsed back into the chair, drained and released once more.

Recovering swiftly, she scooted upright. "Come out, come out, Ricardo. I have to leave at once." That stopped him and, grateful for the cessation of cunning cunnilingus, she quickly composed in her mind the closing paragraph and typed it out, crossing her legs tightly to prevent any further interference.

He rose from the other side of the desk, grinning from ear to ear, his mouth still wet with her ambrosia. He smacked his lips appreciatively. "What you say?"

She ripped the last page out of her typewriter and switched the machine off. She had finished! And it was damn good, she was positive. "I must leave immediately."

His grin faded rapidly. "Why?"

"My brother needs me," she said.

Frowning with disappointment, he swore at length in Spanish. She rose, kissing him on the lips, tasting her own erotic residue. "I'll drive you to the airport. If we have time, we can do it in the back seat in the parking lot. But, Ricardo, please hurry..."

2.

DIRK

From his work bench he grabbed the Hasselblad and snapped in the 50 millimeter, 1.7 lens. Checking the film's ASA rating, he whirled to the nearly nude model lying on the expanse of white paper. The thick paper dropped in one continuous sheet from the giant roll on the ceiling rod two stories above, forming both the backdrop and the floor covering for his setup. With as much professional distance as he could muster, he eyed her through the new lens, feeling a decidedly nonprofessional stirring in his tight Calvin Klein jeans.

She was a sensational find, possessing an exquisite body and a magical, alluring face. Even as she stared back blankly into the camera, she projected a smoldering sensuality, an earthiness that reeked of carnality. Her incredible eyes hinted at untold secrets and a wildly lascivious nature. Black as coal, they dared him to make a move toward her. The invitation was so open, so boldly expressed, that Dirk was having a difficult time keeping his mind on the intricacies of his chosen profession.

He lowered the camera, vaguely aware that the Chuck Mangione tape on his reel-to-reel Tandberg deck was nearing the end. "Toni, let's try a few with the blouse unbuttoned totally."

She smiled seductively and sat up to do as requested. Wearing only white, French-cut bikini panties and a gauzy, see-through blouse of a soft tangerine color, Toni opened the last button, her gaze not wavering from his. Her rounded breasts leapt fully into view, their dark aureoles like another pair of tantalizing eyes egging him own. "How do you want me?" she asked, her voice as sultry as her obvious charms.

He swallowed, wtih difficulty. "Lean back on your hands, knees up. That's it . . . now shift your shoulders . . . more toward me. Yeah . . ." He studied her through the lens. With her breasts pointing high, she looked as if she were offering them to the gods. And what an offering they were—full, round, perfectly proportioned, they reminded him of his sister's—except that Honey's were almost pure white, and Toni's were the color of almonds.

Wanting more highlights on their soft fullness, he adjusted the "barn door" on one of the Fresnels behind him and, satisfied with the results, shot several more exposures. "Okay, slip off the blouse," he said. Pretending nonchalance, he refilled her Baccarat goblet from the rare bottle of 1953 Schloss Eltz Trockenbeerenauslese. Shoeless, he squatted on the white paper to hand over the goblet. She took it with a grateful smile, looking up at him through her long black eyelashes. The come-hither glance piqued further the interest of his bird of paradise. For a long moment he could only stare back in anticipation, his mind racing ahead to explore the mysteries awaiting him. "How are you feeling?" he asked quietly.

"Much more relaxed than I thought I'd be," she replied. "You make me feel quite comfortable, really."

"Good. I told you it wouldn't be difficult." He tore his eyes from her dark-centered breasts and stood, making certain she caught a glimpse of the rising bulge in his jeans. Innocently he busied himself by changing the completed audio tape. The large Palladian windows behind him offered a stunning, panoramic view of the night-lit towers of the World Trade Center. "Any requests?"

"Whatever you like, I'm game for."

"How 'bout a little Jean-Pierre Rampal?"

"What's he play?"

"The flute."

Toni giggled, her breasts bouncing provocatively. Hurriedly he racked up the new reel and switched it on. Soaring, lyrical sounds filled the large, nearly empty studio-loft. "Want any more weed?" he asked. "Snow?"

"Maybe later. That whiff is strong, huh?" She stretched her arms over her head, pushing her treasures up at him. "I can't believe my very first photo session is with someone as well known as you," she said coyly. "Ever since I saw that last layout in *Esquire*, I've always had a fantasy of posing for you."

"See? Fantasies do come true."

"Well . . . sometimes," she laughed.

"Mind removing your panties?"

She hesitated, sudden doubt flooding her young face. *Point of no return*, he said to himself, and smiled encouragingly. Discreetly he turned his back and switched off the overhead spots, giving her time to adjust by herself. Only that morning he had discovered her, standing at a Park Avenue bus stop. With only one look, he had known she possessed that one quality for which he was constantly searching—pure feminine magic. It was an indefinable quality, something he had often tried to put

21

into words but always had difficulty explaining. And yet he instantly recognized it whenever he saw it—a mystical allure, timeless, placeless, it went beyond mere physical beauty and transcended the normal definitions of feminine pulchritude. He prided himself on his ability to discover it, and credited his considerable success to his trained eyes. This beautiful young lady had never modeled before, yet when he had approached her, introducing himself by his card, explaining his desire for a session with her, she readily agreed. All this time he had thought it was his ineffable charm. Now he realized she'd known all along who he was.

He turned back to her and his bird suddenly took wing, fluttering valiantly to be free. Toni lay stretched out on her back, her breasts flattening into soft mounds, her long legs parted slightly, her black bush glistening like a satin pillow; one hand lay on a thigh, the fingers curved toward the unseen opening between her legs. "Perfection," he said softly, and began snapping her pose from several angles, moving quickly from side to side, eventually standing near her head to shoot down the length of her womanly, arousing body.

As he snapped away, her hands moved to her breasts and she touched her dark nipples with intimate assurance, soon standing them to attention like dusky olives. His imprisoned bird jumped fully to life. "Open your legs wider," he suggested, his voice hoarse with urgency.

Slowly she parted her thighs, and he quelled the desire to rush to her feet for a more satisfying view of what he had been longing to see. Instead he finished the roll with varying angles from her upper torso, framing several of the shots of her enticing bush between the hills of her large, puddinglike breasts. Changing to his fully loaded Nikon F3, he pushed down his straining bird and gulped the rest of his wine. He poured another glass and stole a glance at her.

Eyes closed, she had been busy on her own; one finger was tentatively exploring the furled opening to her vagina. Silently he moved to her feet and watched intently her digital dexterity. Delicately she was parting the umber-colored lips, revealing a slash of bright pink. He knelt and aimed his camera, quickly capturing several succulent shots too graphic for the kind of photos he allowed to be reproduced or published, but perfect for his own private collection. The more she probed, the more insistent his cock became, demanding the same personal attention she was giving her own genitals. Not wanting to alarm her, he refrained from whipping it out—but he continued to squeeze it inside his jeans while shooting shot after shot of the ever-widening tunnel in the black-covered valley. Soon he was flat on his stomach, aiming directly into the mouth-watering aperture, grinding his hardness onto the white paper. She had buried her middle finger deep inside to the second knuckle, and now withdrew it, bringing it to her mouth to suck the clinging moisture.

Accidentally he touched her foot and her eyes snapped open, searching for him with an unmistakable, unfocused gaze. It was lust if he ever had seen it. He grinned sheepishly and she opened her legs even wider. "What other equipment have you got?" she asked.

"Lots of mechanical gadgets," he answered, scooting to his knees. "But my best piece is *all* natural."

"Is it healthy?"

"*And* good for you," he said, and placed his Nikon carefully to one side off the white paper.

She rubbed both palms over her thighs, bringing them down on either side of her black-fringed love trench. "Well, for heaven's sake, bring it out. I'm all for anything natural."

Pleased as punch, he unzipped his tight jeans and, with difficulty, extracted his full-grown bird. She raised herself up on her elbows to study it with a distinct smile of approval. "Well, bring it up here so I can test it," she murmured.

Quickly he moved to straddle her trunk. His bird trembling, he waited expectantly for her next move. She took it in both hands; her touch was cool and assured on his heated, hard cock, which twitched as if straining to fly away. With maddening slowness she raised her mouth and repeatedly kissed its swollen head. Watching the exquisite, magical mouth mother his member, he struggled for control, wanting desperately to ram it deep into her throat.

Her luscious lips enveloped the knobby end, and he felt her tongue washing the underside, creating a dangerous tingling in his balls. She sucked it in, taking nearly all of it into the moist warmth of her willing mouth, then pulling it out again. "Not fair. I'm nude and you're not," she pouted. "You promised you'd do *everything* to make me feel at ease."

"Sorry," he mumbled and rose to his feet, shucking his jeans. After stepping out of them, he ripped off his socks and yanked off his Lacoste polo shirt. Nude, excited, he stood over her, his bird flying out from his groin at a hard angle. Her fingers had returned to her love canal, and he suddenly wanted to join them. Reversing his position, he placed his knees on either side of her neck and lowered his head to greet her pussy. Snaking his tongue out, he split her open like a ripe peach. She gasped, and he felt her mouth again clamp down on his prick, as if she were chewing beef ribs.

She tasted to him like Brazil nuts and smelled faintly of musk. The rippled edges of her twat led him directly to the hard island of her clit. Jamming it against his upper teeth, he flicked at it with his tongue, sending her hips into a squirm of delight. As she sucked on him, he teased and tormented her hard love button, pressing his nose deeper and deeper between the undulating walls of her juicy canal. Lost in the heady delight, he could have eaten her for hours.

Toni, however, was panting into his cockflesh, "I want it in me, I want it inside."

Ever desirous to please, he jackknifed and aimed his bird for her love nest. Easing into her was like slipping into a tight, warm glove. For a moment he did not move, loving the sensation of being wetly enveloped, feeling the internal contractions milking at him. Lowering his weight fully onto her, he kissed her lovely face, closing her eyes with his slippery tongue. Gradually he began to move his smothered bird, stroking slowly, drawing it nearly all the way out before plunging it deep again. Over and over he did this, raising ecstatic groans from her.

Raking his back with her fingernails, she clung to him, bucking her hips harder and harder, slamming their pelvises together, urging him on faster and faster. He picked up speed, his knees rubbing raw on the hard floor, his deep moans of pleasure mingling with hers adding a cacophony of vocal accompaniment to the Rampal tape bursting out of the Infinity Reference Standards speakers that had set him back twenty grand apiece.

The tingling in his balls hurled him quickly to the brink. He eased off the pace, wanting first to bring her ultimate satisfaction. He quickly realized he need not have been concerned, for she was screaming with release and he could feel great gushes of her liquids drowning his happy bird. Again he picked up speed, hurrying to his own destination, pleased with himself for achieving his two primary goals: first, to capture her magical essence on film, and second, to fuck the hell out of her.

He was just ready to explode with a magnificent orgasm when an all-too-familiar voice, disturbingly near, cried out, "Dirk, you bastard!"

He flung his head up toward the harsh-toned voice and caught sight of the flushed face of his beautiful sister bending over them. In delighted shock, his bird detonated inside Toni and he hollered in delicious agony, "Aghhh, Honey . . ." As he squirted his last feeble drops into Toni, he watched his sister spin on her heel and stride toward the living area. Her anger was as apparent as her gleaming, deep red hair.

It took several excruciating moments for him to extricate himself from Toni's embarrassed embrace, explaining rapidly as he did that the unexpected intruder was merely his older sister. It was evident that Toni did not believe him. With cold, mechanical movements she gathered her far-flung clothes and marched into the bathroom. Relieved to hear the shower running, he hastily pulled on his Cardin robe of dark blue cashmere and padded toward the gorgeous figure sitting at the far end of the deep-cushioned, suede pillow-couch. In the otherwise dim area, a halo of light from the recessed fixtures overhead encircled her with brightness.

Honey did not look up as he approached, but continued inhaling on the slim, hand-rolled joint. He could smell the sweet, thick aroma of sinsemilla.

"Thanks for coming so quickly," he said awkwardly, not knowing where to begin.

She snorted as if amused, and swung her gaze to him. "I could say the same to you, brother. Some emergency. I bust my buns to get here as fast as I can—fearing the worst, expecting to be met by tragedy and gloom. And what do I find? The pink ass of my horny little brother, frantically waving hello at me. I don't know whether to be relieved or enraged."

"It is an emergency, I swear," he said, and sank down beside her. "I wouldn't have wired you if it wasn't serious, you know that."

She exhaled a tired lungful of smoke, her eyes narrowing as she scrutinized his face. "Well, it certainly can't be too catastrophic if you still have the inclination to get your rocks off."

He hung his head, guilty as charged. "I was trying to keep my mind off it. It's the best way I know how..."

A bubble of laughter welled out of her, husky and warm, yet with a biting edge. "Dirky, why the hell the secret code? 'Snatch'? That's only for life-or-death emergencies, you know that."

"It *is* life or death—at least I think it is. She begged me, pleaded, more with her eyes than her voice. She didn't have time to say anything but, 'Help me, please... help me.'"

"The beauty in your bathroom?"

"No. The girl in the park."

She passed him the joint. "You're talking to a reporter, not a psychic. Take a good hit and start at the beginning ... as slowly as possible."

He sucked in the sweet smoke, held it, and began speaking through clenched teeth as deliberately as he could. "Last Sunday I was in Central Park with my Nikon and the 850 telephoto lens. And this incredibly sweet-faced, super-sensational blonde—no more than sixteen, seventeen—captured and held my eye. She was everything I'm always looking for."

Honey nodded wryly. "I should have known it was a beautiful lady. So what happened?

He exhaled in a rush, feeling a sudden lightheadedness. "I didn't even get to talk to her. Just as she got out the words 'help me,' two thugs who looked like leftovers from a Sicilian gang war grabbed me, started roughing me up.

Tried to take away my camera. I fought like hell. Managed to get away, camera intact. Come here . . . I'll show you."

He led Honey past the large white walls, adorned with huge blowups of some of his favorite models, and toward the fully equipped darkroom at the very rear of the former warehouse space that occupied an entire floor of the building. Inside the cluttered, narrow room he located the eight-by-ten blowups he had made of the blonde, and handed them over ceremoniously. Honey studied them, nodding slowly. "Yes, I see . . . enchanting. Charming. Very."

"I've *never* seen such a face," he said with conviction as he stared at the Botticelli-like angel.

"So what happened then?"

"I ran off, hid, and followed them. The two thugs clamped onto her and walked her really fast into the Pierre Hotel. But when I asked the desk clerk about her, he got very nervous, uptight. Told me there was no one of that description registered and ordered me to leave at once, before he called the security guard."

Even in the dimness, he could see the spark of interest light up her eyes. "And?" she asked.

"That's it. Except that I watched the hotel day and night, practically—until this morning. But I never saw her again."

"That's it? A beautiful blonde in the park says 'help me,' and you yank me all the way from California?"

"I can't get her out of my mind, Honey. She's in deep trouble. I just know it."

"Why?" she asked coolly. "The lady of the bath's a gem too, from all I could see. What's another pretty face to you?"

He struggled to find words for his feelings. "That one in the park was everything. I feel obsessed with finding her. Her life's in danger and I'm the only one who knows. That's exactly how I feel. That girl is depending on me, I could see it in her eyes. She is counting on me to help her. I can't ignore that, I just can't." From the antique brass clothes tree he grabbed some clothes and began tugging them on. He didn't know where he was going, he only knew the magical girl was out there someplace and it was up to him to find her.

"Dirk?"

Honey came to him, a vision of creamy skin, full curves, and burnished hair, a wistful smile gracing her lips. She stopped before him, locking eyes with his and putting her arms around his neck, pulling him close. She held him tightly and his heart raced. His chest burned from the imprint of her breasts. "Of course I'll help you," she murmured. "Just hold me for a moment . . . give your only family a little warm welcome, okay? Then we'll find your mysterious blonde of the park . . . I promise."

3.

HONEY

Within the hour, Honey had checked into the Presidential Suite of the Hotel Pierre. As she tipped the bellman extravagantly for bringing up her bags, she showed him one of Dirk's photos of the lovely young blonde and received a vague, noncommittal reply that he thought he recognized her, but he couldn't be sure. Unconvinced that he was telling the truth, she thanked him, turning on her considerable charms. "By the way, who's the manager here?"

"Evan Bell," the young man replied, easing toward the door. "But he's not on duty until morning. Our assistant manager, Merit Harper, will be happy to be of service until then."

After thanking him, Honey waited until he had departed before calling the front desk and asking that the assistant manager be sent up in exactly a half hour. Hurriedly she unpacked and changed into an apricot-toned peignoir, discreet but enticing in its simple elegance. Brushing the full waves of her hair, she realized that she and Dirk had damned little to go on; if she couldn't get a lead here at the Pierre, she had no idea how she would be able to continue. As much as she wanted to help her dear brother, she would be at a dead end. And that disturbed her greatly. She could not recall ever seeing Dirk so completely obsessed by anything or anyone in his life. His passionate, desperate desire to help the mysterious blonde had touched something deep inside Honey, and she felt compelled to offer assistance in any way she could. But she had to have something to go on, and at the moment she only had the photo of the girl. Not much, she assessed ruefully. Not much at all.

The assistant manager turned out to be a distinguished-looking gentleman in his early sixties, with graying hair, an eager-to-please smile, and an overly polite manner. "Miss Wildon," Merit Harper greeted her effusively as she ushered him into the sitting room of the suite, "it's an honor to have you as a guest. I am a great fan of your articles."

"Why, thank you, Merit. May I call you Merit?" She waved him into an upholstered wing-backed chair.

"I'd be pleased, thank you."

Languidly she settled back into the couch, crossing her long legs underneath the sheer skirt. "I confess, I need your help. I am trying to locate someone—a young girl of spectacular beauty." She leaned forward and handed over the eight-by-ten photo, carefully watching his reaction.

It was guarded, cautious. He looked up with a quizzical smile. "She *is* lovely ... but I've never seen her before."

"Are you absolutely positive? I have reason to believe she was a guest here as recently as last Sunday."

"I'm certain I would remember her," he replied stiffly. "Why, may I ask, are you seeking her?"

Honey flashed him her trademark smile—open, engaging, hinting at future rewards. "I'm afraid I'm not at liberty to discuss that. You may rest assured that it is a matter of utmost importance and extreme urgency. Perhaps even a matter of life and death . . ."

"Oh, dear," he murmured nervously, and laid the photo on the coffee table as if it were a ticking time bomb. "I'm sorry I can't be of help."

She eyed him for a long moment, her journalistic nose smelling clear evasion and coverup. She redoubled her efforts. Standing, she moved casually behind his chair and placed her hands on his thin, sloping shoulders. She felt him tense at her touch and she rubbed his neck. "Merit," she purred intimately, "I find you an enormously attractive man, and I just know you'll help me."

"I'd like to, Miss Wildon," he sputtered. "Really I would. But I don't know how."

She leaned down close, her soft tresses touching his cheek. "I would be so indebted," she said softly into his ear. "You have no idea how much."

He pulled free and stood, turning to her with a flustered, apologetic smile. "Miss Wildon, please . . . I just can't help you."

She came to him and touched the buttons of his pinstriped suit, nailing him with her luminous eyes. "I'm sure you could, if you put your mind to it."

"Miss Wildon, it's late. I have other duties I must attend to."

She pressed closer, her heavy breasts touching his chest. He looked as though he was about to faint. She smiled plaintively. "I'm alone in this big city, with no one to turn to but you. Won't you stay for a bit? I'll make it worth your while . . ."

He drew himself upright, ramrod straight. "Miss Wildon, please. You don't understand, I *can't* help you in *any* way."

"Forget the girl for now. Just help me make it through the long, lonely night ahead ... please?"

He flushed several shades of red. "I can't help you there either, I'm afraid. You see ... I've been impotent for over a decade."

"Oh, poor man," she murmured genuinely. "Perhaps I can help *you*. I'm very easy to be with."

"It's not a psychological problem," he replied uneasily. "I am physiologically unable to achieve an erection. Believe me, I've been to the experts and have tried everything."

"Would you like me to try?"

"We'd both be wasting our time," he said firmly. "Now, if you'll excuse me, I must see to my duties." He backed away. "Believe me, if any woman could help, *you* could. But, alas ... goodnight, Miss Wildon." He fled to the door and, without a backward glance, let himself out.

She stared at the closed door, silently cursing his misfortune. Abruptly a wave of tiredness swept over her and she realized she was still on California time; it was after four in the morning out there. She attempted a call to Dirk to report on her lack of progress, but there was no answer at his Soho loft. Hoping it meant he had found some clue to track down, she slowly disrobed, longing for the randy Ricardo, whom she'd left at the San Francisco airport. For the first time in weeks, she fell into bed by herself and was soon asleep.

In the morning, bright and early, she was up, dressed in a demure Chanel suit of sapphire-blue wool, and knocking on the manager's office door just off the spacious lobby. The moment she laid eyes on Evan Bell, she knew her prospects were decidedly more propitious with him than they had been with the assistant manager. He was a charmingly handsome young man of no more than thirty-five, with laughing gray eyes, carefully coiffed dark blonde hair and a trim, athletic body under his expensive three-piece suit. He greeted her warmly, making no attempt to cover his obvious interest. But when she showed him the photo of the blonde, explaining her quest, Evan Bell turned cool and distant. "No. I've never laid eyes on her. Anything else?"

"Are you certain, positively?" Honey inquired. "This is a matter of vital importance."

"I regret I cannot be of help." He pushed himself to his feet behind the desk. "I hope you enjoy your stay at the Pierre."

With downcast eyes she said forlornly, "If you can't help, I'm afraid I must leave at once."

"Pity," he replied, walking to the door and opening it. "I'll have your bill drawn up."

She rose, gliding to him. "You're most kind. I was so hoping you'd help."

"Regrettably, I can't. Good day Miss Wildon." He ushered her out and closed the door behind her.

With long, angry strides, she crossed the lobby and slipped into a telephone booth, dialing Dirk's number. Again there was no answer. Her anger boiled—both at her inability to get anywhere with the hotel management and at her brother for not bothering to wait for her promised call. Slamming the receiver back into the cradle, she caught sight of the manager leaving his office and exiting the lobby through a side door marked Employees Only. Quickly she followed, determined to get the truth out of him.

The door led to a long, dimly lit hallway. At the far end, the manager was disappearing through a partially open doorway. By the time she reached the door, it was closed. The sign on it read Linen Room. She was about to knock when she heard, on the other side, a muffled giggle from a distinctly feminine voice.

After a glance back up the deserted hall, Honey knelt quickly and put her eyes to the large, old-fashioned keyhole. What greeted her did not surprise her, but certainly raised her interest. Directly opposite the keyhole, the profile of an also-kneeling Evan Bell was buried in the muff of some girl. A maid's uniform was bunched up around her waist, and her rounded, firm ass was being clutched by the eager hands of Bell as he lapped at the brown-haired bush, his feverishly moving tongue sporadically visible.

Just when Honey thought she had seen enough of the arousing display, the couple beyond the keyhole reversed positions and Evan Bell was now standing, his hard prick in the maid's mouth. Honey felt a growing heat within her own loins, and her breathing intensified. But she could tell the maid was a rank amateur in the art, for her ministrations to Bell's appetizing-looking cock were tentative and unsure.

Making up her mind, Honey stood and, without bothering to knock, threw open the door. The pretty young maid, her mouth full of meat, choked in surprise and rose with a squeal of embarrassment, trying to yank down her uniform to cover her fetching nakedness. Even Bell's hands flew to hide his stiff cock, a look of such profound astonishment on his handsome face that Honey had to suppress a laugh. Before she could speak, the maid, red-faced, ran from the small room, which was lined with shelves of stacked and folded sheets and towels. Calmly Honey closed the door after the girl and faced the tongue-tied manager. "Mr. Bell," she said wtih a grin, "I'm so happy I found you before I checked out."

36

"Miss Wildon, I...I..." He fumbled to put his still-stiff dick back into his trousers.

"Don't be shy," she insisted and moved to him, catching his trembling hands. She grazed the moist cap of his hard cock with her hand and locked eyes with him. "Let's help each other, all right?" She brushed his hands away and clasped his thick appendage firmly.

He gasped with pleasure, his confusion and uncertainty apparent. "Miss Wildon..."

"Please, call me Honey. Does this door have a key?"

He nodded and jerked his head toward a large brass key hanging on a nail by the door jamb. She let go of him, took the key, locked the door, and replaced the key on the nail. Evan Bell stared in disbelief as she took off her suit jacket, hung it on the nail, and slowly began unbuttoning her blouse. "You have a beautiful cock, Mr. Bell," she said easily. "Why don't you get undressed so I can see the rest of you?" She tugged off her blouse and displayed her treasures for him. The soft fullness of her pale breasts shone in the light from the single bulb overhead. And still the manager stared, his rigid tool pointing at her like a silent, one-eyed observer.

Smiling at her good fortune, she stepped out of her high heels and unzipped her skirt. Yanking it down, she folded it carefully and placed it on a nearby stack of fresh towels. "Aren't you going to join me?" she asked, standing only in her pale pink, low-cut silk panties.

With a start, as if suddenly awakened from a deep sleep, he began tearing off his clothes, flinging them aside until he too was nude. His chest and thighs were covered with an appealing, downy fuzz. She stepped close, rubbing her nipples over the soft mat of his chest. His thickness below the waist poked into her belly and she kissed him lightly on the lips, one hand behind his head, then sank to her knees.

Taking his iron-hard rod in both hands, she traced its length with her tongue, following the intricate pattern of thick blue veins. She took one of his balls in her lips, washing it with her tongue, and then did the same with the other, finally putting both in her mouth, applying pressure gently. Returning her attention to the blood-red cap, she smothered it with kisses, making it wet and sticky with her saliva, before sucking it deeply into her mouth.

He groaned with desire, his hands kneading her shoulders, and began pumping his hips, driving his peter in and out of her mouth. She opened wide, swallowing it fully, her nose buried in his kinky pubic hair. She could feel the thick head pushing deep into her throat, and could see the rapid rising and falling of his belly button. With expertise gained through years of continual practice, she worked her wonders on his pulsating penis.

When it began to twitch uncontrollably and his balls contracted upward into their fleshy sack, she deduced he was on the brink of coming. Teasingly she let his penis slip from her mouth. Grabbing a few clean sheets from the lowest shelf, she placed them on the floor, then lay back on them to wiggle out of her panties. She smiled sweetly and parted her creamy thighs, displaying the fiery red of her bush. "My turn now," she said.

He sank between her knees and, with an excited growl, flung her long legs up over his shoulders. For a brief second he surveyed her tantalizing pussy, noting the rose-colored petals lining the entrance to the portal of her pleasure, before sticking in his tongue. She was already wet with desire, and that only increased his ardor. Locking feverishly onto her lust-trigger, he pummeled it with his blunt tongue.

Delighting in his knowledgeable ways, she lay back, her hands roaming her body, caressing her breasts, squeezing and releasing the hard nubs of her nipples, losing herself again in the delicious sensations of erotic stimulation coursing through her system.

All too soon, Bell rose up to jam his hardness into her inflamed trench. "You are *so-o-o* beautiful," he rasped, and rammed at her like an overeager schoolboy. She wished he would slow down, but his momentum only picked up. His zestful groans increased also, and she feared he was ready to climax. Placing her hands on his shoulders, she shoved him up, ordering, "Lie down on your back."

Unwillingly he withdrew his cock and flopped over on his back. Straddling him, she took hold of his thick, slippery dick and carefully sat on it, easing it all the way into her demanding box. Firmly in control now, she put her hands on his chest and began to rock up and down with a slow, easy rhythm. Her heavy, pale breasts swayed and he latched on to them fiercely, as if they were handles and he was trying to enter her very soul.

Carefully watching his face, she rode his pogo stick up and down, up and down, not shortchanging her own pleasure, but more interested in how far away he was from climaxing. When his eyes fluttered closed and his thighs stiffened beneath her, she stopped altogether, pulling off him. "No, No," he moaned in agony. "I'm almost there . . ."

She lay full out on him, and as he squirmed under her, trying to push back into her heated, dripping cunt, she ordered him throatily, "Tell me about the girl."

His eyes registered dismay. "I can't . . ."

"You mean, you *won't*," she corrected. "You're holding back something, aren't you?"

"Let me come, then we'll talk."

"If you won't cooperate with me, why should I with you?" She rolled off him and sat up, reaching for her panties.

"Please ... I beg of you ..." he groaned, groping for her.

"Turn about is fair play," she said breezily.

"I ... I could lose my job."

She curled close again, whispering, "No one will ever know but us." She grabbed his hard, wet peter and stroked it. "The girl *was* registered here, wasn't she?"

Eyes closed, he nodded minutely.

She stepped up the tempo on his trembling dick. "What's her name?"

He shook his head, responding grimly, "I never knew."

She applied more pressure and more speed. "Who was she registered with?"

He was silent and she released his dick, letting it flop back with a smack onto his belly. He rushed to take up where she had left off, beating his own meat frantically. "Evan," she said huskily, "I promise, no one will learn that you told ... or that I saw you with that maid. Now, once again, who was the young blonde girl with?"

He thrust his hard cock into her hand. "Her father," he said almost inaudibly. "A multimillionaire recluse who demanded anonymity."

She rose up over him again and, with deliberate slowness, sat once more on his tormented thickness. He sighed and began bucking his hips, driving it into her. She let him continue for a moment, then whispered, "What's his name? Her father?"

"Barnabas ... Havelock ..."

She frowned and bounced. "Never heard of him. What's he look like?"

"I never saw him ... only his men and the girl." He fell to pumping silently.

"Has this Barnabas Havelock stayed here before?"

"No ... please, let's just fuck ..."

"We *are* fucking. Where is this Havelock from?"

"I don't know..." he wheezed.

"Did he leave a forwarding address?"

"I think so ... I'd have to check."

"You promised to tell me if he did?"

"Anything, yes ... anything..."

"Of course, darling. Would you like to be on top?"

Ecstatically he rolled her over and, with renewed enthusiasm, began humping her like crazy. His cock was so hot, his urgency so great, she soon found herself on a hurtling rollercoaster of lust, careening wildly to reach her ultimate goal together with him. Intense flames consumed her consciousness, and with a loud squeal of joy she began to pop a firecracker string of explosive climaxes. His cock contracted within her and suddenly burst, shooting a load of gism deep inside her. Moaning in contentment, he collapsed on her full breasts.

She let him catch his breath, then made a move to extricate herself. "Up, up, Mr. Bell," she said cheerily. "Let's check for that forwarding address."

"Must we leave so soon?"

"Easy come, easy go," she joshed, and reached for her panties.

Feeling energized by her early-morning sexual workout and by the ultimately helpful assistance of the obliging Evan Bell, Honey returned to Dirk's loft in lower Soho, letting herself in with her own key. She was eager to relay the information she had tracked down—including Barnabas Havelock's forwarding address. The large space was disturbingly silent, and no one answered her calls. On the message board by the phone, Dirk had pinned a note that read, *Honey, play back tape on deck.*

Perplexed, she located the tape recorder, switched it on, and hit the play button. Dirk's excited, boyish voice boomed out over the speakers high in the corners, "Honey,

41

sorry I'm not here. I heard from a photographer pal of mine whoe saw my snap of the girl in the park. He swears on his mother's grave that there is an exact double of the girl dancing in a nightclub in Cartagena, Colombia. I know it sounds as weird as hell, but since we've no other leads, I've got to follow it up. Leave a message here and let me know where you'll be. I'll be in touch soonest. Love ya, Honey. You're the best. 'Bye for now."

The tape fell silent and she switched it off, fighting the flood of disappointment and the bubble of anger pushing up her throat. Damn, of all the rotten timing. She punched the record button and spoke crisply into the built-in condenser mike: "Dirk, honestly, at least you could've waited until you heard from me. All I could find out is that the girl is traveling with her father, who was registered as Barnabas Havelock, supposedly some sort of reclusive mega-millionaire. But I made a quick check with Standard and Poors, and there is no one of that name registered on their worldwide directories. Sounds fishy, no? Anyway, his forwarding address is the Taj Ganges Hotel in Varanasi, India. You're lucky I've never been there, or you'd have to take it from here. I'll leave word with your lawyer as soon as I've learned anything. I love you too, baby brother. Ta-ta . . ."

4.

HONEY

She arrived in Varanasi, India, exhausted by the long
flight from New York to New Delhi and the short hop by
a local airliner to the ancient city once known as Benares.
Located midway between New Delhi to the northwest and
Calcutta on the Bay of Bengal, to the southeast, Varanasi
sat on the banks of the sacred Ganges River like a patient
dowager empress.

As it was Honey's first visit to Varanasi, her energy
level picked up considerably on the frantic taxi ride from
the small airport through the teeming city streets, alive
with masses of people. By the time she reached the
Hotel Taj Ganges, all her senses were once again alert,
stimulated by the exotic, strange sights. New locales always
affected her in this manner, and her sparkling blue eyes
swept expectantly over the grand entrance to the hotel,
as if at any moment something so extraordinary would

occur that she would be swept away, eagerly propelled into a new adventure.

Striding purposefully into the old-fashioned, Victorian-influenced lobby, she was only minimally conscious of the stir she was creating among the staff and occupants sipping their afternoon tea in the lobby's high, fan-backed chairs. White women traveling by themselves were rare in this off-the-tourist-path city, let alone white women with alabaster skin and deep red hair. Her smart Ralph Lauren traveling suit of raw aqua silk set off her striking coloring and clung tightly to her voluptuous body. Dark eyes followed her with unabashed interest as she swept to the desk clerk and politely asked for a room.

She was informed that, alas, there were none available. Instantly she regretted that her trip had been so quickly planned that she had not had time to wire ahead for reservations. She smiled graciously at the dark-skinned, middle-aged clerk. "Surely there must be something available," she said, and extracted a fifty-dollar bill from her green leather purse. Discreetly she laid it on the counter next to the registration book. "I would be most indebted if you could locate accommodations for me. If not here, perhaps elsewhere in the city."

He folded the bill out of sight and replied in perfect English, "I will see what I can do."

"You are most kind," she said. "Meanwhile, I am trying to find a dear friend of mine—Barnabas Havelock. I have strong reason to believe he is here in this hotel."

"Barnabas Havelock," the clerk repeated, as if mystified. "We have no one of that name registered."

"Are you sure? He is traveling with his lovely young daughter." Quickly, Honey pulled out of her purse Dirk's photo of the girl, and displayed it.

Immediately the clerk's eyes narrowed in suspicion and

44

he pulled himself up formally. "So sorry, I am unable to help you."

Smelling deception, she studied the man. His whole manner had changed; only moments before, he had been politely deferential. Now he was coldly efficient. She turned on her considerable charms, flashing a disarming, genuine smile. "You do recognize her, don't you? It's desperately urgent that I locate her and her father."

"I have never encountered her," he said crisply. "Now excuse me, I will see to finding you accommodations." He turned and disappeared through a swinging door into an office behind the check-in desk.

Her instincts told her the man was lying through his dazzling white teeth. The registration book caught her eye, and as the desk was unattended, she turned the large book around and hurriedly scanned the signatures. There was no Barnabas Havelock registered. Keenly disappointed, she righted the book and walked back to her bags, which the uniformed doorman had deposited near the front entrance.

With one eye on the front desk, she signaled the doorman outside the large glass-and-iron doors. The turbaned man entered with a subservient smile. "May I be of service?"

"I do hope so," she said, and handed him the photo of the young blonde. "Is this girl staying here?"

"I cannot say . . ."

"Can not or will not?" she asked, her voice tinged with vexation.

"Perhaps if you inquire at the front desk?" He gave back the photo with an apologetic shrug.

At the moment the desk clerk reemerged from the back room and spotted her receiving the photo from the doorman. Immediately the desk clerk frowned darkly and dashed around the counter toward them. The doorman shrank from her and ducked outside the doors like a cowering puppy.

"I must request you to leave our premises at once," the desk clerk huffed officiously.

"Leave? Aren't you finding me a room?" she asked in surprise.

"There are no vacancies."

"And the other hotels?"

"Check for yourself," he replied, and handed back her fifty dollars. Before she could protest, he spun on his heel and marched away. Her anger bubbling just underneath the surface, she snatched up her bags and exited the hotel.

The city was bathed in the saffron glow of the fast-sinking sun as Honey went from hotel to hotel, only to receive the same reply: "Sorry, we're booked solid." With growing consternation she pressed her search through the narrow, crowded streets. No amount of bribery or cajolery produced any results, even at the smallest, grimiest places of public lodging. Not believing her misfortune, and appalled to be in a strange city with no place to stay and the night fast approaching, Honey strengthened her resolve, determined that the next place would have a vacancy. Unfortunately, it too was full, according to the clerk on duty.

Dejected, she stood on the sidewalk, thumbing forlornly through the tourist guidebook she'd picked up at the airport. The air was sultry and still excessively hot. The smells of human refuse and rotting garbage wafted over her; the flies were thick everywhere, annoyingly persistent. Longing for a bath and a cool place to lie down, she reached the sobering conclusion that she had inquired at every hotel listed in the guidebook. She fought back tears of annoyance and, hefting her bags once again, set off down the crowded street, her progress impeded by thousands of milling natives who looked at her with open curiosity. Cunning beggars, peddlers, and fakirs waved their hands at her, jabbering unintelligently.

Ignoring them, she had no idea where she was headed, but she felt that something would have to turn up soon or she would lose the firm resolve that was now the only thing holding her upright. A fresh breeze drew her on. She reached the steep, wide stone steps leading down to the Ganges itself. A sea of black umbrellas and makeshift canopies stretched along the riverbank as far as she could see in both directions. Beyond them, the murky green water floated slowly. Hundreds of devoted bathers splashed in the water. Some of the men were naked except for G-strings, and the women were dressed in saris that clung to their wet bodies. Bony sacred cows mingled on the bank with black-sari-clad women, young-ish men in sparkling white cotton Nehru shirts, and old men with unkempt hair, wearing dirty loincloths.

Staring at the press of humanity, Honey sank to sit on her luggage, unable to find the strength to continue her search. She was thinking of returning to the airport terminal to wait for the next plane out, when a deep, rich male voice spoke beside her: "Excuse me, may I be of assistance?"

Gratefully she looked up into a pair of kohl-black eyes shining with warmth and concern. The dark eyes were set in a face of youthful handsomeness, topped by a complete bald head. She smiled wearily. "I need a place to stay the night, but all the hotels are booked up."

The young man, tall, lean, wrapped in saffron-colored robes, nodded reflectively. "You have been blackballed."

"Blackballed? What do you mean? Why?"

He shrugged and squatted on his haunches beside her, speaking softly. "It is a very small city. Evidently you upset the manager of the Taj Granges Hotel. At least that is what the streets whisper."

"You mean *he* put out the word not to give me a room?"

Gravely the young Indian nodded. "A runner was sent ahead of you to warn the other hotels."

"But why?" she asked incredulously. "All I did was ask after a friend."

Again the handsome young man shrugged. "Privacy is deeply respected here. Perhaps you were too inquisitive."

"Or asked after the wrong person," she muttered, and dabbed at her perspiring face with a clean hankie. In spite of her predicament, she felt at that moment a deep sexual pull toward the young man, and she smiled gamely at his sober countenance. "My name is Honey Wildon. I am an American."

"Mine is Pagala Baba. And I am a holy man."

"A holy man?" she repeated, unable to cover her disappointment.

He stood, his long robes partially open, revealing a lean, firm thigh. "Your search is over. You may stay the night at my humble abode if you would like."

"I'd like," she said sweetly.

The young priest took her bags and, without a word, set off down the wide stone steps. She followed, trying to match his long, barefooted strides. When they reached the rocky shoreline, she had difficulty keeping up with him in her high heels. Slipping them off, carrying them in one hand, she hurried after him over the smooth stones, terribly conscious of the pointed stares of the thousands of curious onlookers who parted before them. On and on the young holy man walked, until she thought he would never stop. Wearily she padded after his sturdy back, absorbed in the strange sights and smells in the last light of day.

Into the increasing darkness they trudged, far beyond

the outskirts of the city, until the crowds on the river-bank dwindled and faded far behind them. At last, just when she felt she couldn't walk another step, he stopped and set down her bags, announcing simply, "This is my resting spot."

She looked around in the dim light, not seeing anything but a wide curve of the slow-moving river, a steep clay bank, and several squat bushes. She turned back to her benefactor, but could not see him anywhere. "Hello?" she called out tentatively.

"I'm here," came his echoed reply, and a softly glowing light suddenly appeared. He stood inside the mouth of a small cave, and she stooped in to join him. The flickering light of a small kerosene lantern revealed the damp red-clay walls, the floor covered with fresh straw, the untidy pallet of heaped clothes. The ceiling of the narrow cave was too close for them to stand fully upright. He placed her bags at the far end, near some sort of altar, and returned to stand beside her. "I hope you will rest peacefully here."

"I'm positive I will," she said with a yawn. "I can't thank you enough."

He smiled knowingly and tugged at his robes. At once they fell from him. A small cloth covered his loins, and his long, lean brown limbs glowed in the soft light. She felt her throat tighten at his physical beauty; with his clean-shaven head, he looked like a statue of a young saint. Carefully he placed his robes on the straw. "It is time to bathe in the holy river," he said, and bent further to leave the cave. He walked out of the circle of lantern-light and vanished toward the water.

For a moment she stood uncertainly, then decided that the idea of a swim was just too perfect to pass up. Not knowing whether he was watching from the dark-ness—and hoping he was—she slowly undressed and stepped out of her panties with studied nonchalance. She stretched her arms over her head, thrusting out her pelvis, and rolled her rounded hips to work out some of the kinks, then ducked out of the cave. Her full figure silhouetted in the light from the cave's mouth, she stepped gingerly toward the water. Gradually her eyes became accustomed to the darkness, and she spotted his white loincloth lying on a rock. Not wanting to disturb his holy ablutions, she did not call out, but walked into the cool water. The bottom was smooth mud, and slippery, but the water was so refreshing that she waded out until it was over her hips, then slipped fully into it, kicking out into a modified side stroke.

The night air was breezeless but balmy, the sky already filling with stars. In the distance, as she swam lazily about, she could hear a flute soaring tunelessly, and farther down the river, toward the city, a line of campfires could be seen, like a string of glowing pearls. Remembering the sight of the murky water in the daylight, she deliberately kept her head and face out of it and eventually paddled back to the shore. Feeling deliciously renewed, she rose from the water and saw the young holy man squatting nude near the entrance of the cave, watching her carefully. As she walked toward him, her heavy breasts swaying, he stood, his limbs still glistening with water. He had not bothered to put on his loincloth, so she made no attempt at covering herself. "That was lovely," she said.

Silently he handed her a piece of clean cloth, and she patted dry her arms and rounded breasts. She glanced down at his groin, now visible in a shaft of light, and her heart quickened. His soft, uncircumcised cock was lovely, thin, long, the color of mahogany; his balls hanging loosely on either side, were large and potent-looking. She wondered if his priestly vows included celibacy. Just as that thought passed through her mind, she saw his brown shaft suddenly twitch, nodding slowly upward. She raised her eyes to his; he was staring at her breasts as if he had never seen such a huge pair before. She questioned teasingly, "What kind of holy man are you?"

"I am a devotee of Brahma, the Creator."

"And what beliefs does that entail?"

"Brahma began the process of creation," he said solemnly. "Together, Brahma and Saraswati begat the whole race of mortals.

"How divine," she purred, and patted the cloth over her thighs, pausing to wipe the fiery red of her pussy pelt. Aware of the increased attentiveness of his cock, and also aware that his eyes followed her every move, she filled her lungs, expanding her breasts before him. "And what else do you believe?"

"Sexual union is an auspicious Yoga, which, though involving enjoyment of all the sensual pleasures, gives release. It is a path to liberation."

"Now *that* is something I too believe in," she said firmly. She dropped her eyes again to his rising shaft; it was thickening nicely and the dark skin was tightening over the plump head, gradually pulling back, displaying more and more of the nut-brown knob. "Is that your prayer stick?" she asked facetiously.

"It's my holy *lingam,* the symbol of Lord Shiva, the Supreme Yogi."

She placed a hand on her pussy, cupping it. "And what is this?"

"That is your sweet *yoni,* the symbol of Shakti, the essence of bliss. She is the love power."

"How true, how true . . . do teach me more."

Wordlessly he took her hand, tugging her gently into the small cave. "In the springtime the rounded hips of amorous women are adorned with silken garments," he said, as if quoting someone, and laid her down on the cloth pallet. Kneeling beside her, he reached for a small wooden bowl. "Languid with passion, they rub sandalwood paste mixed with sweet flowers, saffron, and musk on their breasts." Tenderly he touched each of her nipples with a sticky orange substance from the bowl, and instantly she felt fires burst to life on her breasts. Her nipples expanded greatly, popping up like small telescopes searching for more pleasure. The sweet smell of exotic flowers was everywhere.

"Where there is only worldly enjoyment, there is no release," he said softly, and touched the sticky residue to the opening of her "sweet *yoni*." "And where there is only release, there is no worldly enjoyment. But both worldly enjoyment and release are in the palm of the hand of one who is devoted to the higher being."

From the spot on her labia where he had lightly touched her, the fire of lust broke out like a sudden rash. It quickly spread deep up her love channel, heating the very core of her sexual appetite. She rolled to one hip, facing him. Between his kneeling legs, his shaft now rose straight out from him, pointing its insistent head at her. He handed her the small bowl of exotic aphrodisiac and leaned back on his hands. "Worship my Shiva *lingam*."

She knelt and dipped her fingers into the sweet, warm substance. Delicately she dabbed the stuff on the head of his throbbing cock, smoothing it into the under-ridges and down the length. She noticed that his eyes were closed and that he was breathing deeply and slowly in through his nostrils, exhaling fully from his mouth. She clasped both hands firmly on his holy tool and pulled the foreskin over the shiny brown head, then pushed it back tightly, squeezing until the knob began to turn a deep purple. Back and forth she tugged, feeling the intense heat emanating from the entire length of his shaft.

Eyes still closed, he chanted softly, "Where there is

ecstasy, there is Creation. Where there is no ecstasy, there is no Creation. In the Infinite, there is ecstasy. There is no ecstasy in the finite."

"Amen to that," she intoned, and slowly lowered her mouth to his straining organ. Her tongue darted out, licking the sweet-tasting substance she had applied. His whole body jerked with a spasm of surprise, and she sucked the head deep into her mouth. Worshipfully she took it in, wiping it clean with her tongue. She teased the small slit, scrubbed the bulbous ridges, and traced his length with her lips. When she pulled back to look at his face, he was staring openmouthed, as if unfamiliar with such forms of worship. She winked and lay back on the scratchy bed of cloth covered with straw. Flinging wide her legs, she explored with her fingers the furled edges of her love temple. She was already wet with desire and could feel a demanding urgency building within her.

With the fluidity of a dancer, he moved gracefully between her legs and sat facing her, his long limbs stretched out on either side of her buttocks. She looked over the pale mountains of her breasts and watched him position his brown stick, pushing it down to the very portals of her pussy. He nudged its head slowly up and down along her trembling labia, increasing the size of her heated opening. Gently he eased only the head of his cock into her, and pulled her legs over the tops of his thighs. Scooting his hips toward her, he pushed deeper inside until he was buried to the hilt. For a long while she waited with growing impatience for him to begin moving. She could feel the walls of her vagina undulating over his hardness, and still he did not move.

Raising herself on her elbows, she looked at him. He too was lying flat on his back, eyes closed, a look of such beatific bliss on his handsome, young face that he appeared to be experiencing a profound spiritual union.

Not wanting to disturb any religious ritual, she slowly began rocking her hips, driving his holy hard-on in and out, and suddenly she felt his cock spring to life within her.

Deep, satisfying strokes propelled her into an ecstasy so intense that she felt she was indeed making it with a very holy man. The feelings of pleasure were so all-encompassing that all sense of time and place faded away, all sense of her own body and mind disappeared. She could not separate where she ended and he began, or which one of them was male, which female. All of her was joined to all of him, and the sensation was so overpowering that she felt a unique mystical uplifting, transporting her into a golden haze, a blurring of all her most primal emotions. Soon, waves of climaxes racked their bodies and still they fucked on and on, ever lifting her higher until she exploded beyond consciousness, into the realms of erotic nirvana.

She drifted back to earth on a fluffy cloud, gradually becoming aware of her surroundings and the still-moist warmth glowing like a hot ember between her legs. White-hot sunlight bounced off the red clay of the cave's walls, and through the arched opening she could see the Ganges flowing from the Himalayas, moving steadily, but with a stately dignity. She summoned the energy to roll over, and discovered that she was alone in the cramped confines. Beside the pallet, a wooden bowl held a few dates, a chunk of flat bread, and a brilliantly red tropical flower of a sort she had never seen before. Ravenously she began eating a date, but the river sparkled below her too invitingly.

Crawling out into the sun, she felt at once on fire, her pale skin searing in the solar rays. Squinting in the brightness, she scrambled to her knees and ran lightly to the water's edge and into the water. She was just knee-deep when she noticed with some surprise that she was the object of the astounded attention of a handful of farmers filling wooden buckets with water. She laughed gaily, waving at them and feeling wonderfully alive and invigorated, then plunging into the water to her neck. Motionless, they watched her cavorting in their holy waters and gazed in openmouthed admiration as she boldly rose and walked, full of assurance, her white breasts held high, her hips swaying provocatively, toward the mouth of the cave.

Inside, she had just finished drying off and had pulled on her panties when a shadow blocked the entrance. She drew back with a start, and then relaxed as her handsome Indian holy prince of a lover bent into the cool interior. His velvety liquid eyes held hers, and in that moment their union was as complete as it had been on the pallet the night before. Stooping, he took the brilliant red flower from the now-empty bowl and stood up to place it in her hair, behind one ear. He smiled at her beautiful image. "While you slept so soundly, I went to the city. I have found someone who can help you in your search for your friend."

He stooped again and went out through the opening, reappearing shortly with a young girl in tow. "This is Leaha. She works at the hotel Taj Ganges. And speaks good English."

Honey stared down into the lovely, nutmeg-colored face. The child was no more than eleven, and her huge black eyes were fixed in complete absorption on the dusky rose nipples of Honey's breasts. "Pleased to meet you, Leaha. Thank you for coming such a long way. My name is Honey," she said warmly, and bent to her purse. She brought up the photo of the young blonde. "Have you ever seen this girl before?"

The raven-black eyes locked on the photo and she

nodded slowly. "Yes," she replied. "This last week." Her voice was as melodious as wind chimes.

"Is she still at the hotel?"

"No. She left two days ago."

Disappointment flooded Honey, and for a moment she stared into the child's face, transfixed by her innocent trustfulness. "Did you see her father?"

The child frowned and looked up questioningly at Pagala Baba. He spoke a few words in Hindi to her, and she returned her solemn gaze to Honey. "The man is not her father."

"He's not? How can you be sure?"

A fragile smile graced her small mouth. "Fathers do not do such things to their daughters."

Honey asked with trepidation. "Do what, my dear?"

Again the child looked to the young holy man, and he smiled encouragingly. She ducked her head and whispered, "I was in the closet, folding sheets, when I saw them join in Tantric union."

In surprise, Honey swept her gaze to Pagala Baba. He merely shrugged. Her concern began to mount, and she felt an even more pressing urgency to find Dirk's mysterious blonde. Quickly she rattled off several questions: "Do you know where they went? Do you know the name they were registered under? Do you know if they were traveling with two men? Do you know what currency they paid with?" To each of these, she received a grave shaking of the head. The child knew nothing beyond what she had said.

Hurriedly, Honey began pulling on her clothes. "Leaha, I can't thank you enough for your help."

"I am sorry I do not do more."

"You are a dear, sweet child. Tell me, this young blonde girl—was she happy? Did she seem to be with this older man by choice?"

"Oh, no," Leaha replied quickly. "She was very sad. Cried all the time. I think she was very unhappy. The man . . . he was not pure."

"Pure? What do you mean?"

She locked her eyes on Honey's face. "He has unclean karma. He is evil man."

5.

DIRK

In the muggy night breeze, he hurried across the grassy, parklike Plaza Bolivar, past the stone Palace of the Inquisition, built in 1770, and ducked down a narrow, cobblestone street lit by iron lamps, searching for the small nightclub. Dirk had been in Cartagena, on the Caribbean coast of Colombia, for only three hours, and it had taken him that long to check into the luxurious Hilton resort out on the Boca Grande Peninsula, then shower, change his clothes, and find out where the reported belly dancer would be performing. The oddity of a Middle Eastern club tucked deep in the center of the old Spanish-founded city did not escape him. But since few people he had approached in the city spoke English, there was no one to tell him how such a club came into being.

Sinbad's Cave turned out to be a tiny establishment deep in the bowels of an ancient fort. Inside, the air was blue with smoke and the place was packed to the stone walls with patrons, mainly Columbian businessmen, lounging on mirrored pillows around small brass-topped tables that ringed a small dance floor. Off to one side, in front of a purple tapestry cloth, an authentic band of Middle Eastern musicians played their instruments as two averagely attractive females in traditional harem garb twirled and danced, displaying a great deal of skin but, in Dirk's opinion, not much talent.

He sank to an available pillow against the rear wall and tried to find a comfortable position for his long legs. Already he was doubting the information he had received from his New York photographer pal. The prospect of finding an exact duplicate of the enchanting blonde of Central Park, performing here in such a dingy hole, was almost too absurd to contemplate. But Dirk was so obsessed with finding the magical young woman that he would willingly have journeyed by dogsled to Siberia in the dead of winter to track down any possible lead.

The club's entertainment dragged on, the weird, atonal music loud and irritating, heavy on the beat of odd-shaped drums and wailing, nasal-sounding wind instruments; the parade of women performers danced as if they had been trained in burlesque, and perfunctorily went through their routines with bored expressions on their perspiring faces. The density of smoke increased, as did Dirk's headache. An hour into the show, he was positive he'd seen all the dancers, and not one bore even a faint resemblance to the girl of his quest. He was about to chalk up the entire trip as a damned dead end, when the master of ceremonies—a rotund, swarthy little man dressed only in a beaded vest and baggy orange satin pants—stepped to the microphone to announce in Spanish the main attraction, "Jamilia." Enthusiastic applause and cheers from the spectators greeted the news, as if they had been waiting for this moment.

The lights blinked off, the foreign-sounding music began again, and suddenly, in a white spotlight, a tall figure appeared, swathed from head to toe in gauzy blue veils. She swayed and twirled to the slow music, remaining completely covered except for a small open band across her eyes. Dirk strained forward and felt a stirring in his groin. Unlike the previous performers, this one was obviously talented. Her movements were graceful, rhythmic, highly sensual, and the more she danced, the more she raised his curiosity and his bird of paradise. He could not believe how aroused he'd become in such a short time—especially by a totally covered woman.

The pounding music picked up tempo and she spun faster, holding out the top veil, forming a billowy canopy of blue over her still-covered head. Dipping, swaying, gyrating, she gradually lowered the blue veil, revealing a creamy expanse of bouncing breast packed tightly into a skimpy bra covered with gold coins. An excited, guttural cheer broke from the men around Dirk. With her face hidden behind a smaller veil, Jamilia danced fluidly, slowly lowering the large veil in her hands. Glimpses of her breathtaking figure were possible now. Her slightly rounded belly undulated and rolled. In her navel, a large emerald glistened and twinkled like a small green island of calm in the midst of a windswept white lake. Low on her rounded, swiveling hips, another band of gold coins clinked in rhythm to her erotic movements, a small girdle of tinkling sounds. A full skirt of shiny blue material, split enticingly up the front, swept around her in a full circle and her creamy thighs flashed through, and now and then her perfectly proportioned legs.

One look at the fully rounded figure, the large white

breasts jiggling provocatively, told Dirk for certain that whoever this Jamilia was, she could not be the exact duplicate of his mystery blonde. That beauty he'd found in Central Park had been a mere girl no more than sixteen years old, and though she was spectacular, she did not as yet possess such a full-blown womanly body. However, in the heat of this moment, he was so entranced by the accomplished dancer before him that he did not care; he was dying of curiosity to see her face.

As if Jamilia had read his mind, at that precise instant, with her back to the audience, her hands rose gracefully to the scarf covering her head. With a quick tug, she yanked free the gauzy piece of material and shook loose a mass of striking blonde hair that tumbled past her shoulders, shimmering like spun gold in the bright spotlight.

Dirk bolted upright on the pillow—her hair was exactly the same tone of blonde as that of the girl in the park! He waited breathlessly for her to turn to the crowd of hollering, appreciative men. Her full hips swaying like a flag in a gentle breeze, she slowly came about, her face partially obscured by soft, curly tendrils of golden hair. With an almost impatient toss of her head, she threw the hair back from her forehead and smiled serenely— straight in his direction. He stared, frozen in surprise and delight.

His pal had not steered him wrong. Jamilia *was* the spitting image of the fantasy blond he'd captured on film. In spite of the differences in their bodies, their lovely, angelic faces were identical—the same fine sweep of brow, the same classic nose, the same high, regal cheekbones, the same full, sensual mouth. Dirk's expert camera eye could not be misled; the facial similarities were too strong to be a mere coincidence. Jamilia *had* to be related to his quarry in some way. Entranced all the more, he swallowed his excitement, and his bird of paradise sprang into a full-grown boner. He could not wait until he was alone, face to face, with the magical beauty. He began to sweat with tension.

Immediately upon the conclusion of Jamilia's ripely erotic dance, he pushed himself to his feet and, weaving through the densely packed crowd of raucously cheering men, made his way to the backstage entrance. He pushed through the beaded curtain and bumped into the portly master of ceremonies, who emphatically barred his entrance. Dirk pulled a hundred-dollar bill from his money clip and shoved it into the obstinate man's greasy palm. At once, a more-than-pleased grin broke out on the swarthy face and the rotund man bowed mockingly, pointing to a small, grimy door.

Pushing his rigid dick into a less noticeable position, Dirk knocked and a woman's musical voice called out in Spanish, "Come on in." He opened the door and stepped into a cluttered, cramped dressing room that smelled like the inside of a Moroccan whorehouse—sickly sweet perfume, sweat, and the arousing, intoxicating scent of women. Jamilia stood before a full-length mirror on the opposite wall, wiping her beautiful face with a towel. Her full breasts, heaving in the tight coin-bra from the recent exertion, rose and fell like rapidly inflating and deflating balloons, their creamy skin filmed with perspiration. She swung to him questioningly and his heart hammered even harder. She was even more breathtaking in person. Her large, pale eyes stared boldly into his, and he could not find his tongue to speak.

"Yes?" she asked lightly.

"I . . . I think I'm in love with you," he stammered.

She laughed as if she'd heard that line before. "You're from the States?"

He nodded, transfixed by her mesmerizing allure. She

laughed again at his silence and stepped behind a folding screen of tightly woven latticework. From behind it she asked, "What brings you to Cartagena?"

"I . . . I came to find you . . ."

"Me?" she queried, her blonde head appearing briefly above the screen. "Why?" With a soft clinking sound, she flung her coin-covered bra onto the top of the wood screen.

Just thinking of her womanly body being exposed behind the lattice wiped all other thoughts from his mind, and for a moment he forgot the pressing reason for his visit. With a soft rushing sound, her billowy blue skirt appeared next to her bra, then her heavy coin girdle. She poked her gorgeous head up again. "We don't get many Americans down this way," she commented easily. A bemused but interested smile graced her lips.

Pulling his thoughts together, he fumbled into a pocket of his blue blazer and brought out a slightly crumpled copy of the photograph of his vanished blonde. Hesitantly he took a step forward and held it out.

Perplexed, Jamilia reached a graceful hand over the screen and took it, holding it up to the ceiling light to look at it. At once her face blanched. "Kolina?" she gasped, and disappeared.

"Kolina?" he repeated. "You *do* know her, then?"

With a flurry, Jamilia scooted from behind the screen, gathering a sky-blue silk robe about her nude figure, her lovely face a mask of concern. "Where did you get this?" she demanded hoarsely.

"I took it myself. In New York."

"When?"

"A week ago Sunday," he replied, increasingly concerned by her obvious alarm.

Almost frantically she searched his face, then burst into tears. "My darling Kolina," she sobbed, and kissed the photo. She collapsed into a straight-backed chair and wept openly into her hands. In a flash he was kneeling beside her, his arms around her soft body, pressing her head to his shoulders, his fingers tracing the silken robe on her back. She did not resist his embrace, and he marveled at her open trustfulness. "There, there," he said quietly into her blonde mass of sweet-smelling hair.

She cried for several moments, and with each renting sob, his desire to help her intensified all the more. Finally she pushed away and her tear-filled eyes sought his, imploringly. "You must tell me everything you know about her. I beg of you."

Burning with his own curiosity, he hurriedly relayed the entire story of his encounter with the girl in Central Park, her plea for help, and the two thugs who chased him and whisked her away. He finished with how and why he had come to Cartagena, then quickly added, "Now it's your turn. Who is this Kolina?"

She stiffled a sob. "She's my younger sister. And she's been missing for over a month."

As Jamilia hastily pulled on her street clothes behind the lattice screen, she explained in broken phrases, often interrupted by a new burst of tears, what she knew of Kolina's disappearance. Much to Dirk's disappointment, he learned very little, but he could piece together a general outline.

Jamilia had been paying for Kolina's education in an exclusive girl's school in Switzerland ever since their parents had drowned in a freak boating accident in the Mediterranean, some five years earlier. She and Kolina were very, very close and would meet in Paris each summer to spend Kolina's vacation touring and having a grand time together. During the school term, Kolina wrote to her often, and occasionally, when Jamilia felt especially flush, she would call overseas for a friendly little chat with her sister. She had spoken to Kolina in this manner only two days before the telegram arrived.

The fateful cable from the Swiss school's headmistress had awoken Jamilia one morning over a month ago. Kolina had disappeared overnight from the school's grounds and could not be found. Desperately, Jamilia had flown to Switzerland and spent two frustrating, ennervating, and painful weeks hounding the school, the local police, even Interpol, but no trace of Kolina could be found, not even a single clue as to what might have happened to her. Heartbroken, Jamilia had returned to her high-paying job in Cartagena, waiting in dread each day for some word. Until Dirk had shown up with the photo taken only a short time before, Jamilia had not known for certain that her precious little sister was even still alive.

Protectively, Dirk walked the distraught exotic dancer back to her place within the oldest part of the city. She lived on the top floor of a white stone house surrounded by wrought-iron balconies. Reaching her door, at the top of the narrow stone stairs off a small interior courtyard, Dirk was longing to comfort the beautiful creature on even more intimate terms. But he was too much of a gentlemen to press his own raging needs upon the obviously upset young woman.

Much to his delight, Jamilia invited him inside. Her small apartment was decorated charmingly with handicrafts of local artisans. colorful wall hangings of patchwork appliques, thickly woven wool rugs, stuffed lizards of various sizes; a huge stuffed tortoise, balancing a sheet of glass on its shell, served as a coffee table before a comfortable-looking couch. In an alcove, a large bed was covered with hand-embroidered pillows. Jamilia switched on a pounded-brass lamp and threw open the glass doors to the small balcony, revealing the twinkling lights ringing the harbor. She indicated an array of liquor bottles on a shelf near the kitchenette and told him to help himself while she took a bath. She entered the adjoining bathroom and closed the door.

Listening to the soft sounds of her bathing, he nursed a straight Scotch and stood on the small balcony, seeking a cool breeze and trying to deal with his rising expectations. He felt inextricably drawn to her, as if he were the only one in the whole world who could help her find Kolina. He pledged to himself that he would do everything within his power and resources to reunite the two sisters.

He was thinking of trying to reach Honey with news of the recent developments when Jamilia emerged from the bathroom, her voluptuous figure wrapped only in a large, damp bath towel. Wordlessly she poured herself a small cognac in a large snifter.

He raised his own glass. "To finding Kolina."

"You will help me, then?"

"Of course, Jamilia," he said. "My sister and I have already begun."

She moved closer to him, sipping from the snifter, eyeing him over the rim. "Jamilia is my dancing name. My real name is Barbro."

"Barbro and Kolina," he murmured. "Those are Swedish, aren't they?" He could feel the heat rising within him like mercury in a thermometer.

She nodded. "We were born outside of Göteborg on a small farm. Our father was a professor of economics at the university." Her lovely, light blue eyes welled with tears again. "And our mother was a folk dancer in a professional troop."

"How did a Swedish girl end up belly dancing in Cartagena?"

She smiled wistfully, and for a brief second he saw again the identical image of Kolina in the park. "I was raised dancing," she began softly. "And one year, when I was eleven and Kolina was six, my father taught in Tunisia. I began studying Middle Eastern dancing there. After . . . after the boat explosion that claimed by parents' lives, I needed a profession to put Kolina through school. Because my figure is too full for any other kind of dancing, I went to Egypt and studied more. Blonde belly dancers are a rarity, and I became quite successful. The best offer came from this club here. Blondes are also at a premium in South America."

"Especially such talented ones." He could not control his urges any longer. He bent and kissed her tenderly on the lips. She did not pull back, but rather returned it in full.

When they parted, she looked at him strangely. "Why do you want to help find Kolina? You saw her only for a moment."

"I'm a professional photographer. Beautiful women are my passion. I've never, ever seen a face like hers . . . or yours, for that matter. You look so much like her . . ." He broke off, flustered at his ineffectual explanation, and tried again. "She looked so damned vulnerable, so in need of someone to help her . . ."

Barbro nodded silently in agreement and took his hand, pulling him toward the bed in the alcove. He hesitated, torn by conflicing desires. "Barbro . . . you don't have to do anything for me. I'll look for your sister without any reward from you."

She placed a finger on his lips. "Shhh . . . I want you, Dirk Wildon. You are a good man, a decent man. And I haven't had any man for such a long, long time."

In amazement he stared down at her beautiful face. "I find that difficult to understand. You could have any man you wanted."

She sighed and sank gracefully to the bed, tossing embroidered pillows aside. "Belly dancers are always thought to be promiscuous because their art is so erotic. But my standards are high. Rather than risk my reputation, which would make my life hell in such a place as this, I prefer to remain celibate." She lay back on the pillows and held her arms up to him. "You are a very sexy man. Tall, lanky, like an American cowboy . . ."

Thrilled by her praise, he fell beside her and gathered her to him, whispering into her face, "And you are a very sexy woman . . . full, ripe, delicious, a smorgasbord of delights . . ." She giggled and he kissed her hungrily; his tongue sank deep into her smooth mouth, which tasted of mints and smelled of cognac. Their tongues twisted and coiled around each other like mating snakes. At once his larger snake raised its head and pressed heatedly through his slacks into her soft belly.

He reared up to pull the damp towel from her luscious body and fling it on the floor. By the dim light of the brass lantern, he gazed raptly at the revealed wonders. Her skin was the color of his sister's, creamy white, unblemished, satiny to the touch of his roaming fingers. Her breasts were a treasure trove—full, rounded mounds of pale flesh, pliable to the touch. Her aureoles were pale pink, and her nipples, slightly darker in color, were already as hard as pencil erasers, cylindrical in shape, flat-topped. He lowered his mouth and sucked on one, flicking it with his tongue as her encircling arms pressed him to her. Not wanting to slight a single portion, he traced his tongue across the deep crevice between her breasts and to the other nipple, biting it softly, raising a soft moan of approval from deep in her throat.

She pushed his shoulders up off her, panting, "Get nude, Dirk . . . I want you nude too."

He rolled off the bed and stood, tearing off his shirt, tossing it aside while he toed off his Gucci loafers. As he unzipped his slacks his hard peter bounced into view and she reached out a cool hand, taking hold of it while he shucked his slacks and stepped out of them. While she kept hold of his rigid bird, he struggled out of his socks and was about to kneel again on the bed, when her mouth swooped forward and closed over the end of his pleasantly surprised dick. She sat on the edge of the bed holding his hips with her hands as her mouth encompassed his cock, sliding down on it until he could feel the back of her throat. Stroking her blonde waves, he watched her devour his bird as if it were a sausage of the tastiest meat. His hands lowered to her bouncing breasts and he tweaked her nipples, rolling and pinching the puckered flesh between his fingertips; cupping her full breasts, he held them in the palm of his hand, feeling their weight, their resiliency.

She let his dick slip from her mouth and inhaled one of his balls, washing it around her talented mouth, scrubbing it with her tongue before letting go of it to apply the same attention to the other testicle. His hard peter battered her soft cheek, and he could feel a roaring furnace stoking to life deep in the center of his groin. She pulled back slightly to study his bird, holding it gently in both hands, pulling the skin tightly back from its engorged head, licking the end of it, parting the small opening with her tongue.

He couldn't wait any longer and shoved her back on the bed, crawling between her legs, spreading her creamy thighs wide, opening her steamy portal to paradise for his own minute study. Her bush was the color of tropical beach sand, soft and silky. Her crinkled labia were tinged a delicate rose hue, which deepened in color the further he explored with his eager fingers. Her internal walls were slick with dew and undulated with their own erotic dance. Slowly he lowered his mouth, inhaling the sweet aroma of ripe fruit. She tasted just as sweet, and his tongue dug deep, slicing her open like a fresh fig. He located her love trigger and afflicted it tenderly until her generous hips were writhing.

He scooted his legs around, bringing his demanding cock to her mouth, and as he ate at her delectable morsels of love meat, she sucked his quivering bird deeply into her throat. He pumped his hips gently and caressed the insides of her thighs, clutching at the soft cheeks of her buttocks, pulling her buttocks wide apart, reaming her purple-pink anus, and returning to the tender trench like a homing pigeon. For a long while they continued in the classic sixty-nine position until he felt too close to creaming into her mouth. Wanting to postpone the inevitable as long as possible, he withdrew and, turning her on her side, crawled around her, spooning his hips up to her soft mass of ass, his aching cock pressing between her cheeks, his arms encircling her, his hands grabbing for her large breasts, his face buried in her neck just below her ear.

He pulled her top leg over his thigh and, with the excitement of a school boy on his first fuck, slowly sought her liquid opening with the head of his ready-to-fly bird. He eased into her incredibly tight pussy with a deliberateness and she arched her head back into him, groaning. Deeper and deeper his bird burrowed into the moist meat until he could go no further. With one hand he stroked her full breasts, the other circling low on her rounded belly, down over the kinky softness of her bush, his middle finger seeking out the top of her love trench, locking on her lust button, jiggling it steadily as he plunged, again and again and again, deep into her.

Soon she was groaning lustily, "Do me, Dirk . . . do me good. Fuck me, fuck me hard . . ."

Ever the gentleman, he did as she demanded, giving it to her with all the finesse born of his many years of experience. Many times he was so close to coming that he had to stop moving altogether to prolong their pleasure to its fullest. Again and again he raised her to peaks of passion and still he fucked on, at times slow, at times hard and fast, like a piston in a precision racing machine. The sheets were drenched with their sweat and her juices before he rolled over on top of her. The new position raised her to even further heights of ecstasy and made it easier for his eager bird to ram as deep as possible. She shrieked as she peaked again, and, unable to contain his own climax any longer, he lowered his head between her mountainous breasts and drove for home with the determination of a long-lost orphan. His dick felt three times its normal size and was raw from the workout before it finally detonated deep with in her. With a growl of joy, he shot his load and was surprised at its duration and amount. Drained, he collapsed on her voluptuous body and suddenly realized that when he'd come, he had been fantasizing that he was fucking her sister, Kolina.

In less than an hour they made it two more times. By the fifth fuck before dawn, he was pleading for some rest. By breakfast he was as limp as a wilted daisy. And still she wanted more. He rose to the occasion...but fell asleep in midstroke.

6.

HONEY

Rather than take the train from Zurich, she hired a chauffeured Mercedes-Benz limousine. The nearly three-hour drive to Klosters, high up in the Swiss Alps, near the Austrian border, was filled with scenic, even awesome grandeur. From the deeply cushioned rear seat of the luxurious auto, Honey stared out at the passing panorama of dense virgin woods, craggy, sunlit peaks, and lush green valleys sprinkled with vivid spring flowers. She was filled not only with the peaceful beauty, but also with bitter-sweet memories of her own schoolgirl years in very similar surroundings, near Lucerne. For six years, until she turned eighteen, she had lived and studied there. In many ways, she now felt she was coming home.

Dirk's telephone report from Cartagena had caught up with her in Rome, where, in the villa of a dear friend, she'd been recovering from her Indian sojourn. The news that Kolina had disappeared from a Swiss boarding school called Bon Coeur had immediately sent Honey off on this present journey. Dirk's voice, via transoceanic phone, had been filled with such desperate urgency and insistence that she could not deny him. Besides, the news that Kolina was officially missing only confirmed their previous fears that the girl was in jeopardy, held against her will. That alone was reason enough for Honey to be concerned and to try to help in any way she could. If there were any causes to which she was fervently, irrevocably committed, they were personal liberty and freedom of choice.

The little village of Klosters did not disappoint her memory of it. Though she had been there several times in winter for the area's excellent skiing, this was her first visit in the spring. The quaint little chalets dotting the hills around the town looked strangely naked sitting in plush velvet green rather than amid drifts of snowy white. Flowers were blooming everywhere, draping over balconies, filling window-boxes, even decorating mailboxes. At the other side of town, past the steepled, whitewashed *kirche,* her driver crossed the bridge over the Landquart River and took the road that wound up the side of the mountain, following the carved wood signs for Bon Coeur. Eventually the stone gates of the school itself came into view, and the sleek, long limousine turned off the main road and passed under the arched entrance and up the tree-lined drive. Honey leaned forward in anticipation.

The stately old stone buildings of Bon Coeur came into view, looking much like her own alma mater—refined, monied, full of tradition and respect for academic knowledge. Surrounded by towering pines and century-old maples, the grounds looked like those of an exclusive private club with sweeping expanses of closely mown grass. Stone terraces and benches were scattered about, offering stunning vistas of the Alps and the tiny village in the valley far below. Schoolgirls ranging in age from six to eighteen, wearing a full uniform of short blue-and-green plaid skirt, smart blue blazer, white blouse with dark blue tie, and white knee socks, strolled about the grounds in small groups, or sat under trees alone, studying or just enjoying the sparkling sunshine. Honey had a sudden twinge of memory and felt a sweet longing for her dear school chum, Disa Dichter, whom she had not seen for weeks. When they had been these girls' age, they'd usually been off in the belfry, ringing their own chimes.

She instructed the driver to pull up before the administration building, and as he parked, she removed from her Venetian leather purse a gold Tiffany compact, making a quick survey of her face and hair. Remembering her old headmistress's stern, matriarchal manner had prompted Honey to dress conservatively in a very tailored, midnight-blue tweed suit by Ungaro, with low Charles Jordan pumps. She had even swept up her deep red hair into a modified French roll, leaving wispy tendrils on either side of her face to soften the severity. She waited until the elderly chauffeur opened her door, then slid out with a grateful smile, telling him in French to please wait. She walked up the brick stairs and entered the imposing structure, feeling suddenly very young and yet very out of place.

Inside the high-ceilinged reception area, Honey was immediately approached by a sweet-faced, uniformed schoolgirl with inquisitive eyes, who asked in French, "May I help you?"

Flawlessly, Honey replied in the same tongue, "I have an appointment with Mademoiselle Orleans. My name is Honey Wildon."

The young girl's eyes widened. "The journalist? I just love your columns. We all read them here."

"Merci," Honey replied and was promptly ushered through a side door into a small waiting room. The sweet

young thing smiled shyly. "I'll be right back." She knocked softly on an inner door and opened it, shutting it behind her. Shortly she reappeared, holding the door wide, her eyes playing adult games. "Mademoiselle Orleans will see you now."

Smiling her thanks at the delectable child, who could not have been more than fifteen, Honey breezed into the headmistress's office. The room was lined with books, and opposite the door, in a draped, windowed alcove, stood a large desk. Behind it, in a high-backed leather chair, sat a prim young woman with horn-rimmed glasses, her hands folded tightly on the desktop before her. Honey stopped in surprise. "Mademoiselle Orleans?"

"*Oui*," the young woman replied solemnly, and stood. Her slender figure was covered by a severely styled dress of somber gray, and her auburn hair was pulled tightly up into a small topknot. She offered a hand over the desk without a smile. "*Enchanté.*"

Honey took the cool hand and shook it, trying to read the face behind the glasses, behind the mask of propriety. She laughed lightly. "I was expecting a much older woman. *My* headmistress was old enough to be my grandmother."

Mademoiselle Orleans frowned and sat herself in the chair. "Age has little to do with ability," she said as she waved a hand toward the straight-backed chair in front of the desk. She waited until Honey sank into it before speaking in very precise English: "You must forgive me, but I have many matters to attend to. Your telephone request for an interview was rather vague. Just what is it you want from us?"

Honey crossed her long legs and decorously adjusted her skirt. "I am attempting to track down Kolina Svenson."

The face across the desk flickered with discomfort before it once again became sternly stoic. "Why, may I ask?"

"Because the authorities have been unable to find her and I have every reason to believe she is in great danger."

Again a small frown creased the brow of Mademoiselle Orleans. "Are you planning on writing an exposé on Bon Coeur, is that it?"

"No, this is entirely a personal matter." Honey was not certain, but there could have been a slight softening of the headmistress's stiff formality. "I know Kolina's disappearance was beyond the control of the school, and I wouldn't want to do anything that would be detrimental to Bon Coeur's sterling reputation."

For the first time a small, unsure smile greeted her. "We thank you for your discretion."

Honey returned the smile with a dazzling one of her own. "I was merely hoping that you might be able to recall something that would give me a lead."

A slight, very French shrug moved the slim shoulders behind the desk. "I'm afraid I've given all I know to the authorities, Miss Wildon."

Internally debating her next move, Honey opened her tailored suit jacket, tugging open the cravat of her white silk blouse. "Please, call me Honey. And your first name is?"

The prim headmistress stiffened. "Claude," she answered hesitantly. "But here we are not so quick with first names as you are in your country."

"I mean no disrespect, be assured. I only want to be of help to you and your fine school."

"I do not see how you could help, when all the authorities have failed."

"Try me," Honey replied with an open smile. "Believe

me, my worldwide contacts have already in place a network of feelers."

"Feelers?" Claude Orleans repeated, a slight blush invading her cheeks under the black-rimmed glasses. "I'm afraid I dot not understand."

"Information—people on the look out for the missing girl," she said easily. "Perhaps I could begin by looking at Kolina's school file. That would give me a better idea of the girl."

Abruptly, Claude Orleans swiveled her chair to the partially draped window beside the desk. Disconsolately she stared out for several moments, seemingly on the verge of tears. Honey was thinking of things she might say to console her, when she became aware of the young woman's elegant profile. Backlit by the diffuse light from the window, Claude Orleans possessed a perfectly lovely facial silhouette—a graceful brow, an aquiline nose that would have been at home on any classical statue, a chin that was almost a shade too determined, and a long, swanlike neck. Her body was trim, like a gymnast's.

Honey chastised herself for being so put off by the young woman's initially cold manner that she had failed to note her physical attractions. Claude's skin was as smooth and clear as pale silk, and her auburn hair glowed healthily in spite of the severe style. Her consciousness of Claude's natural loveliness increased Honey's desire to be the young woman's friend. She stood and moved silently behind Claude's chair, placing a gentle hand on her shoulder. "It must be very difficult for you, Claude," she said intimately. "I can imagine how you feel, being totally responsible for all these young girls and suddenly, through no fault of your own, losing one like this . . . and so mysteriously. You must be under a terrible strain."

Claude raised her face, and behind her glasses, her

clear, nut-colored eyes were moist with tears. *"Très, très tragique.* Kolina is a magnificently gifted and intelligent child. And so beautiful she breaks your heart just to look at her."

"Yes . . . yes, I know," Honey murmured.

"You know? But how? Did you ever meet her?"

Honey reached into her suit jacket and extracted Dirk's photo. Claude took it as if it were a religious artifact and, gazing at it, burst into tears. "Sweet, sweet Kolina," she sobbed. "It's all . . . all my fault."

"How could it be?" she comforted, squeezing Claude's shoulder gently. "The police report I read this morning in Zurich verified that Kolina vanished sometime after the evening bed check and the following morning's roll call. It would have been impossible for you to have an inkling as to what might transpire."

With a trembling hand, Claude removed her glasses to wipe the flowing tears from her eyes. "But she was my responsibility. I cannot forget that." Her head snapped up. "Ever."

Honey stared into the fiery brown eyes and at the fragile beauty of her face. Without her glasses, Claude looked so vulnerable, so young, barely older than some of the girls outside the door. A faint stirring erupted in Honey's loins, and she fought to ignore it. "You poor darling," she said, and sat on the edge of the desk. "There are some things in life that are totally beyond our control. We must learn to accept them. *C'est la vie,* no? Let us feel responsible for the matters we do have control over or an influence upon—like finding Kolina."

Claude searched Honey's eyes imploringly, as if wanting desperately to believe, then suddenly grabbed one of Honey's hands with both of hers, raising it to her lips to kiss it. *"Merci,* Honey . . . *merci,"* she whispered into it.

Then, as if embarrassed by her unladylike show of emotion, she dropped the hand and put on the black-rimmed glasses.

Honey reached out and, with the back of a hand, softly stroked the young woman's tear-streaked cheek. "Courage, Claude—like the Maid of Orleans—faith and courage. All will be well."

The young woman melted at once, her strong stern facade crumbling visibly into a welter of emotions. The tears started again, and Honey was moved to lean down and kiss her soft lips. Claude's sharp intake of breath revealed less than did her mouth, which pressed back, returning the kiss in full.

A knock at the door brought Claude to her feet and around the desk like a startled doe. With some amusement, Honey watched Claude covering her embarrassment, firming her back. "*Entre,*" she said in a quavering but determined tone.

The door popped open and the sweet-faced student with the knowing eyes stepped in, surveying her headmistress before turning a bold gaze on Honey. "Pardon, but soon I am going to my English lesson," she said in French. "Will you be needing me for anything more?"

"*Oui,* Brigitte," Claude responded, once more in complete control of her formidable presence. "Will you please find Kolina's file for Miss Wildon? And make yourself available for an interview if she so desires?"

Honey stood and smiled openly at the charming girl. "You're Brigitte Deauville? Kolina's roommate?"

"Yes," the girl said quickly. "How did you know?"

"Miss Wildon," Claude began, all efficiency, "is a renowned journalist whose business is to know things like that. Now, please, take Miss Wildon to the records room and get her Kolina's file and anything else she may ask for." The headmistress turned to Honey. "We may continue our session after you've checked all you want."

"*Merci,* Mademoiselle Orleans," Honey said graciously, and moved to join Brigitte by the open door. "I will be looking forward to that enormously. *Adieu* for now."

Outside the office, Brigitte's posture drooped into a more contemporary slouch and she eyed Honey brazenly as they walked down the hall to the records room. Honey took the opportunity to question the girl about the night of Kolina's disappearance. Alas, Brigitte furnished no new information. Kolina had been in their room when Brigitte fell asleep, and was not there upon her awakening. And no, she could not imagine what had become of her. And no, she knew of no boyfriends or enemies who would be involved. Kolina was loved by everyone.

Kolina's school file offered little that Honey had not already learned. The girl was in the top five percentile of her class scholastically and was involved in numerous extracurricular activities, from playing a position on the field hockey team to winning an all-school poetry prize, to playing the lead in *Hamlet* the year before. As Honey sat in the stuffy records room, which was crammed with cabinets and dusty ledgers, Brigitte slumped against the table, observing her every movement. Occasionally, Honey would raise her head to ask a question and find the girl staring with obvious interest. Brigitte was blessed with rosy cheeks and a pouty little mouth that demanded attention. Her uniform was deliberately designed by the school to cover any budding pubescence, but her manner left little to the imagination. The girl was already more than sexually aware, Honey guessed. It was apparent in her steady knowing gaze. Honey did her best to concentrate on the file before her, but a soft rustling sound broke her efforts.

Leaning against the closed door, Brigitte had removed her blazer and was slowly unbuttoning her blouse under the wide blue tie. Through lowered lashes, her eyes simmered. "I think you are the most beautiful woman I've ever seen," she said, her young voice dripping with sexual innuendo.

"Thank you for the compliment," Honey said, as coolly as she could under the circumstances, "but I'm afraid you have an overly active imagination."

Brigitte threw back her tie over one shoulder and parted her blouse seductively. Her surprisingly mature breasts burst into view, their dark centers enticingly firm, like plums ready to be plucked from a tree.

"Brigitte," Honey sighed in warning from her chair, "you are a fetching bundle, to be sure, but now is not the time or the place. *Je vous remercie,* anyway."

"You are 'chicken'—is that not the right word?"

"Right. Now cover yourself before we find more than we can handle."

"I want you to handle me ... please ... just a little?" She bounced forward and thrust her teasing tits into Honey's face. A firm young hand snaked around Honey's neck, pressing her head forward toward the tempting offerings. Honey had little desire to resist. She stuck out her tongue and sampled one of the plump brown nipples by taking a discreet lick. Abruptly, Brigitte jerked Honey's head closer, jamming the tender young breast fully into her face. The youthful flesh tasted sweet and fresh, but Honey twisted away. "Sometime later, my pet," she said, and stood with great difficulty, her knees quaking with desire. She managed to move to the other side of the conference table, where she looked back with a longing gaze.

Brigitte had flung herself flat on the tabletop and hiked up her skirt over her waist, shoving a hand down her pristine white panties. "I am hot for you," Brigitte panted, her fingers speedily working under the tight white cotton. "See?" she croaked, and snapped down the waistband of her panties to her firm young thighs. Her pussy lay open like a halved walnut, the fringe of soft brown hair like foliage around an oasis. She parted the tender lips even further with her fingers. "Eat me . . . I'm begging you . . . eat me before I cry."

With a resolve she had difficulty calling into play, Honey shook her head sadly and remained on her own side of the table. "Brigitte," she admonished. "You are only making it hard on both of us. Cover yourself at once, before—"

The door behind Honey flew open and the headmistress stepped into the room, carrying a fat file folder. A squeal of astonishment and anger broke from her open mouth. "Brigitte!" she hissed. The girl jumped from the table, frantically trying to cover herself. Immediately contrite, she pulled her blazer over her still-open blouse and, ducking her head, ran past the startled headmistress and disappeared down the hall.

Claude Orleans turned an icy glare on Honey and, head held high on her long neck, sputtered in rage, "C'est incroyable!" With that, she spun on her heel and stalked out of the room, slamming the door behind her.

Moments later, Honey knocked on her office door and, without waiting for a reply, walked in. Claude Orleans whirled from the window where she had been weeping. "How dare you come in without my—"

Honey shut the door forcefully behind her, cutting off Claude's outburst. With a mischievous glint in her eye, Honey snapped the lock on the big oak door and marched to the desk. "Claude," she said, "I am innocent of any wrongdoing. Brigitte is a precocious, forward young lady who flung herself at me. What was I to do?"

"Leave the room at once."

"Now or then?"

"Both," Claude snapped.

"Well, I didn't, and I won't," Honey fumed. "You are a blind fool if you don't think that kind of thing goes on at a girls' school. My first lover was my roommate, and we still get it on whenever we're together. She taught me more about about love and sexual pleasure than anyone I've had since, and it all began at a girls school exactly like Bon Coeur. Surely you are aware that it is normal and healthy to—"

It was Claude's turn to cut in, and she did so with a vengeance. "I am not concerned with your disgusting escapades away from this school. What I am deeply concerned about is how you conduct yourself while you are here . . . as a *guest*. I have never been so thoroughly mortified by anyone's actions before. I am deeply disappointed that a woman of your position—"

Honey couldn't take it a moment longer. She strode around the desk as if to strike Claude. Instead, Honey grabbed the young woman's shoulders, pulled her close, and kissed her fervently and feverishly on the lips. Claude struggled in her embrace, but Honey would not let her squirm free. She pressed her breasts into the taut, slender frame until she began to feel Claude soften and respond.

With a groan of surrender, Claude threw her arms around Honey, and her torso collapsed with a growing passion. They hugged each other, kissing each other's faces, their breaths quickening, scorching the air between them. Honey caressed Claude's back and trailed a hand down to stroke the soft buttocks beneath the gray jersey skirt. Honey skilfully laid her back over the desktop, bringing up a thigh and pressing it on Claude's mons veneris. Even through the layers of clothing, Claude's pussy felt as hot as a volcano ready to erupt. Wanting to fire it even more, Honey slipped a hand up Claude's leg, over and around inside the knee, up the thigh to the top of the stockings, across the swatch of silky skin to the front of Claude's panties. Honey was surprised to find that the headmistress's choice of lingerie was more daring than her outer garments. The panties were of lace, and skimpy, very French and soaking wet over the crotch. Excited by the discovery, Honey poked a friendly finger under a side of the panties and had just reached her goal when Claude clamped her thighs tightly together.

"My students," she panted.

"Screw your students," Honey rejoined.

"I wish I had the nerve," Claude confessed in the throes of the embrace.

"Try me instead." Honey stood and reached for her purse on the edge of the desk. From its depths she brought out her trusty ivory dildo—a piece of traveling equipment she was never without. She licked one bulbous end of the nine-inch piece of ancient artwork, which looked like a Pompeiian phallus, and rubbed it wantonly over her own pussy mound, her tongue flicking her parted lips.

Claude stared in shocked amazement, her brown eyes blinking, however, with more than casual interest. "I couldn't . . ." she breathed.

"Oh, yes you could," Honey teased, and placed a spread palm on the upturned mound just beneath the gray skirt. She applied pressure and leaned down to order firmly, "Get up, my sweet pussy. We're moving to the couch." She tugged Claude up and propelled her toward the leather couch in front of an overflowing bookcase.

With the sureness born of long practice, Honey unbuttoned Claude's dress, despite her protests, and slipped it over her pale, slender shoulders, letting it drop to the carpet. Claude stood, a vision of trim desirability in tiny red lace panties, black garter belt, dark stockings, and a mere wisp of a bra that Honey tore away with one quick motion. Claude's breasts were not large—mere handfuls, really—but they were so perfectly shaped that they looked as if they'd been painted by da Vinci. Their nipples were tiny pink seashells, and yet they stood out from the muscular mounds with demanding tumescence. While hurriedly tearing off her traveling suit, Honey lowered her mouth to suck on one of the delectable tidbits, and could feel Claude shaking with almost uncontrollable lust. That only raised Honey's fires, and she quickly finished undressing, stepping out of her heels and stripping off her pantyhose to stand nude and proud.

Claude drank in her beauty, her eyes growing to twice their usual size. With a cry she fell on one of Honey's large breasts like a babe long denied a feeding. While she sucked, Honey backed to the couch and lowered herself to the soft, cool leather cushions, bringing Claude down on top of her. Wrapping her long legs around the headmistress, Honey pushed against Claude and they ground their mounds together as if they were two stones grinding flour. Still clutched in one of Honey's hands was the ancient ivory dildo Disa had given her so long ago. She rubbed it down Claude's backbone and over the slim but exciting derriere, and up and down the crevice between her buttocks. Claude writhed with delight and brought her head up to engage Honey in a fevered session of French kissing.

Soon Honey was on top, kneeling between Claude's thighs, removing the drenched bit of red lace from her hips. Along with the panties came the garter belt and eventually the silk stockings. Now Claude was just as naked as Honey was and the latter gazed down reverently at the revealed wonders. Claude's delta of Venus was like a rosy croissant hot from the oven. Honey swooped to it with her mouth and funneled the lips open with her nose, followed close behind by her tongue. The headmistress tasted of baked apples, naturally sweet, full of delicious juices and steaming with heat. Honey lapped lustily and locked on the small protuberance which was the very core of Claude's sexuality. Tonguing it, she simultaneously ran her hands up Claude's trunk, landing on her small, tight breasts, flicking her long fingernails over the hard buttons of her nipples. Claude was moaning and swooning with such abandonment that Honey could tell the young woman was close to coming.

Honey rammed the hard bone of the dildo deep into the flaming trench, and Claude squealed, arching her back, then drove her pussy down on the old ivory, plunging it up to Honey's fingertips. Holding tightly to the double-headed dildo, Honey maneuvered herself over the free end, pulled it out a bit to allow herself a fair share, and inserted it into her own moist pussy. Then, her hands free, she pressed one on her own clitoris, seeking Claude's with the other. Rocking up and down, she drove the old white bone in and out of both their twats, feeling her own glorious sensations while providing Claude with a surfeit of sensual splendors. Claude was grasping her shoulders, gasping for air while totally unladylike sounds came from her throat. Her head was thrown back on the cushion, her eyes closed as if she were having the lesson of her life. Spasms started wracking her body and she increased her movements, her eyes glazing over and rolling back in their sockets. With a series of grunts she began climaxing, and continued to do so until Honey caught up with her. Together they came again and again, rocking and rolling on the ivory centerpiece like two bitches in heat.

It was some time before they cooled down enough to take stock of themselves. They discovered with shock that Claude was due at a faculty meeting in less than five minutes. Rapidly they disentangled themselves and flung their clothes on, grinning at each other like two conspirators in a Tangiers marketplace. Claude was hastily repiling her hair into the tight bun when Honey thought of something in Kolina's file.

"Claude, my pet," she purred as she stepped, stockingless, into her low pumps, "what was this poetry prize Kolina won last year?"

"Very prestigious and very deserved. Sponsored by Chateau Bouscaral."

"The famous French winery?"

"The Marquise Bouscaral endorsed the generous grant that makes the reward possible," Claude explained as she tried to smooth her wrinkled skirt. "And the Marquise herself invited Kolina down to her chateau on several occasions. She was most gracious and attentive to the poor child. As was her son."

"I don't remember anything in Kolina's files, here or in Zurich, about the Bouscarals knowing Kolina."

Claude turned to her with a look of astonishment. "But I am sure I mentioned that to the police."

Honey kissed her tenderly. "Not to worry, my pet. I'll follow through. *Irons-nous faire un petit tour?*"

7.

HONEY

In the Bordeaux region of France, Chateau Bouscaral sat like an ornate centerpiece in the vast vineyards that marched in neat rows up and down the rolling landscape. As Honey drove the rented Citröen up the curved drive, she felt as though she were stepping back in time—into the days of grandeur and pomp of the French aristocracy. The sprawling, many-winged, single-story chateau, built in the mid-eighteenth century, was capped at each end by tall, conical-crowned turrets. The simple, long, low lines of the tan stone chateau and the stately, formal gardens in front bespoke of titled wealth handed down through the same family century after century.

She was greeted at the massive, hand-carved doors by a petite maid in traditional black dress with white apron and cap, who politely led her through the opulently appointed entrance hall lined with exquisite Flemish tapestries. Each room they passed through was filled with immense artistic riches: Persian drinking bowls, Chinese wine vessels, a huge wooden horse ridden by a man-sized dummy; Honey recognized the latter as models used by seventeenth-century Italian painters. Inside a drawing room decorated in a decidedly feminine style she was told to wait, and the maid discreetly withdrew. Left to her own devices, Honey wandered about the lovely room, admiring the relatively modern masterpieces adorning the walls; among her favorites were a de la Resnaye and a large Picasso from his blue period.

Her reverie was interrupted by the arrival of the *grand dame* herself, the present-day driving force behind the successful, much-honored winery, Marquise Berengere-Marie Bouscaral. Honey was surprised at the youthful vitality of the aristocratic-looking woman. Tall, slim, silver-haired, the Marquise held herself with the erectness and bearing of a woman who enjoyed fully her exalted position in life. Wearing an "at home" long gown of heavy pink satin, she glided into the drawing room like a queen, gracious and regal.

"Miss Wildon," she greeted Honey in a lovely, deep voice in faintly accented English, "it is indeed an honor to welcome you to Chateau Bouscaral."

Honey took the proffered hand covered with sparkling jewels, as she replied, "Madame La Marquise, I am the one who is honored. Thank you for receiving me on such short notice."

Briefly they exchanged pleasantries; Honey's hand was held by the Marquise as if it were one of the rare crystal decanters lining the glass shelf near them. At last the *grand dame* let it go, almost reluctantly, and moved to an embroidered wall cord, which she pulled to summon tea to be served. They sat on moire-silk-covered Louis XV chairs before a pink marble fireplace that was ablaze with a small, neatly laid fire in spite of the bright sunshine outside the open French doors leading to a garden terrace. Sipping tea from bone china cups, they chatted about inconsequential matters: the fine spring weather, the difficulty of finding suitable help, St. Laurent's new Parisian collection, mutual friends they discovered in common. In a very short time, Honey felt quite at ease and she sensed the feeling was reciprocal. She decided the moment was right to get to the pressing purpose of her visit.

"Madame La Marquise," Honey began with her trademark smile, "forgive me for leading you on. I am not here to write about your superb winery—although someday soon I would love to do just that. What brought me here was something most urgent, and I would be extremely grateful for any help you might be able to give."

A look of concern spread over the regal visage of the older woman. "I am at your service," she intoned. "Pray, do tell me how I might help."

Honey took a deep breath and plunged in. "I have recently come from Bon Coeur in Klosters. I understand you are acquainted with the recipient of last year's school poetry prize, Kolina Svensen."

"Oh, my, yes," the Marquise replied with a broad smile. "Lovely child, and quite talented. She was our guest here at the chateau on several occasions."

"When was the last time you saw Kolina?"

"My, let me recall . . . I believe it was over the Christmas holidays. Yes, I'm sure of it now. The Baron de Rothschild was also a guest for New Year's, and he was quite taken with her. Kolina is a true delight. Everyone who meets her is enchanted at once."

Thoughtfully, Honey studied the beautiful, unlined face before her. "Have you been in touch with her since then?"

"No. Why do you ask?"

"Because she has been missing for over a month."

A bejewelled hand flew to the Marquise's face like a dove. "Oh, no! How tragic. How unfortunate. Do tell me the circumstances."

The Marquise's alarm was so genuine that Honey knew at once she was not fabricating her reaction, and Honey rapidly filled her in on the scant details of Kolina's disappearance. She downplayed her own fears about the girl's being in serious danger, but hinted that she suspected foul play. Upon the conclusion of the brief summary of events, the Marquise's intense blue eyes filled with tears and she was speechless for several moments. Finally she rose, gathering her long skirts in one hand to leave. "You must excuse me, Honey, this news has upset me greatly. Please, I insist you be our guest for the evening. The maid will show you to a room. Dinner will be promptly at eight. My son, Yves, will be back from Marseilles by then, and we can enlist his aid in finding the poor child. Until then, my dear." She swept out of the room, wiping her eyes.

The guest room to which Honey was led by the docile-eyed maid was on the second floor of one of the round turrets. The gilded woodwork glowed in the sunlight from casement windows that overlooked the sweeping drive and the sea of vines beyond. A huge canopy bed stood in the exact center of the round room, surrounded by sheer curtains of peach-colored silk. Her suitcases had already been fetched from her car and unpacked; her clothes were hung in the walk-in closet and folded neatly in the drawers of the large rosewood armoire. Looking forward to meeting the Marquise's son, Honey took a leisurely bath in a large, claw-footed tub in the adjoining bathroom. The fixtures were of solid gold, and the array of oils and bath salts on the dressing table offered a wide variety of delectable aromas. Upon rising from the mountains of rose-scented bubbles, Honey was pleasantly intrigued to see the young maid enter to dry her off with a luxuriously large bath sheet.

Not used to such amenities, but definitely enjoying the experience, Honey stood watching the young woman, who ever so gently rubbed her dry. As if polishing a marble statue, the maid caressed Honey's bounteous curves, paying special attention to her large, full breasts. Honey could not help herself; the soft touch on her alabaster skin, conmbined with the serious, intent gaze of the pretty young maid, stimulated Honey's nipples and they jutted up, hardening to an obvious state of arousal. As if used to such occurrences, the maid stoically continued her duties and knelt to deal with the lower portion of Honey's anatomy, carefully wiping down each long leg and even spreading apart her toes to dry between them. At last the young maid returned to the center of Honey's ripe figure, wiping her buttocks. Finally, kneeling before Honey's fiery red bush, the young woman brought up a corner of the large towel and dabbed at the labia. Her excitement growing, Honey spread her legs wide, allowing freer access, wondering just how far the young thing was prepared to go.

The more the maid wiped at Honey's lower set of lips, the damper the towel became. As if giving up a lost cause, the maid dropped the towel and from beneath her apron brought out a small onyx-handled brush and proceeded to comb out the soft triangle of red hair, plumping up the bush into a bonfire of beauty. While Honey trembled with rising heat, the young maid surveyed her handiwork and, satisfied, redeposited the brush beneath her apron. Dried, teased, and coiffed, Honey waited with bated breath for the next domestic duties of the serious-eyed maid. Alas, the young woman rose from her knees and asked politely in French, "Will that be all, Mademoiselle?"

Honey could barely find breath to answer. "Unless you want to eat my cunt," she rasped in English.

"Pardon? I do not speak your language," the maid replied, again in French, with a saucy toss of her head.

Not wanting to press her demands or insult the Marquise's hospitality, Honey sighed, "*Très bien. Merci.*" Reluctantly she pulled on her traveling robe and, with a sad smile, walked unsteadily from the bathroom.

A few minutes before eight, Honey, elegantly gowned in a striking black and white dress by Givenchy and refreshed by a long nap in the canopied bed, entered the large, formal dining room. The Marquise was already seated at the head of a long, white-damask-covered table laden with crystal and silver. Bowls overflowing with spring wildflowers of the region had been placed strategically about. Honey bent to kiss the lightly powdered cheeks of the Marquise.

"*Très, très jolie,*" the Marquise praised Honey's stunning beauty, and waved her graciously into the chair on her left. "My son will be down shortly. Do you mind waiting?"

Honey said she did not and they sampled an exquisite champagne, nibbling on fresh caviar from Caspian sturgeon, *foie gras des Landes,* and smoked Scotch salmon on toasted crisp wheat bread. Shortly, Yves Bouscaral strode into the room in formal velvet dinner clothes, a man in his mid-forties who was obviously at ease with himself and the world around him. Ruggedly built, with gentle brown eyes, he appraised Honey warmly, kissed his mama devotedly, sat opposite Honey, and began at once to get soused on all the lovely home-grown wines that accompanied each course, and for which Chateau Bouscaral was renowned worldwide.

By the dessert, raspberries with *crème fraîche,* Honey was also feeling the heady effects of all the scrumptious wines, but her impatience had grown because the Marquise had yet to bring up the subject of the missing Kolina. Even though the lovely older woman had drunk just as much as her son and honored guest, she remained alert, loquacious, witty, and decidedly charming. It was not until the rich, black demitasse coffee was served that the Marquise inquired of Yves if he had been aware that Kolina was missing from Bon Coeur.

"Mon Dieu," he cried, with just a shade too much shock. Abruptly his flushed cheeks drained of color and he reached for a newly opened bottle of champagne. Pouring a healthy glassful, he looked across at Honey, who was eyeing him suspiciously. "Tell me, Miss Wildon, why are you involved in this messy business?" His words were slurred, his tone cool.

She smiled as best she could. "I am a friend of her sister, Barbro," she lied. "She asked me to help, as the authorities are getting nowhere with the case."

"Ah, Barbro," he muttered, and nodded into his wine. "Kolina showed me her photograph once. Is she still shaking her belly in Lima?"

"Cartagena," Honey furnished, not trusting the man's responses. She proceeded to question him about his relationship with Kolina, and about the last time he had seen the girl. Although all his answers agreed with those of the Marquis, Honey had the distinct impression he was witholding something. Her many years as a seasoned journalist had helped her develop a keen sixth sense—"a built-in shit detector" was how she termed it—and it now warned her that Yves Bouscaral knew more than he was letting on. The scent of the hunt quickened her blood, but she feigned sleepiness and, thanking the Marquise for a lovely meal, bade her *bonne nuit,* to retire upstairs to her turret room.

Naked, she lay between the cool silk sheets of the large

canopied bed, thinking back over Yves's evasive responses and waiting patiently until the chateau was silent. Not until the nearly full moon was high in the sky, flooding one side of the round room with a ghostly white light, did she deem it safe to follow through on her plan. Quickly she slipped out of bed. Pulling on an almost gossamer robe, she padded barefoot down the steep, winding stone stairs of her separate bedroom tower. Moving swiftly down the darkened hallways, she made her way to the west wing. As she passed through the all-glass solarium connecting the wing to the main building, her luscious curves were silhouetted starkly against the moonlight.

Reaching the door to Yves's suite of rooms, she paused long enough to fluff her waves of titian hair off her face, then tried the doorknob. Damn, the door was locked from the inside. Undaunted, she tapped with her knuckles and pressed her ear against the hardwood. She could hear a startled male voice whispering, then the sound of an inner door closing. Honey smiled to herself—the chateau was even more alive at night.

Momentarily the door opened a crack and Yves's pale face poked out. His jaw dropped in surprise. *"Qu'est que c'est?"* he croaked.

"Mon cher, I cannot sleep," she purred, and leaned against the door, shoving it open easily. As he stood aside reluctantly, she slipped by him and shut the door quietly behind her. She leaned against the door, one knee slightly raised, a rounded thigh shaping her sheer robe, her full breasts straining at the loosely tied bodice. "Perhaps you could give me something to make me sleepy," she suggested.

Even in the flickering light of the single fat candle by his rumpled, king-sized bed, she could see Yves blush deeply. His embarrassment touched her and she thought perhaps she might have misjudged him. He seemed so disconcerted, standing there fidgeting with the belt of his heavy, full-length robe. She crossed to him to ease his worries, and placed a cool hand on his fevered brow. "Relax, my pet," she said softly, while pressing her heavy breasts into his chest. "I'm sure that with the proper care my insomnia will be cured. Just hold me for a moment."

She waited for him to put his arms around her, and was disappointed to feel him shrinking from her. She stood on her tiptoes to kiss him gently, smelling the wine and a lime-scented cologne. Still, he did not respond as planned, and she pulled away with a little pout. "Pardon, Yves, I was just feeling a little lonely ... what a lovely big room this is." She made a slow tour of the room, pretending to be admiring the heavy antique furnishings and the suits of shining armor in the corners, but the whole while trying to decide behind which door leading off his bedroom stood the hastily banished bed partner. She also used her expressed interest in his room as an excuse to display her lightly covered body to its best advantage.

Breasts pointed to the ceiling, she stretched up to touch the cold nose of a boar's head hanging on the wall; she bent, ass projected at him, to rub the fur on the head of the polar bear rug, and near him, she leaned gracefully over his writing desk to study the first edition of Flaubert's *Madame Bovary* thus "accidentally" showing a copious amount of snow-white bosom. She managed to get her robe caught on the corner of a chair and it parted briefly to the waist, flashing the red beacon of her loins before she hastily covered herself. She ended up sinking onto one hip on his bed and looking back at him seductively over one shoulder.

He wasn't even looking at her! He had crossed to the window and was staring out as if the moon were more attainable than she was. "Yves," she called softly, and when he turned, she added in a husky voice, "Come here, at once."

Obediently he did so, and stood beside the bed. She reached up and, taking one of his hands, pulled him to a sitting position. "Yves, I know you think me terribly brazen and forward," she began, all contriteness. "And I admire your sensitivity. Forgive me for forcing my attentions on you. You are so terribly attractive, and my stay here is so brief . . . I couldn't resist the temptation."

He smiled nervously. "Miss Wildon . . ."

"Please, call me Honey."

"Honey . . . you are too beautiful and too intelligent to choose me indiscriminately. What is the real reason you seek my attention?"

"*Touché,* Yves," she said good-naturedly. "Very perceptive. I'll be just as direct as you are. You're holding something back about Kolina. I want to know what." She smiled genuinely. "But if you want to fuck all night, that's okay too."

He laughed. It was open and unforced, and elicited a similar one from her. Warmly he put his arm about her. "I like you, Honey."

She snuggled into his shoulder, finding the feeling mutual. "Well, then, do you want to talk first or after we get it on a few times?"

He grew serious again and withdrew his arm. "To be perfectly honest, I would prefer neither. But since you are here and since I am disturbed about the news of Kolina . . . I'll make a deal with you. I'll give you what you want and you, in return, give me what I want."

"I'm game . . . *if* I'm capable of returning the favor."

He smiled mysteriously. "Oh, I'm quite certain of that. Is it a deal, then?"

She studied his face, trying to determine just how kinky he was. Well, she decided, whatever it was, it most likely wouldn't be the first time for her. She figured she could handle anything he had up his sleeve . . . or anywhere else, for that matter. She smiled widely. "It's a deal, Yves. You talk. Then I'll see what's on that twisted little mind of yours."

Instead of expressing pleasure at the bargain, as she was expecting, he became somber-faced again and stared toward the moon-drenched window. "What I am about to tell you is only speculation. I have no way of knowing if it could be true. But I always suspected Kolina would run off one day . . . with some man." He swiveled his gaze to her. "She was quite precocious, I'm afraid. She proudly told me once that she had been sexually active since she was twelve."

"So what?" Honey said with a grin. "So was I."

"But I'm certain you showed much more discretion and restraint. Kolina was always infatuated with someone —*obsessed* would be a better word. She could easily have run away with her latest."

Honey nodded, digesting the information. "Is that all?"

"Yes. I'm afraid it is not much, but a deal is a deal, no?"

She laughed. "I've a funny feeling I've been had."

"Not yet," he replied, and nodded to the center door opposite them. "Go open that door."

Getting into the spirit of the exchange, she bounced off the bed and flew to the indicated door, flinging it open, expecting anything but what she discovered on the other side. Crouched nude, down where the keyhole had been, a muscular youth pumped on his thick, hard cock. He jumped up in surprise and Honey gulped at his size and mammoth physical attributes. He looked carved out of

99

granite, and his chiseled face bore a rugged handsomeness. But Honey could not take her eyes off his rock-hard prick, which jutted out from him like a thick log. It was his most impressive feature.

"Honey," Yves called jovially from bed, "meet Philippe. Now come here, you two."

Accompanied by the rugged, grinning youth, Honey strolled back to the bed, making her movements as provocative as possible for Yves's enjoyment. Once again, however, she noted that he was not watching her; this time his eyes were caressing the handsome hunk next to her.

"Philippe is one of my grape-pickers," Yves was explaining. "His family has been in service to my family for over two hundred years."

"*Enchanté*," Honey said to the brawny youth, who could not raise his eyes from her snow-white breasts. She grabbed his sturdy pole. Unable to get her fingers fully around it, she pumped it up and down as if shaking hands. Philippe laughed boyishly and palm-patted each of her breasts, as if playing patty-cake.

"Philippe," Yves ordered sternly and rose from the bed, speaking in French. "Take off her robe."

Eagerly the lad yanked at her gossamer robe, pulling it from her shoulders. Approvingly, his hungry eyes swept over her. She noticed that Yves also had removed his robe and stood watching the two of them. His cock was flaccid and uncircumcised and looked like a deflated balloon hanging between his legs. Yves swept a hand toward the bed, commanding in French, "She has been a naughty girl, Philippe. Ravish her."

In a split second, Honey found herself hurled to the bed on her back and the horny, immense Philippe straddling her belly, one heavy thigh pressing down on either side. His meaty, callused hands held her wrists over her head, flat back on the velvet quilt. His blood-thickened prick poked at her fleshy breasts like a battering ram.

Not as turned on by the sudden activity as she would have liked, she decided that if Yves was giving the orders, she could still express her own will. Bucking her hips, trying to throw off Philippe's weight, she rolled back and forth energetically, displaying surprising strength.

Her efforts were so great that, at one point, the hefty lad was hurled from her torso onto the mattress. "Philippe!" Yves admonished from a nearby armchair, and the youth renewed his efforts with a look of grim determination. Easily he regained the upper hand and was soon forcing his big dick to her mouth. She made him work for his rewards, but soon set about sucking as much of his enormous appendage as she could. With his tight cheeks resting on her breasts, he thrust again and again into her wide-open mouth, but still she could get less than half of him in. She concentrated instead on tormenting his joy knob until she was evoking sharp cries of pleasure. Athletically he swiveled himself around, and supporting his weight on his hands and toes, his body a rigid plank above her, he dove into her moist, sweet meat.

Honey took the moment to cast a glance at Yves. He sat in the cushioned chair not far from the side of the bed, watching them as if they were his own private, wide-screen entertainment. In one hand he grasped his puny but stiff pecker, attacking it with determination. The vision of a finally aroused Yves, in addition to the wonders that Philippe's tongue was working within her, set Honey off into a paroxysm of electrical jolts. Her pussy began to feel as sticky as a melting caramel candy. She grabbed the stiff pole jabbing at her chin, and angled the apple-sized head into her mouth.

"Fuck the bitch now, Philippe," Yves gasped from his chair, and his young stud leapt to the task.

Poised between her legs, he grinned at her and, with the force of a Hercules, jammed his hot prick into her cunt. She gasped at his hugeness and felt as if his heated pole were splitting her apart. Philippe lowered his granite body upon her and pumped and panted, sweated and swore with passion. And all the while, Yves pampered his plump little prick, and Honey, who could only hang on for dear life, felt as though she were being broached by a blimp.

Her flaming funnel began twitching with unreleased tension, and a few more batterings from the magnum prick brought her quickly to a series of explosive climaxes and she began squealing her delight. Almost at once Philippe cried out, "Now, Yves," and he reared back, pulling out his massive meat, and proudly watched his own cannonballs of gism bombard her fleshy breasts. "Bravo, Philippe," Yves bellowed, and Honey rolled her head toward him just as his plump balloon popped with a dribble of white frosting. He sighed happily, "You gave the sweet bitch what she wanted."

It was some time later—after a repeat performance by Philippe, with Yves watching from the foot of the bed—that Honey was able to extricate herself from the room. Weakly she made her way back to her own room, not bothering even to pull on her robe. She felt drained and, indeed, ravished—but, oh, what a lovely sensation! Something was nagging her, however, and as she let herself into the turret room, she realized she still felt that Yves Bouscaral had not told her everything he knew. She decided to call Dirk in the morning and set him on the case. She was going to take a much-deserved day off.

Much to her delight, her canopied bed was not empty. The somber-eyed maid who had helped with her bath lay nude atop the covers. The white moonlight bathed her lovely, slender body with a luminous glow. The pretty young maid smiled betwitchingly from the pillows. "I've been waiting a long time," she said softly in French.

"Then we have much to make up for," Honey said silkenly, and settled down beside her. The maid's breasts were pert and pink, her candy box full of sweet goodies, but Honey was so exhausted she could hardly move. Discouraged but still game, she rolled on her back, opening her legs and patting her red pelt of fur. "Forgive me, sweet one," she yawned, "but I'm afraid this one will have to be all on you. In the morning, I promise, I'll return in kind."

Honey drifted gently to sleep, the obliging young maid lapping at her tender twat like gentle waves upon a beach.

8.

DIRK

In the absurdly ornate lobby of Portugal's Bussaco Palace Hotel, Dirk fidgeted in the telephone booth, waiting impatiently for his call to be connected to Paris. Through the booth's beveled-glass doors, his eyes, however, were locked on the rugged Frenchman across the rococo lobby, sitting by himself, reading a newspaper and sipping brandy.

Eventually the hotel's operator broke in on the line to explain in halting English that his party had been reached. "Honey?" Dirk said quickly into the antique receiver. "You there?"

"Yes, luv," came her lilting voice. "Where are you?"

"Where'd you expect? I got here this morning."

"Have you located Yves?"

Dirk swiveled his head to stare out the glass doors at the man across the lobby. "Yup, he's here, all right. How'd you know he'd be coming?"

"A little maid told me," she giggled. "I would have followed him myself, but I'd already made contact with him. He'd know for certain I didn't believe him. How was your flight from Cartagena?"

"Hated to leave, hate more to be here. This place is weird. Looks like it was designed for some fantasy pavilion at Disneyland."

"The Bussaco Palace is one of the world's best kept secrets," she laughed. "Used to be the hunting lodge for Portuguese kings. It's one of my favorite hideaways. Broaden your horizons, baby brother."

He ignored her sisterly dig. "What are you doing in Paris?"

"Waiting for my darling Disa to return from Munich. I'm hoping she'll be able to help. She knows absolutely everybody who's anybody on the continent."

"I still don't know how I'll learn anything new from this Yves fellow," he sighed. "If *you* couldn't get the truth out of him, how do you expect *me* to?"

"Use your imagination, Dirk," she said lightly. "And, as I said before, don't be so damned provincial you forget to broaden your horizons. Call me as soon as you make contact."

"Are you telling me everything I should know about this fellow?"

"Dirk," she teased, "for pete's sake don't be such an old fuddy-duddy. Yves is perfectly harmless, but he's lying through his teeth."

Dirk was about to respond when he spotted the subject under discussion rising and moving swiftly across the lobby toward the stained-glass front entrance. "Got to run, sis. Yves is on the move. I'll call you soonest. Ciao." He hung up, grabbed his camera bag, and exited the booth, moving rapidly after the disappearing figure.

Outside, on the broad front steps of the bizarrely designed hotel, he hesitated, looking in all directions before spotting Yves Bouscaral scurrying down a path leading into the densely wooded hills that surrounded the former royal hunting lodge. Dirk hurried after him, past the rock-lined reflecting pool graced by several white swans, and into the thick stand of trees. The sunshine of northern Portugal was diffused by the overhanging branches, and the farther Dirk progressed along the winding dirt path, the dimmer the light became. The crisp smell of pine increased as the trail wound steeply up into the hills.

For a long while Dirk followed the path, working up a fierce thirst and not catching so much as a glimpse of his prey. Then, rounding an outcropping of slate, he pulled up short. Up ahead, in a small clearing, the path was bisected by gravel road that followed the crest of the ridge. On the road was a black Rolls touring car, looking oddly out of place in the rustic surroundings. But it was the human factor that held Dirk's interest. Yves was meeting with a man just emerging from the rear seat of the chauffeured Rolls. Dirk ducked behind a tree trunk and quickly opened his camera case, pulling out his Nikon F3 and his 350 mm 5.6 mirror lens. Hastily he assembled the tools of his trade and, after checking the ASA of his film, began snapping a series of pictures of the two men.

Wishing he were closer so that he might hear some of the exchange, he studied the figures framed in his viewfinder. It was more than obvious that Yves was greatly agitated, for his hands and arms waved angrily in the air as he spoke. The other man, whose face was obscured partially by a gray fedora, was replying with an equal amount of Gallic exuberance, shouting back, gesticulating wildly. Yves stomped away, then whirled, hurling still more invective. The other man whipped off his gray hat and slapped his thigh with it in disgust. Seizing the moment, Dirk focused on this man's face and snapped away, his automatic film advancer whirring softly in the still air. Whoever he was, this second man had a face that Dirk would never forget; a pencil-thin mustache made a precise black mark just below the man's nose, giving him an evil, decadent appearance, and his eyes were mere narrow slits of anger.

Abruptly this second man spun to the Rolls and climbed in the back seat again, slamming the door. In a shower of dust and gravel the large black auto shot forward, careening out of sight at the top of the ridge. Yves stared after the departing Rolls and, with a defeated shrug, turned back to the path, heading straight down toward the unseen cameraman. Dirk plunged into the bushes and squatted, waiting for the man to pass. Yves was muttering to himself in French as he stalked by, barely three feet from where Dirk hid.

Dirk followed him back toward the hotel, wondering what could have been so secret about the meeting of the two men that it couldn't have been held in a more public place. The hotel itself was so far from the normal tourist route that it was fairly isolated. And the nearby village of Mealhada was so small, Dirk doubted that such a rendezvous as he had just witnessed would have raised an eyebrow among the natives. Whatever the reason for the clandestine encounter in the woods, it only increased Dirk's growing interest in Yves Bouscaral.

His quarry returned to the front of the hotel and stood with apparent uncertainty on the front steps. Dirk, still in the woods, skirted along the edge and found a suitable spot for further pictures of the man. With the afternoon sun striking the façade of the former palace, all of its intricate details were starkly lit. The many-storied structure was a humorous tangle of battlements, buttresses, towers, turrets, outside staircases, gargoyles, and arches.

The ornateness diminished the lone man on the front steps and made an interesting composition for the photographs. Dirk was so intent upon his camerawork that he almost missed Yves dashing down the steps and into a waiting cab. The local taxi—a small, battered Renault—sped away toward the village.

By the time Dirk could get a cab of his own and reach the sunbaked town, Yves was nowhere to be seen. Cursing his luck, Dirk roamed the narrow streets, checking the many eating and drinking spots that catered to the hotel guests. The sun was setting behind the high hills before he found parked in front of a cafe the taxi that had whisked Yves from the hotel. The driver was a friendly fellow who responded to Dirk's twenty-dollar bill with a desire to help. He pointed down the street toward a stone building and winked lasciviously. "He there," the cabbie said, and winked again.

Dirk nodded his thanks and trotted to the indicated building. He opened the front door and stepped inside. Darkness greeted him, and the disturbing smells of sweat and dirty clothes hung in the heavy, moist air. At first he thought it was a laundry, but as his eyes grew accustomed to the gloom, he couldln't figure out where the hell he was. A small windowed booth off to one side held a baldheaded figure who was beckoning him over. Dirk approached, conscious of how quiet the establishment was. The bald man behind the small counter, whispered, "You want locker or basket?"

"What is this joint?"

"Bathhouse. You want locker or basket?"

"Give me a locker," Dirk replied, and pulled out some local currency to pay the entry fee. He was pointed through a side door, where he entered a long, dimly lit corridor lined with many doors. Dirk kept going and walked into a locker room. An old attendant dressed in white handed him a towel and a padlock, nodding toward a row of metal cabinets. Dirk chose one in the far corner and disrobed hurriedly, wrapping a towel around himself and stuffing his clothes inside the locker. He told himself he'd make a quick tour of the place, and if he didn't spot Yves, he'd wait outside for the guy. Already he was feeling extremely uncomfortable.

As casually as he could, he started on a hurried survey of the mazelike hallways. In almost no time he discovered that the bathhouse was more of a local gay cruising joint than a legitimate establishment. Though there were steam and sauna rooms and a bubbling, tile-lined hot pool that could easily have held twenty, most of the activity was taking place in the darkened recesses off the halls. The grunting and groaning, slurping and sucking sounds as he passed told him more than he wanted to know. Every man he ran into in the halls made some sort of pass at him. One beer-bellied guy, whose extra-large towel kept slipping off, even started following him, making cooing, clucking sounds.

Dirk had had enough. Trying to find his way back to the locker room through the crisscrossing halls, he cursed silently. *Damn Honey,* he thought. *She knew all along what Yves liked—that's why she insisted I take over from here. Well, there's a limit to how far I'll go to help Kolina . . . damn right there is.* Dirk was still grumbling to himself when he turned a corner and ran smack into Yves Bouscaral.

"Pardon," Yves apologized, and a sly grin formed on his ruddy face. *"Sprechen sie Deutsch?"*

"English," Dirk replied. "And you?"

"French . . ." He paused suggestively. "Come to my room?"

"Room? They've got private rooms here?" Dirk asked caught off guard.

"*Very* private. Come on."

Yves turned and walked away. A few steps up the hall, he turned to see if Dirk was following. His face fell as he saw that Dirk was hanging back, but Dirk squared his shoulders and started forward with a grin, wishing he were somewhere else.

Yves led him to a door off one of the side halls. Inside was a tiny room containing only a narrow cot covered by a white sheet. Dirk stood just inside the open doorway and wondered what to do next. Yves was trying to close the door behind him, and he pushed Dirk gently aside to do so. Dirk smiled weakly.

Yves was at the cot, searching under the mattress with one hand. "Would you like some cocaine?" he asked.

Unhesitatingly, Dirk said, "Sure."

Yves brought out a small leather case and zipped it open. Inside was a small mirror and all the necessities. Expertly he proceeded to lay out four healthy lines of snow on the mirror. He handed a tooter and the works to Dirk, who inhaled almost gratefully. The rush was instantaneous—sharp, clear, like a blast of supercharged energy. The second line skyrocketed him even further. Savoring the sensation, he returned the case. "Good stuff."

"Peruvian flake," Yves said, and precisely snorted the remaining two lines. He packed away the case and slid it back under the mattress, sinking to sit on the edge. "You are a very attractive man. Very American."

"Ahh . . . thanks, I guess . . ."

"What brings a Yank to this part of the world?" Yves asked in a friendly manner.

Dirk stared at the man, trying to determine how to proceed. Yves was masculine, warm, and seemingly quite at ease with his homosexuality. Dirk, on the other hand, was just as assured of and comfortable with his own heterosexuality. The problem he was confronting was simple—he wanted something different than Yves did, and therefore he concluded he'd have to be direct. "I came here to find you."

Yves looked surprised. "Why?"

"I want information about Kolina Svensen's disappearance."

Yves blanched and sat straight up. "I don't know what you are talking about."

"Come off it, Yves. I'm not out to hurt you. I just want to find the girl."

"How do you know who I am?" Yves asked, suddenly on guard.

"That's not important," Dirk said. "What's important is that Kolina is returned safely. That's all I want."

Yves looked away. "I cannot help you."

"I think you can. You know something about Kolina that will help locate her. Surely you don't wish her any harm."

Yves shook his head sadly. "Of course not."

"Then help me . . . help her," Dirk urged.

Yves snorted bitterly. "Ironic, no? I bring you in here to get something, and it turns out you want something more urgent."

Dirk moved toward the door, telling Yves, "I'll meet you in the cafe across the street. And don't try to run away. I'm a very determined man."

Dirk retrieved his clothes from the locker, pulled them on, and sped out of the bathhouse. Relieved to be outside in the fading sunlight, breathing the fresh mountain air of the tiny village, he crossed the dusty street and plopped down in a chair in the nearly empty outdoor cafe. Eyeing the only door to the bathhouse, he ordered a cold bottle of local beer and gulped it down. He was on his second when he spotted her: a black-eyed, black-haired, buxom young lady of no more than twenty-one, sitting by herself in the deepening shadows of the awning-covered patio. She had the face of a Goya painting, bewitching in its sultry magnificence, enticing in its sensual magic. And she was eyeing him covertly over a glass of what looked like sangria.

A fire of unquenchable proportions burst to life in his groin. He smiled his most engaging, nonthreatening invitation. Much to his delight, she returned it in kind before glancing coyly away. He was about to move to her table when Yves, once again debonairly dressed, strolled out of the bathhouse and started directly across the street toward him. Cursing the rotten timing, Dirk shrugged apologetically to the mystically beautiful presence in the far corner, and turned wtih a wry expression to greet the gay Frenchman.

Bouscaral sank into the opposite chair with an air of resigned amusement. "No hard feelings?"

Dirk shrugged, muttering, "Not yet." In spite of the circumstances of their meeting, he could find nothing to dislike about the man. If Honey had drummed one thing into his head over the years, it was that an individual had the right to freedom of choice. Therefore he couldn't fault the man merely for his predilections. He glanced at the large-breasted lady in the corner and reluctantly returned his focus to his tablemate. "Okay, Yves, tell me what you know."

Bouscaral took out of his blazer a slim gold cigarette case, and fished out a cigarette. With some irritation, Dirk watched him light it with a matching gold lighter, inhale deeply, and exhale, blowing the smoke to one side. Yves smiled. "I'm afraid you've overreacting to this girl's disappearance."

"Meaning?" Dirk asked testily.

"Easy, my friend." Yves puffed for a moment, then began in a confident manner, "Kolina is in no danger.

On the contrary, she is having the time of her life. I know for a fact that she's run away with a man she adores. It is merely an affair of the heart. Passion, that's all. Surely you can understand passion."

Dirk thought for a moment, then took a wild stab in the dark. "This guy wouldn't be the one you met with up in the hills early today?"

Yves's casual facade crumbled like a dry sand castle, his ruddy complexion going pale. "Absolutely not," he rasped, and pushed himself out of his chair. "*Au revoir,*" he said as he strode briskly away.

Dirk cried after him, "Dammit, you're a big fuckin' help."

The Frenchman paused long enough to shrug and smile. "So were you, Yank. So were you."

In less than an hour, Dirk was back in his cluttered and garishly tiled hotel suite at the Bussaco Palace, reporting to Honey by phone. From the bed, he said into the receiver, "The problem is, the bastard won't say who Kolina is with."

"Sounds like another coverup, doesn't it?" Honey commented, the excitement of the chase evident in her tone. "Very suspicious, Yves flying off for a sudden rendezvous just after I ask him about Kolina. My hunch is, this stranger he met in the hills is somehow connected. How soon can you get me copies of the photos you took? Dirk? You there?"

On the bed, on top of the buxom, black-eyed beauty from the village cafe, Dirk pumped away, his head buried in the pillow next to the receiver, above her soft shoulder. "Yeah. I'm here," he croaked, enjoying the sensation of talking to his beautiful sister while fucking a gorgeous college student from Madrid. "What'd you say, sis?"

"Am I keeping you from something?" Honey asked, laughingly.

"No," he replied and adjusted his knees, pushing apart the young woman's firm thighs, opening her pussy lips even wider. "I'm doing just super, Honey."

"I asked how soon I can get those photos?"

"They're on the way," he grunted. "When's Disa arriving?"

She laughed. "Flying in from Munich on Wednesday."

"Ah, the fabulous Disa," he mused aloud, and visualized the beautiful blonde with whom he'd never managed to score. "Give her my best."

"I'll do more than that. I'll give her *mine*. Say, I'm sorry I failed to mention that Yves goes for men. Must have slipped my mind."

"Yeah, sure," he growled and banged his way deep into the wet warmth of the young woman's hot oven. "Well, like you always say—to each his own." The receiver fell away unnoticed and he lost himself in the pure exhilaration of coming. By the time he recovered enough to remember the phone, Honey had disconnected.

9.

HONEY

The moment Honey showed her the copy of Dirk's Portuguese photo, darling Disa Dichter exclaimed, "Why, that's Yves's older brother, Henri Bouscaral! But of course I know him," Disa continued in her spirited manner, tossing her blonde mane like a proud lioness. "He is the black sheep of the whole Bouscaral family. Honey, he's *very* decadent. Very heavy into kink. It is his *idée fixe,* his obsession."

"What kind of kink?" Honey asked, her interest in the man more than piqued.

"Absolutely *everything,*" Disa winked.

Honey smiled. "Well, then surely you, Disa, of all people, would know where to begin looking for him."

Disa considered the question only briefly before bursting into a smile reeking of illicitness. "But of course. Nadez will know!"

"Nadez? Who's that?"

Disa frowned with mock alarm and locked arms with Honey, drawing her into an intimate embrace. "Sweet Honey, you have been out of the social scene far too long. Nadez is renowned in my circles. Absolutely *everyone* who's in the know calls her the Queen of Kink."

Honey trilled a laugh of delight and kissed the wickedly beautiful face before her. "What are we waiting for? Let's visit this kinky queen *tout de suite!* Where does she hold court?"

The afternoon of that very same day brought Honey and her cherished former school chum to the lovely harbor city of St. Peter Port, Guernsey, on one of the tiny Channel Islands a dozen miles off the French coast. Overlooking the blue sea, quaint cottage-styled houses rose, tier upon tier, up the steep hillside ringing one of the most beautiful natural harbors in all Europe. Enchanted by the view, Honey read in her guidebook: "Though more French in history than English, the island natives pledge their allegiance to England as a result of the conquering invasion of the United Kingdom by William, Duke of Normandy, in 1066." From their luxury hotel suite she surveyed the harbor filled with fishing boats and dozens of pleasure yachts, thinking that the locale was so innocent-appearing that it would be the last place in the world she would look for the Queen of Kink.

True to form, however, Disa had her finger on the pulse of all that was decadent and risqué in the world. Relishing her assigned task as go-between, she curled like a jungle cat on the large bed and dialed the unlisted number for Nadez's infamous establishment. As Disa gave the secret password over the phone, Honey stood by the windows, admiring once again the lithe but full-breasted body of her longtime lover. Disa was a delicious vision of tawny skin, lean limbs, and masses of champagne-blonde hair piled with fetching disarray on top of her head. The beloved only child of a German multimillionaire industrialist, Disa had always spent enormous sums of money frivolously and indulged her every whim. And Honey adored her, loving her vivacious, carefree spirit and her tender devotion.

Disa hung up the receiver, glowing with success. "We have an appointment at eight sharp tonight," she cooed, and kicked off her high heels. "Now come here, you beautiful vixen. We have a great deal of catching up to do."

Honey fell into her arms with growing urgency. They wrestled and rolled on the big bed like two schoolgirls, giggling, kissing, and tearing off each other's clothes. Soon they were naked, passionately embracing, their aroused nipples brushing together. As they reexplored the familiar but still stimulating territories, their lovely bodies were perfectly matched. Both were long-limbed, with large full breasts; their mounds of Venus, between curvaceous thighs, were well defined. Only the colors of their hair and skin were strikingly dissimilar; Honey's deep red tresses contrasted vividly with Disa's light blonde masses, and Honey's satiny skin was the color of fresh milk, while Disa, who frequented the world's most exclusive nude beaches, was tanned all over a light golden brown. Their muffs also were quite different; Honey's was a vivid, bright red, as full and luxurious as a fox pelt, while Disa's was scantier and a soft, golden yellow.

Honey now dipped her face into the luscious lower lips of her playmate and licked the ambrosia that had already formed. Disa tasted as sweet as an aperitif. She wrapped her strong legs around Honey's neck, urging her with writhing hips to deeper explorations. Honey obliged, parting the happy valley with her teasing tongue and locking on the hard nubbin of lust she knew so well. Like a volcanic rock in a sea of rolling liquid, Disa's distended clitoris responded at once to Honey's lingual liberties. "Oh, my darling," Disa squealed, and pumped her pussy against Honey's mouth. "Why has it been so long?"

Honey raised her head, licking her lips. "Because, dear one, you are rarely in one spot long enough for me to track you down."

"And you," Disa sputtered as she pulled Honey up to her soft breasts, "*you* insisted on being a roaming journalist instead of enjoying the fruits of your poor father's labors. With his estate, you could live like a princess for the rest of your days."

Honey bubbled with laughter and pushed Disa's head down to her own love delta, which was rapidly filling with volatile fuels. "Eat me, you wicked, lazy bitch."

"My pleasure," Disa replied, and dove into her partner's pussy with a vengeance, her eager tongue darting into the moist darkness like an anteater searching for delicacies. On and on she snacked until Honey's love channel was so filled with raging lust that Disa's tongue was swimming.

Wallowing in the netherlands of sexual ecstasy, Honey yanked Disa's hips around so she could give as well as receive pleasure. Mouths pressed to each other's pussies, the two rapidly rode to their mutually satisfying climaxes, in a series of gut-wrenching explosions that left them gasping in delight.

Shortly before eight, refreshed from their late-afternoon tryst and a subsequent nap, Honey and Disa rode by cab to an isolated mansion on a windswept bluff not far from Victor Hugo's former abode. From the outside, Honey could detect nothing out of the ordinary. The large Tudor-style house looked discreetly normal, elegantly refined. A single Rolls Royce Silver Cloud was parked in the maple-lined drive that swept up before the imposing, ironbound front door. Disa knocked with a special code, and shortly a small window flew open and a pair of beady eyes surveyed them. Disa smiled bewitchingly and spoke the passwords: *"Aux grands maux les grands remédes."*

Instantly the wide, heavy door opened inward and they stepped into the flagstone-paved entry. The door was closed behind them by a thin man dressed in formal butler's attire. Silently he led them down a nearby hallway into an antique-furnished reception room. Flocked gold wallpaper and crystal chandeliers aglow with lighted candles added a festive atmosphere to the room. The hall door shut behind them and they were alone. From somewhere deep in the house, a Chopin piano etude filtered to them. With keen anticipation they stared at one another and waited.

"Welcome, my beauties," a deep female voice greeted them with a thick Russian accent. In surprise, Honey whirled around just in time to see a secret panel closing in the wall behind the unexpected arrivee. The woman was huge, well over six feet tall and weighing at least two hundred and fifty pounds. In spite of her large proportions, she possessed an hourglass shape emphasized by a tight black Merry Widow corset. Her mammoth breasts overflowed the tight covering, and on her hefty thighs, black garters held up black net stockings. Her lower legs were encased in knee-high, laced-up black leather boots with stiletto heels. In one hand she carried a short riding crop and in the other a goblet of an odd-colored liquid. It was impossible for Honey to discern what the gargantuan woman's face looked like, for it was covered from brow to just below the nose with a full black leather mask. At once Honey was intrigued, and she felt a delicious tingle rising between her legs.

Disa stepped forward as if greeting an old friend.

"Madame Nadezlida Filaretovna, I would like to present a dear friend, Honey Wildon."

The woman strode to them with surprising grace, her large round hips swaying like a chorus girl's. "Are you Honey Wildon, the writer?" she asked in a gruff voice quite at home in the lower registers.

"Yes I am," Honey hastened to say.

"No writers allowed," the madame said, and turned to Disa with a friendly grin. "But you, my sweet, are always welcome."

Honey pulled herself up to her full height. "I am not here as a writer," she protested. "I came to ask you a personal favor."

The beefy madame swung her masked head back to stare openly at Honey. "I do not trust the duplicity of writers."

"But I assure you on my parents' graves, I have not come here as a writer but as a woman who needs your help."

"*My* help?" the madame questioned in obvious amusement. "All my people come to me for help."

Honey smiled warmly. "But I do not seek sexual help, only information. About one of your regulars. Henri Bouscaral."

In the holes of the mask, the madame's eyes narrowed. "I *never* divulge anything about any of my clients."

"Even if it might mean saving an innocent child?" Disa broke in, all golden charm and enticing persuasion. "Honey, show Nadez the photo."

Hastily Honey displayed Dirk's snapshot of Kolina and explained her fears that the girl had been kidnapped and was being held against her will by Henri Bouscaral. The madame looked to Disa for confirmation. "Is this true?" she asked. Disa agreed readily, adding that she wouldn't have brought her there if Honey were not trustworthy and loyal. The madame eyed Honey with new appraisal and took a sip from her long-forgotten goblet. "If you want information, you must pay dearly for it."

"Anything you ask," Honey replied, opening her purse.

The madame laughed heartily. "Not with money, but with your body. You must prove to me that you are truly an aficionado of all kinds of pleasures. Only then will I speak of Henri."

Honey tossed a titillated glance at Disa, who shrugged, smiling her agreement. "It seems only fair, Honey. Madame, I will leave her in your very capable hands and go myself to partake of your palace of fine arts." She hurried to the hall door and threw a wink at Honey. "Enjoy yourself, *liebchen*. I'll meet you back at the hotel." With that she exited.

Honey shrugged at the huge madame and decided what the hell. There was very little that she hadn't tried, and even less that she hadn't enjoyed. "Where do I begin?"

"By stripping at once."

Honey, eager to prove her worth, pulled her Pucci dress over her head and stepped out of her heels, displaying her perfectly formed breasts with a bold grin. "What next?"

As if surprised at the suddenness with which her request had been met, Madame Nadezlida Filaretovna stared at the flawless body before her. Her eyes widened with wonderment in the mask holes, and a stubby pink tongue ran over her thick lips. Slowly, deliberately, she made a complete tour around Honey and returned to face her with a pleased grin. "What a pretty package you are, my sweet. A welcome addition to any house. Follow me."

Knees quaking with anticipation, Honey managed to move after the heavy body crammed into the tight corset. Nadez touched a concealed release in the gold-flocked wall, and a hidden panel slide back noiselessly, revealing a narrow passage. The big woman squeezed into the opening, and Honey followed. At once the panel closed behind them. A flight of stairs led downward, and the farther they descended, the warmer it became. On a lower level, the madame stopped, turned to her captive audience, and pulled a small half-mask over Honey's face. "This is your first test. Remember, I will be watching your every move."

Honey smiled gamely. "I'm looking forward to proving my worthiness."

Nadez pushed a spot on the wall and another panel opened. Honey stepped through the doorway and found herself in a steamy communal shower. People were soaping and lathering each other's bodies, the men's pricks as hard as the white bars of soap, which were in plentiful supply. Almost immediately, Honey was surrounded by slippery, rubbing bodies. She was sandwiched between two men—one tall, with a rigid cock the size of a good-sized cucumber, the other short but possessing an even larger tool, fat and brown like a potato. The men soaped her ripe body with loving care, not missing a centimeter of her fair skin as they slid their hard members up and down her limbs. Loving the tactile sensation, Honey returned their amorous attentions and, grabbing their cocks, jerked them to an easy climax.

She eased away from them and, pushing through the wet tangle of human flesh, exited the shower at the far end, to find herself in a warm room whose walls and floor were covered entirely in soft gray carpet. Thick white towels were folded neatly on a bench next to a standing young man whose towel was draped over his stiff pole as if it were hanging from a special wall rack. Playfully she grabbed the towel from his pleasing prick and began drying herself. The masked young man slipped behind her and gently bent her forward over the bench. She gasped with pleasure as she felt his hot, hard meat slip with ease into her still-wet channel. Simultaneously toweling her luxurious locks dry, she pushed back onto his driving dick and felt herself rocketing upward into the fleecy clouds of lustful enjoyment. She placed her hands on the bench and, her breasts swinging beneath her, rode his pounding peter for all she was worth. Soon he creamed into her with such a load that she felt her ditch overflowing. He pulled out and patted her ass with a friendly "Thank you." She swung upright, still unsatisfied, and wiped the damp towel between her legs.

The other door leading from the gray-carpeted room brought her into a dimly lit corridor of many doors, each containing a small sign labeling the room behind it, as well as a small window through which one could view a portion of the goings-on. Brimming with curiosity and unfulfilled desires, she made her way down the hall, glancing both at the signs and through the small windows.

Shaking her head in wonderment, but not as yet inclined to partake of anything she had observed, Honey reached a carpeted staircase and climbed it. At its top she found a large room filled with medieval torture devices. Flickering torches cast a gloomy light over the damp brick walls, revealing a number of naked, heated bodies in various stages of orgasmic delight. One fat man who looked like a judge was laughing loudly while being birched repeatedly by a tiny woman who swung the thin stick with enthusiasm. Another man was being fist-fucked by an aggressive young woman, and still another man had his cock wrapped in leather thongs tied to a revolving wheel, which was pulling him off. The ecstatic grin on his face assured Honey that he too was enjoying the hell out of his "torture." One woman was hanging from the ceiling by her heels in leather stirrups, and she was blowing a man lying beneath her on a large block of ice. A guy with overdeveloped muscles, like a Greek statue come to life, was beckoning to Honey, his small hard cock bobbing at her.

Entranced by his welcoming smile as well as his body, she sashayed over to him and he pointed to an oddly designed leather sling chair hanging from the ceiling on slender silver chains. Definitely curious, and remembering that she was being tested by Nadez, Honey clambered into the contraption, which had a hole in it for her ass and vagina to hang down. The cool leather sling was more comfortable than it looked, and she was just adjusting her position when it rose in the air, lifting her upright, her sexual organs swaying in the breeze. Below her on a small table, the body-builder lay on his back, holding his dinky dork upright. Slowly she was lowered over him until she felt his tiny tool enter her wide-open pussy.

Gradually the sling chair began to swing in a slow circle, revolving her around on the muscleman's meat. The sensation was so unique, to be floating in the air while being serviced, that she began to feel her labia moistening with joy juice. The guy's dick may have been small, but it was positioned perfectly; each revolution of her cunt brought his cock in contact with her clitoris, raising the temperature of her pussy to unbelievable heights. Hanging on to the chains holding her sling chair, she swung around and around, feeling dizzy not only from the constant circular motion, but also from the lusts raging in her furnace. Abandoning herself to the absolute bliss of the moment, she threw back her head and hung on, her eyes closing with rapture.

The intensely pleasurable agony kept building within her, and she longed to be free to jump up and down on his deliciously delicate dork. But she was a captured prize and could only hang on for the duration of the funhouse ride. Each maddening slow revolution inched her closer to climax, and the exquisite sensation soared her higher and higher. Just when she thought she would go insane from the intensity of the experience, she suddenly reached her longed-for goal. Shrieking her relief and delight, she began to come, whirling round and around, flooding the budlike head of the small prick embedded in her.

She was not released from the confining leather sling until after the muscleman had also climaxed with a healthy spurt. Shaking dizzily, she climbed out of the sporting chair and kissed the man gratefully. She staggered out of the room and walked directly into a large, darkened orgy room carpeted with writhing bodies.

Drained but still game, Honey piled onto the amorphous mass of flesh and soon felt greedy, wet mouths on every part of her body, as well as exploring fingers and toes. Hard pricks pushed into her soft skin everywhere, and she found new energy coursing through her aroused system. Latching on to the first available pussy, she began eagerly to suck at the tender lips. In no time her liquids were flowing again, and she longed for one of the hardened cocks to be inside her. Almost at once her wish was granted twofold. One shoved into her pulsating pussy, another inched into her anus. A different mouth was chewing on each of her breasts, and her own mouth was eating the tasty cunt hovering over her face. Honey's sensual circuits were soon overloaded. She felt as if she were one large orifice, filled to overflowing with an immensely enjoyable ardor.

She had no idea how long she had been indulging her desires, but when she finally managed to extricate herself and stumble out of the room, she caught a glimpse of the rising sun through a leaded-glass window. Sweet exhaustion blanketed her as she showered in still another area.

Emerging from the drying area, she was pleased to see a smiling Nadezlida Filaretovna standing like the Rock of Gibraltar before her.

"My apologies, Miss Wildon, for not trusting you," the madame said jovially. "You are a true connoisseur of kink. Come with me, please."

Bolstered by the praise, Honey followed her down the stairs into a private dressing room, where her own clothes were neatly hung. As Honey pulled on her dress, Nadez lit a cigar and puffed thoughtfully. "You ask after Henri Bouscaral," she began in her thick Russian accent. "What is it you wish to know?"

"Merely where I might find him," Honey said breathlessly. "I only want to help the girl, not bring any harm to him."

Nadez nodded silently and blew a ring of smoke in her direction. "I have no idea where the Prince of Kink is. But perhaps I can tell you where you might eventually find him. There are two things I know he has on his schedule of worldwide pursuits, two areas he has often mentioned that he would like to experience."

"Any clue would be a help, Nadez."

"The first is a trio of Chinese acrobats in Shanghai, a set of triplets widely known for their sexual athletics. I only know them by name—the Mee-Lan triplets."

Honey quickly made a mental note and stepped into her heels. "And the second possibility?"

"Henri often said he wanted to partake of this year's debauching of the Sisters of the Moon," the madame replied. "A strange order of nuns whose convent is in the mountains outside of Sofia, Bulgaria."

"When does this debauching take place?"

"Every ten years, on the first full moon of May."

"Why, that's in less than a week," Honey exclaimed, and spontaneously kissed a plump cheek of the Queen of Kink. "Thank you, Nadez. I thoroughly enjoyed my evening at your establishment."

The mountain of womanhood laughed heartily. "*That* was most obvious. I never saw a newcomer get into the swing of things with so much enthusiasm. Please, come again. You are welcome anytime, my beauty."

10.

HONEY

Nervously she patted her cheeks, making certain the false beard and mustache were firmly in place. Hiking up the belly pad that helped transform her decidedly feminine body into a closer facsimile of a man's, Honey joined the line of men on the rocky path. The chartered bus from Sofia had just dropped them off at the end of the state road. Now the rest of the journey was to be on foot. As the winding path was steep and treacherous, Honey was glad she'd been able to locate a pair of sturdy walking shoes in her size.

The boisterous pilgrims soon quieted down as the trek up the heavily wooded mountainside became more arduous. Soon they were strung out single file, with Honey laboring near the tail end, just in front of the more elderly men. She was dressed in baggy old clothes she'd purchased that very morning in Bulgaria's capitol city of Sofia: a large checked sports coat worn over a garishly patterned

Hawaiian shirt and plaid wool pants. On her head she wore a floppy slouch hat, her hair tied up with a scarf under the short-cut, scraggly brown wig. Spirit gum held the itchy full beard and mustache in place. Thus far her odd disguise had drawn little attention, and she'd been readily accepted by the stalwart group of men as merely another sexually curious male.

Much to her disappointment, she had yet to see Henri Bouscaral among the long line of men. She had studied Dirk's Portuguese photos carefully, in hopes that she would be able to spot Henri on this strenuous journey to the Convent of the Sisters of the Moon. But there were so many busloads of men trailing up the path to the remote location that she had yet to see anyone bearing even a remote resemblance to the world collector of sexual oddities. Undaunted, however, she forged up the path, intrigued by what lay ahead and determined to find the man who most likely had Kolina under lock and key.

Before leaving Paris for this hasty journey, Honey had quickly researched the convent, of which she'd never heard until Nadez's brief mention. Not even Disa, with all her knowledge and experience in worldwide sexual matters, had been aware that such a place existed. Founded in the seventh century, the Convent of the Sisters of the Moon was the last enclave of fervent believers in its particular sect. Even ten years since 1584, the sisters honored the memory of their own who had been repeatedly gang-raped by marauding Turkish soldiers. On every tenth anniversary of the event, the gates of the isolated convent were thrown open for one twelve-hour period, and any man who so desired could enter to have his way with the nuns. As the unpublicized event was held only once every decade, and as the convent was located high up in the remote mountains near the Valley of Roses, and as Bulgaria, which obviously did not promote or condone such atavistic customs, was locked deep behind the Iron Curtain, few had ever heard of the strange custom. But enough had, Honey now assessed, for the long line of men who had come from all over the world stretched far out of sight before her.

The sun was setting behind the mountain range by the time Honey wearily reached the imposing stone walls of the ancient convent. Perched on the edge of a craggy cliff, they rose above her like a medieval fortress. At the base before the closed wooden gates, the men sank to the hard earth to muster their strength for the more athletic activities ahead. The itching of her false beard was driving her to distraction, and her leg muscles ached from the long climb, but she forced herself to move slowly down the line of expectantly waiting men. Walking as masculinely as possible in front of them, she kept her hands folded across the large padded belly, hoping that her breasts could not be detected in all the loose clothing. Carefully she searched for a single familiar face.

The men were of all ages and all nationalities; some were well dressed, others poorly, some had brought hampers of food and wine, others stared longingly as if they hadn't eaten in weeks. But in all of them she discerned one similar trait: a certain randiness that brightened their eyes, making them all look like schoolboys playing hooky in hopes of a little nooky. And still she did not spy Henri Bouscaral.

As more men were straggling up the path, she turned her attention to them and sat with her back to a large rock, grateful for the respite from the rigorous trek. Again she wondered at the wisdom of Dirk's going to China in search of the infamous Mee-Lan triplets while she came to this desolate but picturesque part of the world. But time was of the essence, and if they were to help Kolina, one of them had to make the trip to this convent so far off the beaten track. The luck of the draw had made it Honey, and now she debated how to enter into the fast-approaching rape of the Sisters of the Moon. If the Prince of Kink was in the vicinity, she would find him, regardless of what might lie behind towering walls. Over the rim of a distant mountain the full moon began to ascend in the ever-darkening sky, like a mammoth, glowing breast poking out over a blanket.

A mournful bell began to toll the hour—six o'clock. The men began scrambling to their feet, pushing and shoving to be the first at the gates. Before the last stroke of the bell had faded into the surrounding, tree-shrouded hills, a small door in the tall wooden gates opened and out stepped a stately, maternal-looking woman robed all in white, her head covered by a strangely shaped hood. She raised her hands for silence and waited almost sternly until the men stopped their multilingual jabberings. Only then did she proceed to read in Bulgarian, her voice loud and firm, from a yellowed parchment scroll.

A distinguished-looking gentleman near Honey whispered in English to no one in particular, "What's she saying?"

Another man, whom Honey could not see, responded, "She's blessed us, and is now reading the rules for the evening."

"Rules?" another man grumbled under his breath. "No one told me of rules. I thought everything inside was fair game."

Still a third man, old but lively, piped up in broken English, as if he were an old hand at the coming attractions, "You sign your name in your own blood and must agree to fuck at least ten of the nuns in the twelve hours before sunup. Before you can leave, they count your beads."

"What beads?" the man nearest Honey growled.

"One rape, one bead. The raped nun gives you a rosary bead," the old know-it-all said proudly. "You must have ten beads to get out. Otherwise they lock the gates on you. A decade ago, I lost a friend in there for months and months. When they let him go, his cock had been split open."

At once Honey felt trapped. Her hasty research had turned up nothing about being *forced* to rape the nuns, let alone *ten* of them. If it had not been for the press of men around her, she would have turned to leave right then. But as it was, before she could squeeze away, the gates were flung open and with a raucous, lusty roar, the stampede was on. Honey was swept forward in the rush to get inside.

Once beyond the gates, the line re-formed as men laboriously signed the agreement, puncturing a thumb with a sharp quill and using their own blood as ink for their signatures. Honey was about to seize the opportunity to slip away when she thought she spotted Henri Bouscaral just leaving the signing booths and running into the inner courtyard, from where already she could hear the enraged and terrified screams of the attacked nuns. Not wanting to lose him, she stood her ground, moving up to the wooden table that held the bloody list of names. When it came her turn, she pricked her thumb without so much as a wince and signed Dirk's name with a bold flourish.

Like the other men before her, as soon as she'd signed the document, she bolted toward the arched doorway leading to the inner reaches. Once there, Honey pulled up in astonishment. The rough stone pavement was littered with nude women who looked even more naked because of their totally shaved heads. They were being attacked, raped, and skewered with surprising authenticity and fervor. She noticed that the Sisters of the Moon were primarily young peasant women, their bodies on the heavy side, with ponderously full breasts and meaty thighs. Though this once-a-decade event had been booked for centuries, the young nuns were kicking and clawing, screaming and shrieking like stuck pigs—as if the very Turkish soldiers of yore had returned to defile their sacred order.

Honey felt extremely uncomfortable, standing there watching. But then she noted something that abruptly changed her attitude. One of the hefty young nuns who, only moments before, had been one of the loudest and toughest resisters, upon the completion of the sexual attack suddenly became as docile and as affectionate as a lamb. She was kissing and stroking her attacker with obvious gratitude, her face radiant with a beatific glow. Almost reluctantly the sweaty, besmirched nun handed over a single bead from the small leather pouch tied around her neck, and waved a sad farewell. At once she was leapt upon by another randy attacker, his hard cock flailing at her like an angry eel. The young nun began to scream shrilly, putting forth a valiant effort to hold him at bay.

Beginning to understand the curious psychology behind the debauch, Honey pressed her search for the elusive Bouscaral. Darkness was rapidly descending, and flaming torches stuck into iron sconces on the walls lit her way. Everywhere she looked, another nun was being ravished or being chased; she even stumbled over some thrashing bodies in the winding corridors of the dungeonlike nunnery. But more and more the nuns' physical resistance and theatrical protests were vanishing into the night. Some of the bolder nuns were running in packs, turning attacker, hunting down elusive males. As the night progressed, Honey kept discovering men, nude or seminude, hiding, cowering in a quiet corner, trying to catch their breath before another onslaught. None were Henri Bouscaral.

The moon climbed higher into the night sky, covering

the ancient convent in an eerie white light. Shrieks and screams, as well as satisfied grunts and groans, echoed down the stone corridors and filled the crisp air. Honey continued her search, aided by the light of one of the torches. She would come to an inky black doorway and thrust in the flame, revealing momentarily the humping white ass of the attacking male, then his startled face as he turned to glower at the intruder. She hurried on, aware that the halls were beginning to reek of sexual excess.

She entered a long dormitory lined with iron cots and, thinking she was alone, located a solitary cot off in an alcove and fell flat on her back, welcoming the relief to her aching muscles. A heavy tiredness swept over her and she was just drifting off to sleep, planning on pursuing her search in the early daylight hours, when she heard a distant sob from under the cot. With some alarm she peered over the edge and spied a Wagnerian-sized, nude young nun whimpering in the shadows. Honey reached in to comfort her, and the young woman's teeth latched fiercely onto her hand. Honey let loose a decidedly unmasculine howl of outraged pain.

The mouth of the bald, naked nun popped open in shock and she scrambled out from under the bed and trembled in confusion against the wall, staring wide-eyed at the imposter on the cot. Her weighty breasts, ribboned with fine blue lines, heaved before her like bellows. Her bush was the color of strong tea and as thick as the forest outside. Still in considerable pain, Honey rubbed the bitten hand and tried to put the girl at ease with a friendly, forgiving smile. Abruptly the young nun, who looked all meat and potatoes, dropped to her chunky knees. Bowing her shiny head in a supplicating manner, she began babbling in her mother tongue. The words were unintelligible to Honey, but the tone was not—it was terrified pleading if Honey ever heard it.

The terrified nun touched a responsive chord deep within Honey's heavy concealed breasts. Brilliant but cold moonlight streamed through the arched window, cutting a wide swatch across the broad back of the kneeling young woman. Tenderly, Honey patted the nun's shoulder, as if telling her not to cry. The bald head rose with disbelief. Honey indicated the cot's mattress and the young nun slowly eased up to sit down next to her. Up close, Honey could see the natural beauty of the nun's tear-stained face. Though somewhat flat-cheeked, the young woman had lovely big brown eyes, like those of a heifer, and a delicious mouth shaped like a rosebud. Hurriedly the shy nun began to speak again in her guttural language, and Honey had the distinct impression that the girl was onto her disguise. Wanting to silence her before someone else might hear, Honey leaned into the moving mouth and kissed her firmly.

At once the young nun threw her beefy arms around Honey, returning the kiss with ardent passion, pushing her meaty breasts against her. Honey felt an insistent heat erupt with surprising force inside her, and the young nun squirmed mightily. They fell back onto the cot, kissing as if they'd just invented the game. The nun's tongue scraped the inside of Honey's mouth, and her milkmaid hands began fumbling with the front of Honey's pants. Concerned to be so openly exposed, Honey pushed back the Rubenesque body, all the while kissing and sucking at the nun's milk-white jugs.

Feverishly, Honey lowered her face, tracing with her tongue the healthy swell of the nun's belly and moving deep into the valley between the snow-white thighs that towered on either side of her bewigged head like glaciers. The young nun's bush felt as coarse as winter wheat, and Honey nuzzled through it in search of the hidden entrance. A seepage of warm fluids led to the most tightly closed pussy Honey had ever encountered. Gently, with her expert tongue, she cracked apart the trembling lips and tasted the creamy sauce. Gradually the sealed lips began to flow, opening up like an early spring primrose in a snowbank. The hefty thighs clamped tighter around Honey's head, and the young nun began to writhe on the narrow, hard cot, her lusty grunts increasing in frequency and volume.

Well inside the inner recesses of the nun's tight cunt, Honey's tongue slammed into a solid wall—a thick, unbroken hymen. The virgin nun panted as if she were about to be broached, and tightened her viselike grip on Honey's ears. Honey, in turn, wrapped her tongue around a thumb-sized clitoris and began attacking it. The young woman grunted with a voracious appetite and began to pump her broad pelvis. Honey crammed a hand inside her pants and began diddling her own clit.

Suddenly a gruff male voice exclaimed. *"Merde!"*

With a start, Honey jerked up her head from the clamping thighs. In doing so, she lost both her wig and scarf. Her deep red hair tumbled to her shoulders as she stared in shock at Henri Bouscaral! The Prince of Kink stood glowering, dressed only in a long black satin cape, his purplish-red prick sticking out between the folds like an inquisitive dolphin.

The young nun screamed and Honey dove out of the moonlight, grabbing her headgear from the cot. Hastily she pulled them on, just as Henri leapt upon the already primed nun, like a fanatical priest exorcizing the very devil out of her. He gored and stabbed, the young woman shrieking shrilly. Honey could not tell whether the big virgin was crying out in fear or lust, but not wanting to hang around, she scooted along the wall and ran for the doorway, thinking she would wait just outside the door until Bouscaral emerged.

Tucking her hair up under the old hat, she dashed into the corridor and straight into the white-robed arms of an even bigger nun. Built like a biker, this one held her so tightly that Honey feared her belly padding would break open. She struggled briefly before realizing the futility of the effort and went limp in the heavily muscled arms. Unceremoniously she was half dragged, half carried to a small cell lit dimly by a glowing lantern.

Inside the dank smelling room, Honey was confronted by the stately nun who had earlier welcomed the marauders outside the gates. She now stood behind a small table, her matronly face set sternly. She held out her hands and demanded something in her native tongue. Honey, feigning innocence, shrugged questioningly. Again the mother superior spat out words in several languages, until Honey recognized the French word. She knew then what was being demanded—they wanted to see how many rosary beads she had collected since she'd entered the gates. Stalling for time, Honey pretended to search the pockets of her baggy clothes. There was no escape. Her only way out of the tiny cell-like room was blocked by the massive nun behind her. Impatiently the head nun snapped her fingers, demanding again to see the beads. Honey, with a sheepish grin through the fake facial hair, turned her pockets inside out, demonstrating that they were empty.

A string of oaths broke from the astonished mother superior, and she railed openly, then beckoned the bigger nun forward and spat out an order. At once the bigger nun, who had a face like a slab of roast beef, began pulling the white habit over her massive shoulders and tossing it on the table, standing nude, like an enormous avalanche of white flesh. Her breasts were so huge and heavy they hung far down on her obscenely swollen stomach. If Honey hadn't thought it highly unlikely, she would have sworn this fat nun was nine months pregnant. The obese

140

nun, whose pussy fur couldn't even be detected in the heavy, waxy rolls of fat that hung from her waist like sacks of laundry, promptly lay down on the table and opened her stumplike legs. The mother superior pointed at Honey, then at the gaping nude thighs. Her meaning was more than clear—the head nun wanted this "man" to perform his sworn-in-blood task. Honey shook her head defiantly, and from the table the big nun reared up partway, as if ready to strike out with a clenched fist.

Honey stood her ground and kept shaking her head. She pointed instead to the mother superior and pumped her hips, indicating that she wanted to fuck her instead. A look of astonishment came over the older woman's face, followed by one of resigned acceptance. She hurled an order at the nun on the table, who heaved herself off, grabbed her white habit, and slunk out of the room as if she had just been sent to the showers. Honey swept an arm up in the air several times, gesturing to the older nun to take off her robes.

A gleam of unholy lust burst alive in the matronly nun's eyes, and she tore off her white habit, exposing a reed-thin, but surprisingly well-preserved body. Her small breasts lay like pancakes on her prominent ribcage. Almost coyly she lay down on the wooden table and parted her slender thighs. Honey glimpsed a wiry pad of hair and formed a quick plan. Stepping boldly forward, she began unzipping her baggy plaid pants, as if ready to draw out her cock, then leaned down and blew out the lantern's flame. The cell was plunged into total darkness, and Honey whipped out her trusty dildo, which she had wisely thought to bring along. Moistening it with her mouth, she put it in her fly and stepped up to the open thighs. With her fingers she searched the area before her, found the tight trench, and pushed her bogus cock into the crevice.

The mother superior of the Convent of the Sisters of the Moon was none the wiser. Though the dildo was larger than most of the infidels who had forced their way with her in debauchings of bygone decades, the ersatz appendage now shoving into her was as real as her memory of the authentic article. Grimly she gripped the table and passively allowed herself to be raped by the strange, bearded man who had never taken off his clothes. However, the more his stiff, big, and slightly cold cock plunged into her, the more she could not deny her internal reactions. In a very short time she was reeling with earthly sensations. Wildly she began cursing aloud the infidel's talented tool, in hope that she would be spared the humiliation of such forbidden pleasures. But alas, her curses unconsciously slipped into praises, and she lost her ability to understand what was happening to her. The flames licked at her very heart and she felt transported upward on hot wisps of smoke, higher and higher, until the very face of Ormazd, lord of light and goodness, materialized before her internal eye, surrounded by an intense white light. Weeping, the nun reached up her arms to embrace her lord and instantly exploded into a conflagration of brilliant heat. She screamed with joyous release and became one with him.

Honey, amazed at the wild transformation of the stately nun, bent down, kissing her parched lips, and pulled out the ancient ivory instrument of pleasure. In the darkness, the nun clung to her shoulders, weeping with hysterical sobs of pure joy. Gently, Honey pushed away and pocketed the dildo, zipping up her pants, thinking only to locate Bouscaral before he exited the convent. As she turned to leave, the still-panting nun grabbed her hand and gratefully poured into it all of her rosary beads.

Honey pocketed them and hurriedly left the dark cell, returning at once to the dormitory. The virgin nun was not there, nor was Bouscaral. Nor could she find him anywhere in the now-subdued convent. The sun had risen, and in the courtyard men staggered about in exhaustion. Small groups of elderly men were collapsed like broken wine bags around the perimeter. Hastily, Honey completed her search and ruefully concluded that the Prince of Kink had once again disappeared. Heavy with disappointment and fatigue, Honey presented at the front gates the more than twenty rosary beads received from the mother superior, and was ushered outside as though she were the all-time champion. Feeling that she had failed in her quest, Honey began making her way down the steep, rocky trail.

11.

DIRK

The famous Longhua Pagoda, one of China's great architectural treasures, dating back to the Sung Dynasty, looked to Dirk like a giant "French tickler" condom, all pointy edges and ruffled ridges. Surrounded by blooming peach trees, the tall, ancient pagoda rose above the busy streets of Shanghai and made a pretty picture in his viewfinder. Idly he snapped a shot, not all that interested. He had been in China's largest city for three days and had yet to discover a single clue that might lead him to the world renowned Mee-Lan triplets.

Ever since his arrival he had been making discreet inquiries, knowing full well that he was putting himself in danger of being kicked out of the country. The communist regime more than frowned on tourists seeking prostitutes, opium, and gambling, all of which had been plentiful in the old days, but were now strictly outlawed. Still, Dirk was undeterred.

Each morning he had checked the registers of the tourist hotels to see if Henri Bouscaral had registered. Visas were tightly controlled, and Dirk knew it would be extremely difficult for Bouscaral to check in under a false name. Each day Dirk had wandered the jammed streets full of thousands of bicyclists, and had toured the city's sights, hoping against hope that he would stumble across someone who knew of the acrobatic threesome. Each night he had been forced to retire to his room alone as the city seemed to close up entirely, offering no stimulation to one such as he, who was used to an active nightlife. By this third day he was bored out of his mind, and his bird of paradise was raging from disuse. Dirk could not remember going three days in his entire adult life without getting laid. All he could think about was the mysteriously beautiful Kolina and her ravishing sister, Barbro, and beat his meat mercilessly.

Then, quite unexpectedly, on the evening of his third day, an elderly, neatly dressed Oriental approached him just as he was about to retire to his hotel after another futile day of searching. "Excuse me, sir," the Chinese said politely in perfect English, "but I think I may help you."

"How?" Dirk asked suspiciously, aware that the city was ripe with agents of the government.

"If you would be so kind, follow me."

"Where to?"

"To that which you seek." The elderly man turned and moved off down the sidewalk, which was clustered with curbside barbers and cobblers just closing up their stands.

Eagerly, Dirk fell in behind him, checking carefully to see if they were being followed. There was such a crush of people, scurrying to their homes on foot or by bicycle, that it was impossible to ascertain whether anyone was paying more than usual attention to the tall, lean American. In his short stay, Dirk had become quite accustomed to being the object of an almost childlike curiosity. Grinning, friendly faces had often clustered around him on his daily tours of the city, and he had grown quite fond of their openly expressed good humor. Now, however, he wished he were smaller and less conspicuous, for he had an undeniable feeling he was onto something important. Slouching as much as his six-foot-two frame would allow, Dirk hurried after the elderly man.

He was led far from the hotel, down to the Bund, the waterfront, which, by the time they reached it, was almost devoid of people. Giant freighters and boats of all sizes and descriptions filled the famous harbor, and strident whistles announced departing craft. In the gathering dusk, lights were twinkling on, ringing the waterfront like sparkling jewels. And still the old Chinese man scurried on, with Dirk on his trail. Deeper into the warehouse district they moved, and Dirk began to feel a growing sense of unease. Doubt flooded him. Was he actually being led to his goal, or to some sinister trap? Several times he tried hailing the little man, calling to him to slow down. But the gentleman, dressed in a muted gray Mao suit, did not even turn around. He ducked around the corner of a large wooden structure and disappeared.

Dirk approached the corner and stopped, staring down a pitch-black alleyway, the hairs on the back of his neck rising with suspicion. The little Oriental was nowhere to be seen. Dirk hesitated, debating with himself. Should he or shouldn't he? Though he knew modern-day China was relatively free from crime and violence, his caution was getting the best of him. He was about to turn away when the cultured voice of the little man called out from the darkness, "This way, please. Do not worry. All is well."

Dirk squared his shoulders and walked slowly into the alleyway. He had progressed only a few steps when he heard someone moving beside him. He whirled just as a karate chop crashed into the back of his neck, sending him sprawling to the pavement and into oblivion.

Slowly, tediously he climbed the steep ladder back to consciousness. A single lightbulb glared over his head, and he found himself lying on a metal floor. He eased his head into a roll to look around, and was pleased to note that he was experiencing no pain other than a slight stiffness in his neck. His eyes darted around the metal walls, which were held together with large rivets, like boilerplate. The bare room was small and looked like a cabin on a freighter of some sort. He experienced a flash of fear—was he being Shanghaied, as in olden days? Was he being held prisoner? He pushed unsteadily to his feet and swayed dizzily for a moment before his head cleared. Urgently he checked his pockets; his wallet and passport were missing. That sent him into a tailspin of remorse. Why hadn't he listened to his inner voice of caution? He tried the handle on the single door. He was locked in. He began pounding on the iron door, shouting, "Open up, dammit!"

He ceased his racket to listen, pressing his ear against the cold metal. Not a sound. No engines throbbing, no sense of motion anywhere. Frantically he looked around for something to attack the door's large hinges, but there was nothing in the room except himself. He flashed on Honey's beautiful face admonishing him for taking such an unnecessary risk. And he longed for just one more opportunity to hold her in his arms. Cursing his own foolishness, he slumped against the door in remorse.

A sound broke into his self-castigation. Someone was opening the door! He stepped back with a clenched fist raised, prepared to attack. The door swung inward on its rusty hinges, squeaking loudly. Dirk steeled himself. To his astonishment, a tiny, grandmotherly woman poked her gray head around the door with a friendly smile. "You okay?" she asked politely.

He nodded and was about to bombard her with questions when she motioned to him to follow. She withdrew, and he could hear her cotton shoes swishing down the outside corridor. He stuck his head out, checking both ways before stepping over the raised rim of the doorjamb and hurrying after her. The woman was gowned in a richly embroidered robe of bright scarlet silk, and in her tightly bound gray hair a black lacquered comb formed a small crown on the back of her head. They were, indeed, on a ship of some sort, but there were no indications in the small compartments he passed that it had been used recently. Not a personal item could be seen anywhere. It looked like a ghost ship.

On and on he was led, through the bowels of what was apparently a large ship, until she stopped outside another closed door. She bowed to him formally and opened the metal door. This one did not squeak. A soft glow of light spilled out and he looked in. The walls were covered in rich tapestries that looked hundreds of years old, and on the floor lay an exquisite rug of blue and gold. On a small ebony table before a couch of yellow satin pillows lay his wallet and passport. He scooped them up and checked his money supply. Not a single bill was missing. Perplexed, he turned toward the hatchway. The little grandmother had vanished.

"Hello?" he called out. "Anyone here?" Silence greeted him. In the corner of the room, below a hanging paper lantern, he noticed another table. On it was a slender-stemmed pipe and a small box of wooden matches. He sniffed the bowl of the long pipe and grinned in recognition. Opium. The real stuff. Not one to let such an opportunity slip by, he struck a match and lit the black, sticky residue, inhaling deeply on the pipe. The heady effects of the powerful drug were instantaneous. He settled his long frame on the yellow satin couch and puffed away, realizing he was taking further risks, but too curious to stop.

Time slipped steadily away and he was so stoned that he had little desire to move; his limbs seemed extraordinarily heavy, and visions of Oriental concubines began invading his awareness. Lovely, black-eyed, raven-haired beauties in traditional robes appeared as if from nowhere and pulled him to his feet. Gently they eased him out of his clothes and, naked, he towered above them, grinning down on their perfect beauty, trying to determine whether they were real or only figments of his overstimulated imagination. A soft robe of blue silk was placed around his shoulders and he was tugged forward, one girl on each hand, another behind him, pushing steadily. They moved him directly to one of the large, gold-threaded tapestries, and as if by magic, it parted, revealing a large, opulent room.

The sweet smell of burning incense invaded his nostrils as he was maneuvered into the luxuriously furnished room. Priceless Oriental antiques were everywhere; it was a room truly fit for an emperor. At the far end he was lowered with delicate precision to a raised platform covered with silk pillows, and one of the lovelies stuck an orange segment into his mouth. Its sweetness was astounding. Another was bathing his feet in warm water, massaging them with a musk-scented oil. Still another was arranging pillows behind his head, propping him up to a partial sitting position. Grinning like a fool, he watched through lowered lids the dreamlike proceedings, trying to figure out whether he was blissfully stoned or in the midst of a fantasy come true.

Lute music began playing from somewhere nearby, and as if on cue, the three black-eyed beauties ceased their

150

ministrations and gathered before him in a row, bowing subserviently, each a mirror image of the one next to her. In time to the delicate music, one by one they parted the sashes of their richly hued robes and dropped them to the carpet. He stared in wondrous delight at their perfectly formed bodies. Their breasts were small and set high, and the coal-black triangles between their trim thighs sparkled with a healthy sheen in the faint light. They turned away from him, displaying their straight, strong backs and the sweet curve of their asses, like rounded scoops of almond-flavored ice cream. Dirk's bird began to sit up and take notice.

The lute was joined by several other Chinese instruments he could not name, and the music picked up tempo. The trio of beauties joined hands in a circle on the vibrantly colored carpet and, with a tantalizing smile in his direction, quickly formed a living, inverted pyramid. One girl stood holding on her slightly bent thighs one foot of each of the other two standing girls. The two on the sides arched way back, each held only by one hand of the girl underneath. Their black-haired pussies protruded like chocolate-covered cherries. The two on top leapt lightly to the carpet and at once fell forward onto their hands, kicking their feet up and rising into a handstand on either side of the girl in the middle, who once again held them balanced—this time by one of their legs. Dirk applauded madly.

Still more athletic formations were exhibited, each more difficult than the one preceding. The trio were remarkably elastic, able to bend and contort their slender, lovely bodies into the most unbelievable shapes and positions. Regardless of the permutation of bodies being displayed, there was an underlying sensuality in all their movements, as if the exhibition were for one purpose only: to arouse the viewer to a state of erotic tension. His bird was standing rigid underneath the blue silk of his robe and straining to be released, to fly into at least one of the black bird nests before him.

Teasingly the trio flipped over into a row of backbends, their plump, ripe cunts aimed directly at him, their trim thighs wide open, the luscious lips of their pussies like a matched set of halved walnuts. The girl in the middle remained in that position as her two sisters moved to either end of her. One placed her mouth over the exposed pussy, the other placed her crotch over the upturned mouth of the backbending one. Soon they were in the sweetest daisy chain, linked together in a circle with their mouths on one another's pussies. Dirk could not stand the tension any longer. He opened his robe and took his bird in hand, stroking it up and down as he stared into the tangle of sweet meat.

When the talented trio came up for air and saw him pounding vigorously on his rigid prick, they frowned at him as if he had broken a house rule. They crawled up on the silk pillows beside him, tugging off his blue robe. They laid him out flat and took his hands away from his swollen dick. One girl's hand grasped his fluttering bird near the base, and directly on top of that hand another girl clutched it, then the third on top of that one. Rhythmically they began to stroke up and down, their lovely faces serious as they concentrated on matching movements. He reached out a hand and fingered the loose lips of one, finding her tight and moist. Encouraged by her docile reaction, he reached for a second helping and found this one the exact duplicate of the other. As the triplets pumped on his peter, he fingered two of their cunts. The third looked at him sorrowfully and he snapped his tongue at her, indicating that he wanted to lick her silly. Obligingly she scooted around and hunkered down over his face.

His tongue darted into her, parting her outer lips and getting down to business. She tasted like ripe melons.

Fingering, tonguing, his cock twitching in their hands, Dirk felt a growing urgency to satisfy more basic needs. But the trio knew what they were doing; theirs was an ancient, honored art and they were a marvelous, well-oiled machine designed expressly for the purpose of pleasing a male. Just when he felt on the verge of showering them with semen, they would change positions or tactics or rhythms, easing him down on the other side of ecstasy and gently but steadily raising him back up again. One would suck on his dick, another on his toes, another on his fingers. Then they would change; rolling him over, one would tongue his asshole while another would wash his balls in her mouth, and the third would take both his thumbs and jam them into her open portal of pleasure.

And his bird kept growing larger and larger, turning beet red, its engorged head a deep purple, pulsating with every pounding beat of his overstimulated heart. He felt that he was being tortured, tormented, that the lovelies were deliberately trying to drive him mad. Even when one slid her juicy cunt over his dick and began athletically to bounce up and down on it, like a pogo stick, he could not help thinking that this too shall pass ... and it did, for when his balls began to contract, signaling an approaching climax, the girl would slip off and shove his screaming peter into a cool liquid, sending him plummeting away from coming. On and on they worked on him, until he had no thoughts, no feelings except in the hot head of his perplexed and pleading bird. It was as though the trio had turned him into one giant throbbing cock, and he began to moan with the agony of it all.

Regardless of how much he ate at their jelly rolls, or how deeply he fingered their moist channels, the triplets gave no outward sign of arousal. Steadily they went about their business, impervious to their own pleasures. He began to writhe on the silk pillows, pleading for release, his senses satiated, his bird becoming numb from the workout. At last one of them let him enter her pussy again and he banged into her, bouncing her up into the air, their pelvises crashing together. Nearer and nearer he approached the elusive goal, and he feared he would be teased away from it once more.

Closer and closer he felt the tidal wave building, and he lapped frantically at the dripping lips perched over his face, his middle fingers dived deep into the last girl's pudendum. The tension-filled ecstasy was overwhelming, mounting steadily until he felt he could not take any more. Higher and higher his lust climbed, and then peaked, balanced precariously on the very edge of the precipice. Instinctively the trio of beauties stopped all their movements and he hung suspended on the unbearable brink. All at once, he blew up in an enormous explosion of semen. Over and over, he sailed snowballs of gism everywhere and still he kept coming, bucketsful it felt like, and he was drenched from head to toe with the most satisfying climax of his life. It was so complete, so all-consuming, he immediately blacked out and sank into the silky skin surrounding him, drained to the last drop.

When he came to, he was back in bed in his own hotel room. Confused by the sudden transition, he tried to ease his head off the pillow, but did not have the strength. His entire body felt used and abused. He raised the covers to look down at his poor tortured bird. It lay coiled on his thigh like a sleeping snake, but it was the strangest color it had ever been—an almost green tinge at its head, while the rest was a sickly, pale purple. Exhausted, he rolled his head into the pillow, smelling the delicious aroma of the triplets nearby. On the pillow next to him lay three slightly bruised gardenias and a bill printed neatly in English.

It read simply, *For services rendered by the Mee-Lan Triplets—three thousand dollars.*

And that sum was exactly what was missing from his wallet.

12.

HONEY

"I didn't have a chance to show them Kolina's picture," Dirk reported with a rueful smile.

"What?" Honey exclaimed. "You went all the way to Shanghai, spent three grand for a tryst with the triplets, and failed even to get around to your purpose in being there?"

His lightly freckled face flushed and he ducked his sandy blonde head, looking like a guilty little boy. Purposefully she looked away from him and down over the crowd encircling the paddock. She and Dirk were sitting in the bright afternoon sunshine on the outside terrace of the members-only lounge of the exclusive Royal Hong Kong Jockey Club. She had arrived in the city the morning before, but Dirk just had returned from his fruitless sojourn in Shanghai. She swept a stern gaze back to him. "You dummy, I thought finding Kolina was paramount to you."

"It is," he replied defensively. "I told you I was half drugged on that opium, and never even had the opportunity to question them." He fiddled nervously with the binoculars hanging around his neck by a leather strap.

"Well, if that doesn't beat all," she muttered, and took a sip of her cool gin and tonic. Below, the packed grandstand roared en masse at the start of the fifth race. She watched a bay thoroughbred charge into a comfortable lead. "My lucky number seven is ahead," she noted aloud, with little enthusiasm.

He glanced down at the track, following the race's progress around the large oval, and mumbled, "I can't get used to them running clockwise."

"And I can't get used to your attitude," she sighed. "There I was, in the mountains of Bulgaria, busting my ass to help you while you're off dorking around with some dippy triplets."

"They were sensational," he said emphatically. "Well worth the price *and* the trip. They would've blown even your mind, they were so talented. How was I to know I wouldn't get to speak to them?"

The cheering crowd below broke into sustained applause. Number seven had won. It didn't seem to matter to Honey as she said, "Dirk, you're not going to like what I'm about to say, but say it I must. I think we've reached a dead end and should call it off."

"Not on your life, sis," he burst out. "You can quit if you want, but not me. I'm going to find her if she's thirty-five by the time I do."

"But we don't even know for certain that she's being held against her will. Yves Bouscaral thinks she's highly promiscuous and given to mad crushes. Granted, he could be saying that to protect his older brother. But if she is by chance with Henri, it may be through her own choice, because she's enamored of him—an older man and all that."

"You haven't seen her in the flesh," he said. "Well, I did, and she was frightened and seeking help. I didn't imagine that. That was real."

Honey reflected for a moment, realizing she was treading on very thin ice; when Dirk got worked up about something, hell or high water wouldn't persuade him otherwise. She reached across and gently took his hand. "Dirk, you are a dear and generous man to take up her cause. Even as a kid, you were always for the underdog. But face it, we're licked. Where could we possibly look next? Henri Bouscaral has unlimited funds and could be anywhere in the world."

"*We* have unlimited funds, thanks to Wildon Enterprises," he replied forcefully. "And by God, I'll spend every last cent of my share to find her."

"I have no doubt you will," she said, and fished her winning ticket stub out of her purse. "Be a pet and go cash these in. We may need the bread by the time we've located her."

An infectious smile broke out on Dirk's boyish face. Impulsively he leapt up and leaned down to kiss her on the cheek. "Thanks, Honey. You're the very best."

"Well, at some things, yes . . ." She laughed with him and watched him lope away toward the betting windows. At that moment her love for him swept over her with such force that she felt tears welling.

No one in the world meant more to her than her baby brother. She had seen him through many a crisis, and vice versa, but nothing had seemed so important to him as this latest obsession. Even his physical appearance had changed drastically; he was gaunt and paler, a tense nervousness had invaded his gray-blue eyes, and he seemed to have lost his sense of humor, becoming short-tempered and testy. Those changes underscored how seriously he was taking this mission. It pained her to see him in such a state, and she vowed to herself right then that regardless of how futile his quest seemed, she would help him to the bitter end. After all, he was her only family, and one thing she had learned over the years: blood *was* thicker than any other bond. At least to the surviving Wildon clan.

She dabbed at her eyes with a Flemish lace handkerchief that had belonged to her mother, and was returning her attention to the racing form when suddenly Dirk reappeared, running toward her with an alarmingly white face. "She's here!" he croaked breathlessly, and tugged on her arm. "She's here, Honey! In one of the boxes. Down there. Come look!"

"Kolina?"

"Yes, for God's sake, who else? I walked right by her and almost didn't see her. Can you believe our luck? It's holding true, huh? Come on, take a look before she disappears again!"

Honey popped to her feet, hurrying with him to the terrace railing. "Is Bouscaral with her?"

"I didn't see him, but the same two thugs are. The ones from Central Park," he said in a rush, and pointed. "Down there, third box from the center aisle. See? That incredible blonde. That's her. That's Kolina Svensen or I'm a complete jackass. Here, take a good look at her through the glasses." He whipped the binoculars from around his neck and thrust them into her hands. "What should we do? We can't let her get away again."

"Cool it, will you? And stop jostling me, I can't focus." She slowly adjusted the lenses, bringing into sharp detail the breathtaking face of Kolina. Dirk's imagination had not played tricks on him; this was the girl from his photos and one of the loveliest, most enchanting presences Honey had ever laid eyes on. Kolina possessed an irresistibly beautiful face, huge innocent blue eyes, a complexion of pure peaches and cream, a graceful jawline, and a pert, saucy nose. Her hair was the color of white beach sand, and what little of her figure Honey could see was surprisingly voluptuous for a girl barely sixteen. "No wonder you're ga-ga over her," Honey murmured, still observing Kolina under the magnifying lenses. "She *is* spectacular."

"I told you, I told you, didn't I? She is pure magic," Dirk rambled on, beside himself with exhilaration. "I can't believe our luck, Honey. Of all the places in all the world . . ."

She said as she lowered the glasses, "Now the question is, what the hell do we do about it? We can't just barge down there and kidnap her."

"Why not? That's what that damned Bouscaral did."

"We don't know that for sure," Honey said with sisterly caution. "He's an extremely powerful and wealthy man. We don't want to take any chances."

"Well, think of something!"

"I'm trying to," she replied, and marched back to their table to down the rest of her drink. The sight of the two bodyguards on either side of the blonde had given Honey pause; no telling if they were armed. They certainly looked like the kind who would be—all gristle and sweat. Probably loyal to boot, and dumb as hell. Swiftly she examined the options as Dirk remained at the railing, his eyes glued on his beloved Kolina. Even his posture indicated the extent of his ardor; he was bending over the railing like a wet noodle. Honey promptly formulated an idea and returned by his side. "Here's what we'll do . . ."

Moments later, the brother-sister team put into action her daring plan. With Dirk watching from a distance, Honey sidled into the empty box next to Kolina and her guards. She sat next to the iron-pipe railing separating the two boxes and made certain the two thugs caught not only her eyes, but an eyeful of her figure. She was wearing a fetching afternoon dress by Halston, a simple clinging sheath of emerald jersey, cut low in front, exposing a healthy swell of snowy bosom. Her deep red hair was swept up under a wide-brimmed straw hat, and square-lensed dark glasses covered half her face. After tossing them a disarming smile, she pretended to be absorbed in her racing form, and then looked over to the guard sitting just on the other side of the metal railing. "Excuse me," she purred in halting French, "but I need some help. Would you be so kind?"

He indicated that he would be more than happy to oblige, and she leaned across the railing into him, pointing to the confusing statistics in her racing form. Heads bent together as much as her wide-brimmed hat would allow, they computed the chances for her chosen horse to place in the next race. The other guard, on the far side of a bored-looking Kolina, was watching them with obvious jealousy. Honey flashed him a come-hither smile, and he bounced abruptly over to them, kneeling down between them to offer his expert advice. Honey plied her considerable charms on them, brushing a full breast into one, touching the other's knee with an intimate but innocent gesture. She kept bending forward over her racing form, her breasts spilling out of her tight dress like fresh cream. The two thugs, whose accents told her they were from Marseilles, were so taken by her that she moved into the next phase of her plan.

Urging them to come with her to place the bet on their mutually chosen horse, Honey managed to get them out of their box. Unfortunately they brought Kolina with them. As Honey walked in front of them, she spotted Dirk, his face hidden in a newspaper. A few steps farther on she glanced casually over her shoulder and spotted him following several paces behind. Upstairs, just before the lines winding out from the betting windows, she approached the first-aid room. With a sudden swoop she latched on to the nearest guard and, giggling suggestively, dragged him into the room. Fortunately it was empty. The startled man put up little resistance, and even less as she pressed him against the wall, rubbing her heavy breasts into him and reaching for his basket of goodies. Before he could blink, she had his dick out in her hands and had sunk to her knees, placing it in her mouth like a babe at its mother's tit.

She was just working his member up into a healthy-sized hard-on when the second guard stuck a sour face into the room to see what the hell was going on. He was so surprised to see her sucking away that he stepped into the room to castigate the first guard. Not missing a stroke with her mouth, she reached for the newcomer's hand and pulled him toward her. In one deft movement she unzipped him and pulled his cock out also. As the two men stared down in pleased astonishment, she began alternating her attention, first sucking on one, then on the other. Back and forth she went, her mouth like a metronome, her hands caressing and tugging and stroking. Their cocks, like their bodies, were a perfect matched set—thick and stubby. Their short, powerful legs were splayed wide, and their barrel chests were heaving under their tight suitcoats. Each had a sweaty hand jammed down inside her dress, cupping one of her breasts, tweaking and pinching her distended nipples.

With a burst of air through his squashed nose, the first guard came in her mouth. Immediately, as he pushed his thick dick back into his pants to zip up, she inhaled the second cock, washing it with the semen of the first. This guard, however, was more dedicated to his chosen profession. At once he growled at the first to go check the girl. Honey, realizing that Dirk must have had enough time by then to speak to Kolina alone, did not bother to finish off the second guard. Pretending a coughing fit, she gagged on his cock and, gasping for air, stood, wiping her mouth apologetically. He frowned in disappointment and made a grab for her pussy. She let him have a quick feel before pushing him away. He muttered in French that she was a damned whore and she laughed gaily, hurrying out of the room, losing herself quickly in the milling mob lined up to place bets.

As planned, she met Dirk in the private lounge reserved for members. "What'd you do in the first-aid room?" he demanded as she reached his table.

She winked. "That's irrelevant. Did you get to Kolina?"

Glumly he nodded and took a healthy swallow of his Scotch and water. "Just as I expected. She *is* being held against her will. She recognized me at once and ran right to me, begging for help."

"Why didn't you whisk her off right then? I sure as hell gave you enough time."

"I was going to, but Bouscaral showed up," he growled, and downed his drink.

"Henri's here? Where?"

"How the hell should I know? He just appeared and grabbed hold of her and hustled her away. Goddamn, Honey, we were so close to getting her. And now she's lost again. Maybe this time forever."

She patted his shoulder, speaking softly. "Nothing's forever, Dirk. We'll find her. And this time we'll get her away for good." She pulled him to his feet. "Come on, let's go thank our host, the Major General, and get back to the hotel. If Bouscaral's in Hong Kong, he can't go far, can he?"

* * *

They returned to the Shangri-La Hotel in Honey's rented Bentley limousine, and as Dirk hurried into the phone booth to begin checking with the other five-star hotels, she went to the front desk. "Do you have Henri Bouscaral registered?"

The polite young man checked his registry. "Yes we do, miss. Are you here for an interview with him?"

"Well, yes I am," she said quickly. "Tell me, what is he looking for?"

"A governess for his niece, I believe. But he's requested that only French-speaking women apply."

"*Tres bien*. Would you make an appointment for me? My name is Claudine Fortel."

Honey did not tell Dirk of the propitious new opportunity until they were upstairs in the double suite of adjoining rooms she had booked earlier for them. As she hurriedly undressed in her bedroom, she shouted through the open door, explaining her new plan, concluding with, "So I've got till six tonight to become Claudine."

Dirk rushed to the open doorway, obviously upset. "I'm not going to let you do this, Honey. It's too dangerous. You have no idea what this jerk is like."

Dressed only in her French-cut panties, she pawed through her closet of traveling clothes. "I should wear something sedate, shouldn't I? Don't want him to think I'm too worldly."

"Dammit, Honey," he railed. "You're not going through with this."

"Don't be such a pussy," she teased, and yanked out a black crepe dress with a matching box jacket. "This should do. I doubt he'll recognize it as an original Yves St. Laurent."

He ran to her, jerking her around by the arm to face him. "What about the guards? They'll recognize you in a flash."

She smiled sweetly. "I plan to dye my hair. What do you think of a seal brown? Or should it be stark black?"

"Bouscaral is a goddamned pervert," he shouted. "A kidnapper and a raper of innocent girls. Who knows what else? He's the Prince of Kink, remember?"

"I'm perfectly aware of all that," she said softly. "You're a sweet thing to worry about me. But don't, okay? I know what I'm doing. Just think of Kolina. If I can land this job, I'll be perfectly situated to help her escape." One arm covering her full white breasts, she kissed him on the lips and brushed back a lock of stubborn hair from his forehead. "It's too good an opportunity to pass up. It's our lucky day, Dirk. I won back on lucky number seven the three grand you blew in Shanghai, and you found Kolina again. And now this lucky chance. We're on a roll, baby, we're on a roll. Let's go for it."

13.

HONEY

Two hours later, Honey had completed the major portion of her physical transformation into Claudine Fortel. In the luxuriously large bathroom of her hotel suite, she had dyed her dark red hair a deep seal brown and, after it had dried, pulled it back tightly off her exquisite face, sweeping its healthy thickness into a flattering French roll, leaving wisply tendrils around her face to soften the severity. As her brows and lashes were naturally a deep auburn, she left them that way and had applied a minimal amount of makeup, a mere hint of cheek blush and a pale lipgloss.

Standing before the full-length mirrors, still clad only in her pink bikini underwear, she narrowed her eyes and surveyed the results with growing satisfaction. "Goodbye, Honey," she murmured to her image. "Hello, Claudine." She was about to dress when she thought of one additional matter—something that would give her away to the more intimate viewer. Slipping off her panties, she scissored away her fiery red bush and then, lathering her entire mons veneris, carefully shaved it as clean as a baby's. Satisfied that there was little else that hinted at her former self—except her voluptuous figure—she struggled into a brassiere two sizes too small, pushing and mashing her full breasts into the uncomfortable confines.

A short time later she emerged fully dressed and fully transformed, a pair of hastily purchased black-rimmed glasses adding the final schoolmarmish touch. Smoothing the trim skirt of the sedate black crepe dress, she walked primly into Dirk's adjoining suite and waited silently for him to turn away from the window. She cleared her throat to attract his attention and he swung to her, his eyes growing wide with disbelief. "My God . . ." he sputtered.

"No . . . *mon Dieu*," she replied with a half smile. Gracefully she pirouetted for him and with amusement watched the color return to his amazed face.

"I . . . I can't believe it," he muttered finally, shaking his head.

"Tres, tres bien," she replied, even her voice taking on another quality, more reserved, less confident. "If it meets your approval, I'll be off. Claudine Fortel has a most important interview in less than ten minutes."

"What if he checks your passport?" he demanded suddenly.

"I'm leaving all my ID here. A terrible misfortune, losing it all, is it not? I just can't imagine what happened to it—one minute it was in my purse, the next it had disappeared. Thieves, perhaps?" Honey smiled knowingly and started for the door.

"Wait," Dirk said urgently, and moved to her. "I still don't like the smell of all this. You are putting yourself needlessly into danger."

She paused, one hand on the hall doorknob. "Dirk,

relax. It's all part of the game, no? I didn't graduate *summa cum laude* from Wellesley for nothing. Smarts I have. Now if our luck holds, we'll have Kolina away from him before dawn." She stood on her tiptoes and bussed him lightly on the lips. "I love you."

"Damn, I wish I could go with you," he said sourly.

She laughed. "You he'd recognize for sure. Now stop stewing. I'll be fine. I'll be back as soon as I know anything." She blew him a kiss, opened the door, and stepped out.

In the elevator on her way to the top floor of the grand old hotel, Honey herself had a brief moment of concern, but then brushed it aside; there would be no way for Bouscaral to know that the false-bearded face he had glimpsed in the Convent of the Sisters of the Moon was indeed the same as Claudine Fortel.

Her knock on the penthouse door was answered by one of the bodyguards she'd serviced in the Jockey Club's first-aid room. Introducing herself with the bogus name, she surveyed his face, trying to determine whether he suspected anything. Other than an approving leer as he gave her the once-over, there was nothing to indicate that he was onto her disguise. He ushered her into the sitting room of the huge suite and told her to wait, before disappearing through an inner door. Moments later he reappeared and told her Monsieur Bouscaral would see her now.

Sedately she walked into the master bedroom and stopped. Henri Bouscaral turned to face her. Tall, thin, elegantly dressed in a black velvet suit, he was disgustingly handsome in an almost sinister way—neatly trimmed black mustache, carefully coiffed but thinning hair, steely black eyes that studied her in a coldly detached manner. No smile of welcome, no greeting to set her at ease, just a frozen mask of decadence. At once he began questioning her in French: Where was she from? Did she have any immediate family? Where was she educated? Had she ever taught before? What was she doing in Hong Kong? Was she free to travel?

To all these questions and more, Honey replied in fluent, flawless French, supplying answers that were close enough to the truth, yet artfully concealed her background. She said she was the only child born to now-deceased French parents in the United States, reared and schooled in Switzerland, that she had taught for several years at a private girls' school in Canada and that she had come to the Orient to broaden her horizons. Bouscaral observed her carefully through half-lidded eyes, offering no encouragement, nothing but a coldness that bordered on the sinister. She inquired about the salary, the duties she would be expected to perform, and who her pupil would be.

To this he replied, "The daughter of my brother who died last year in Africa."

"How unfortunate," she said in French, with a sad bow of her head. "Will you be staying in Hong Kong for a while?"

"No," he said abruptly and picked up the phone receiver. In rapid English he asked the front desk to have his bill drawn up, and then hung up, returning his steely gaze to her. "The position is yours."

"Merci," she said, and silently congratulated herself on a successful subterfuge. "When do I begin?"

"Immediately. We leave at once."

"Leave?" she asked in surprise. "For where?"

"That is none of your business."

She hesitated, stalling for time. "I must return to my room for my things."

"That will not be necessary," he replied sharply. "I will furnish all you need."

170

"But that is impossible," she protested. "I have many—"

"*If* you desire this position," he interrupted sharply, "you must do everything I say, without comment. Is that understood? I will not tolerate disobedience."

"But my personal belongings . . ."

"I will have them sent to our next destination." Abruptly he turned and threw open the door, calling to one of his men for the bags to be carried down.

Within all too short a time, Honey found herself being hustled out of the hotel by a rear entrance and into one of the several chauffeured Rolls limousines parked with motors idling. With a guard on either side of her, she was able to catch only a glimpse of Kolina slipping into the front limo along with Bouscaral. With one last, regretful look back at the Shangri-La Hotel, Honey was whisked away. Their departure had been so swift, she had not had a moment alone to notify Dirk of the sudden turn of events. A clammy uncertainty gripped her.

At the Hong Kong International Airport, she was placed aboard Bouscaral's private Learjet in a rear compartment with the guards, isolated completely from Kolina, up front with the decidedly decadent Frenchman. The jet took off with a powerful whine of its twin engines, and soon the city's lights had faded far behind them.

The flight was long, with several fuel stops along the way. Throughout, Honey sat between the two guards, who dozed on and off and, when they were awake, rarely spoke to her or acknowledged her presence. Occasionally she would drift off to sleep, only to wake with a pounding heart. Once one of the guards tried to fondle her and she had to put him in his place by threatening to report him to his employer. That threat seemed to work, for the other guard roundly berated him for taking liberties.

171

Thus a silent, tense truce was formed, and she refused to speak with either of them after that.

Then, just as dawn was spreading its glorious colors in the east, the Learjet landed on a green island of moderate size. There she was placed in still another limousine with the two guards. Their limo followed Bouscaral's through the quaint town, and at once she recognized the place as Papeete, Tahiti.

Far beyond the outskirts of town, the limousines pulled off the main road and into a walled compound set on an isolated peninsula. A series of pink stucco bungalows ringed by towering, swaying palms bordered a broad expanse of golden sand. She was shown to her quarters— a separate building that lay some distance from the main house. Exhausted by the tense flight she was told by the guard who accompanied her that she would have until four that afternoon by herself. Grateful for the solitude, she collapsed on the bed and promptly fell asleep.

She was awakened by a soft tapping on her door. A native servant greeted her with several flat boxes and brought them in before withdrawing silently. The boxes contained several changes of clothing, demure in style, somber in color. After bathing, Honey tried on one of the dresses, a simple suit of dark gray, and found that it fit almost perfectly, if a little tight through the bustline. Reluctantly she once again forced her breasts into the small bra, dressed, and left her bungalow shortly before four. The tropical beauty of the locale and the beach's balmy breezes did little to assuage her nervousness as she walked to the main house.

Her knock was answered by Henri Bouscaral, wearing loose white beach clothes, who icily led her to a small, book-lined study, the windows of which overlooked a portion of the stunning beach. He sat behind a large

172

desk and began speaking in officious, pompous tones: "There are several rules you must agree to obey before I will let you start teaching my niece. One, you must never, ever ask her a personal question. Two, you must force her to work hard. Kolina is a very lazy girl and needs strict discipline. Three, if her French has not improved measurably within the week, you will be dismissed. Do I have your agreement on these?"

"Do I have any choice?"

"Do not be impertinent," he barked.

She reached deep for a subservient smile. "I do not mean to be. This is all so new. Forgive me. Of course I agree to any rule you stipulate. You are the boss, no?"

"That is correct." He stood and called out loudly, "Kolina, come in here at once."

Shortly an inner door opened and the girl stepped into the room, a defiant pout on her enchanting face. Almost arrogantly, she eyed Honey as he introduced them. Honey smiled warmly and greeted her with, *"Enchanté."* The girl mumbled the same and, as if bored already, stared out the window to the sparkling blue waves.

"Ma cher," he said quietly to her, "you must be respectful of your new teacher and try very hard to be a good girl."

Kolina replied angrily, "But why must I study French? I can understand every stupid thing you say."

"Silence," he ordered, and stared her down with his cold eyes. "Do not forget your breeding, or your punishment if you fail to live up to my expectations."

"How could I forget?" she wailed. "You won't let me. *Ever.*"

He smiled apologetically at Honey. "See? She is a very spirited, high-strung girl. You will have your hands full." With that, Bouscaral called in one of the guards and strode out of the room. The younger of the guards, a pasty-faced bulldog of a man, stood against the open door with his arms folded across his barrel chest.

Honey smiled again at Kolina. "We will be good friends very soon, I just know."

"How do you know?" the girl shot back. "You won't last a week. Henri will send you away like all the others."

"There have been others before me?"

"No personal questions," the guard growled.

"Pardon," Honey mumbled, and returned her attention to the lovely young blonde. The girl was obviously under great stress; dark circles underlined her large blue eyes like dirty thumbprints on the fair skin, and she had a nervous habit of running a hand through her hair, sweeping it back from her brow continually. Honey sat on the edge of the desk. "How many years of French have you had?"

"Six," Kolina snorted. "I know more than enough, but Henri wants me to be busy all the time with meaningless tasks."

"You speak it very well," Honey praised. "Your accent is lovely."

"*Merci,*" the girl replied with some surprise, and began studying her new teacher with a different attitude. "May I call you Claudine?"

"But of course, Kolina. Let us begin with some simple conjugations . . ."

With a bored, put-upon sigh, the girl began her first lesson.

In the isolated but beautiful location, the following days blended together into a dreary sameness for Honey. Twice a day she met with Kolina under the ever-watchful eye of one of the guards, or sometimes that of Henri himself. For those two-hour sessions, Honey drilled and tested the

174

girl, working her hard but with gentle persistence. Honey discovered that Kolina was an extremely bright and capable young woman, with an inquisitive mind. It took several sessions before Kolina began to trust that Honey was not merely an extension of the authoritarian Henri. Gradually the girl's sullen wariness began slipping away, to be replaced by an openly expressed fondness and dependency. Honey, however, maintained a professional though warm distance, not wanting to raise Henri's suspicions that she was usurping his domain. She knew she was being watched carefully at all times, and made no attempts at getting the girl off alone.

Nights were the longest for Honey, who would retire to her bungalow alone. She worried about Dirk and feared he would be crazed with anxiety from not hearing anything. There was no telephone at the compound, and the only times she was allowed to go into the town of Papeete for toiletries or a bit of shopping, she was always accompanied by one of the guards, so her chances of slipping away to send a cable or mail a letter were nonexistent. She thought of many alternate ways of notifying her brother, but discarded each as too risky. Her meals were taken either alone or with the rest of the traveling entourage of servants. She kept to herself, speaking to no one unless she was first spoken to.

Then, on the afternoon of the fifth day, she found a logical way to get Kolina alone. The compound had several modern facilities, including a sauna. Honey had been allowed to use it by herself once in a while, but it wasn't until she saw Henri driving off with one of the guards that she knew her chance had finally arrived. She waited until she and Kolina were a half hour into their session before suggesting that they take a sauna together and continue the lesson there. At once Kolina agreed to the idea, and as they approached the sauna room, she saucily told the guard to get lost. He pointed out that he was not to leave them alone, and Kolina became quite angry with him. "Am I to tell Henri you insisted on seeing the two of us naked?"

The guard grew flustered, not knowing how to respond. Honey took the opportunity to push Kolina into the small dressing room off the sauna, where she firmly closed the door in the startled guard's face. Kolina immediately shed her clothes as if they were contaminated, and stood in all her nude glory for Honey's approval. Long-legged, high-hipped, the girl possessed large, beautifully formed breasts. Delicately tipped with small pink nipples, they looked oddly out of place on the girl's otherwise lissome body. The soft patch of blonde hair between her legs was like a small pillow of color on her pale, fair skin.

Honey tore away her gaze, not wanting to embarrass the girl. "You are truly lovely, Kolina," she murmured in French, and began unhooking her own brassiere. Her large breasts tumbled free, and she noted the girl's eyes growing wide with astonishment and envy.

"Why do you wear such a small bra?" Kolina asked ingenuously. "If I had big breasts like yours, I wouldn't wear a bra at all."

"I usually don't," Honey admitted, and stepped out of her skirt.

"So why do you now?" the girl persisted.

"Because I don't like the way the guards look at me."

"Those pigs," Kolina muttered with an angry glance at the closed door to the hall. "Honestly, they give me the creeps sometimes."

Honey nodded. "Me too." She tugged down her panties and again noted that Kolina was staring, this time open-mouthed.

"Why do you shave your thing?" the girl asked boldly.

Honey laughed, running a hand over the hairless mound between her alabaster thighs. "I like the sensation."

"What's it feel like?"

"Smooth. Try it. It's all right. I don't mind."

Hesitantly the girl reached out a hand and stroked the area, sending a shiver of delight up Honey's spine. Kolina locked eyes with her and whispered, "Would you shave mine for me?"

"If you want, but are you sure your uncle would approve?"

Instead of replying, Kolina withdrew her hand and, growing pensive, opened the interior door to the sauna, holding it for Honey to enter first. Inside, the dry, hot heat was a refreshing change from the sticky tropical humidity. Silently they stretched out together on a thick towel thrown over the wooden slat bench. For a long while, neither spoke. Finally Kolina whispered, "He's not my uncle."

"I know."

Kolina propped herself up on one elbow. "You do? How?"

Honey rolled toward her, whispering, "Remember the photographer in Central Park—the tall young man with the friendly eyes? The one you recently saw again at the Jockey Club?"

Kolina nodded, holding her breath. Honey brushed a lock of the girl's white-blonde hair off her face. "That's my brother, Dirk."

"But he's a Yankee."

"So am I. And I'm here to help you."

Speechlessly the girl stared, as if trying to absorb the astonishing news. Honey continued softly, not knowing how much time they had alone, "Are you being held against your will?"

"Yes . . . yes . . ."

"Have you tried to get away?"

"At first. But as you see, I'm watched continually."

"Would you let me help you escape?"

"Yes, of course, but how?"

"Leave that to me," Honey replied gently. "Just promise you won't let on to Henri or the guards that I am not what I seem. Or that we're planning something."

Kolina nodded energetically, then dropped flat on the bench, her pert young breasts already filmed with perspiration. "How do I know this isn't another of Henri's tricks?" she complained, staring at the ceiling. "He's always pulling things like this."

Honey placed a friendly hand on the girl's flat stomach. "I swear to you, I am your friend. I will do everything in my power to help. You must believe me. We may not get another chance to be alone."

The girl rolled her head, her large blue eyes searching Honey's with almost desperate urgency. "I want to believe . . . truly I do . . ."

Honey could not resist the temptation any longer. She leaned into the enchanting face and kissed Kolina softly on the lips. She heard a sharp intake of air from the girl, and then felt her slender arms encircling her. "Sweet Kolina," she murmured into the girl's moist neck. "I love you . . ."

"And I you," Kolina whispered passionately. "What's your real name?"

"For now, it's better that you don't know. You might mistakenly call me by it."

"I understand," Kolina said firmly, and rubbed her hardening nipples against Honey's already inflamed ones. "I want to make love to you," she panted into Honey's ear.

"And I to you . . . but we'd be taking a great risk. Henri

178

or the guard—" Her words were cut off by the sweet young mouth on hers. For a long while their kisses grew in intensity, their tongues snaking in and out of each other's bodies with their hands, slicking the thin film of sweat from firm breasts and tender thighs. It took Honey little time to realize the girl was more than knowledgeable in all areas of lovemaking, for Kolina's movements and responses were assured and experienced. That only increased Honey's ardor for the sweet young thing. Throwing caution to the hot, dry air surrounding them, Honey willingly followed the girl's expert lead. Their knees pressed up between damp thighs, pushing into the tender flesh of their crotches.

Though the temperature inside the cedar-lined sauna was already extreme, it did not begin to match Honey's internal heat. The long, lonely nights of total abstinence had left her like dry tinder, ready to explode at the slightest spark. And now the enchanting, almost mystical beauty of the virginal-appearing young woman in her arms, combined with the girl's expertise and firm, pliant flesh, set her off into spasms of incandescent bliss. Kolina's nipples in her mouth tasted like candy, and her skin was so smooth it seemed polished by thousands of worshipping hands. As Honey trailed her tongue down the soft curves of the healthy young breasts, Kolina's sweat-filmed skin tasted both salty and sweet.

As the girl traced her fingers over Honey's bounteous breasts, Honey, in turn, maneuvered herself around to bring her face down to the damp mat of blonde hair. She licked the pretty little navel, then worked her way down through the sparse blond hair and between the girl's pristine thighs. She was concentrating so hard on the contrasting texture of fair skin and fair hair that she was startled when Kolina darted a deft tongue deep into her wet slice. Honey moaned and, with her hands, spread the girl open even further. Like a fresh peach, juicy and sweet, pink and dripping, Kolina's cunt looked heavenly. There was a delicacy about the coloring, a perfect symmetry to the two halves, a girlish ruffle to the ridges. Honey parted the outer lips with her fingers and stared down into the lovely inner pair, undulating and waving at her like a welcoming flower of dewy flesh. Eager to taste the hidden delights, Honey lowered her tongue and, making a cone of its tip, dipped into the succulent, swollen trove. It was like diving into a jar of strawberry preserves, sweet and satisfying.

As Kolina worked her own tongue deep into her teacher's honeypot, Honey's tongue sliced into the trough of tender flesh. With the girl flat under her, Honey, on her knees, bounced up and down on Kolina's stiff tongue, perfectly placed on the exact center of her most sensitive spot. Kolina's clitoris was a tiny nub of firmness in the fleshy folds. Perspiration rolled off them like a tropical shower, pooling on Kolina, making her as slippery as an eel. She writhed and twisted under Honey, and moaned, squealing softly, but she never missed a stroke with her talented tongue.

Buried to her ears, Honey slapped her heavy breasts down on the girl's belly, her hard nipples raking the slippery skin like metal prongs. Inside, she was a pyrotechnical display, fireworks bursting with ever-increasing brilliance of color and design, heat and desire. Showers of sparks flew outward to every pore of her inflamed skin; the very soles of her feet seemed afire. The conflagration intensified, the hot, dry air burning her nostrils and scorching her throat with each gasping lungful. The moment of truth approached with the suddenness of a desert storm. Lightning flashed and cracked before her eyes and struck deep within her valley of love. She crammed her exploding cunt down onto the upturned mouth and lost herself in the blessed relief of the lengthy thundershowers that flooded down her delta of lust. Almost at once, Kolina erupted with her own bursts of passion, and Honey, overjoyed at the mutual climax, collapsed on the firm flesh. They melted into one another and rode out the delicious aftershocks.

Not long afterwards the pair emerged from the dressing room, fully dressed and demurely proper. The guard glared at them, growling his displeasure at the length of their stay. Kolina breezed past him with her pert nose in the air. "I was conjugating a very difficult verb," she told him and, with a sidelong wink at Honey, pranced down the hall.

Honey watched her tight young buttocks twitch out of sight. Still reeling from the magnificent release, she smiled sweetly at the guard and gave him a small shrug of remorse for keeping the girl so long at her studies. Moving after her pupil, Honey realized that she was hooked all the more on the beautiful girl. Now, more than ever, she was committed to helping Kolina escape. Even if it meant risking her own life.

14.

DIRK

Consumed by the double loss of his sister and Kolina, Dirk had frantically attempted to locate the missing duo in Hong Kong, only to be informed that Henri Bouscaral's private jet had departed for parts unknown. Plagued with guilt for having placed Honey in jeopardy, he had to hang about the luxurious Shangri-La Hotel, hoping that she would contact him there.

Anxiously he had waited for an entire week, rarely venturing out for fear he would miss word from her. Each day dragged by tediously. He did not shave for the whole period, and ate little; booze offered no consolation, nor did the wide variety of drugs available on the black market, or even the beautiful Oriental call girls whom he occasionally had sent to his suite. Usually, fucking would take his mind off anything—but not this time. Even when he was in the lusty saddle of some exotic Chinese whore, his mind dwelled on his own part in placing Honey in danger.

At the end of the maddeningly frustrating, draining week, Dirk gave up. After leaving explicit instructions with the hotel management on how to track him down if word from Honey did arrive, he flew to Paris to locate Honey's old school chum, Disa Dichter, whom he had not been able to reach by phone or cable. He had hopes she would have an idea where Bouscaral might be. Once in Paris, he was further disappointed to learn that Disa was not in the city; she had flown to Alaska with her new beau, a Canadian timber baron. Dirk set off at once for Alaska.

In Anchorage he learned that Disa and her boyfriend had left by private helicopter for Skagway. Immediately, Dirk flew there and went straight to the former boomtown's ritziest hotel. To his relief he found that Disa and her traveling companion were still registered, but had departed only moments before for the railroad station, for a jaunt to Whitehorse. Dirk ran the entire nine blocks, arriving just as the old-fashioned, narrow-gauge train of the White Pass and Yukon Railroad was pulling out of the station. Throwing caution to the winds, he raced after it, jumping on the observation platform of the rear coach at the last possible moment.

Winded by the sudden burst of athletics, Dirk now pushed his way into the passenger car. It was jammed beyond capacity. There were young backpackers eager to make the trek over the Chilkoot Trail, made famous by the Klondike Gold Rush of 1898, camera-toting enthusiasts out to capture some of the spectacular scenic wonders, backwoodsmen returning to the wilds after venturing into civilization for necessary supplies, families of American and Canadian tourists who were out for another day's adventure into the hinterlands, and local natives who used the quaint old railroad as means of getting to their homes and places of employment.

With great difficulty, Dirk inched forward through the mob, scanning the surrounding faces for a glimpse of Disa. After much shoving and many apologies, he managed to make it through one passenger car and squeezed into the next. It too was excessively crowded, and he began his worming act all over again. Halfway through that car he bumped into the conductor, who asked for his ticket. Pleading a foulup by his travel agent, Dirk was able to purchase a round-trip ticket to Whitehorse and once again set off on his search.

In the next car forward, he spotted, far up in front, a familiar blond mass of ringlets. "Disa!" he hollered over the surrounding heads, not caring what they thought of him.

"Who is it?" came her loud query.

He could barely see her looking around. "Dirk Wildon," he shouted, shoving toward her.

"Dirk!" she squealed in surprise, raising a hearty laugh from the crowd. "What on earth are you doing here?"

"Looking for you," he replied. By this time, all the occupants of the car were into the reunion, and made every effort to allow him access to his objective. Determinedly he made his way until Disa was only separated from him by three layers of people. "Honey's missing," he reported gravely over the heads.

Disa's lovely face registered deep shock. "Missing? What do you mean?"

With a final effort he was able to squeeze through the crammed aisle, and he grabbed her in a hug of relief. A congratulatory cheer from the car's occupants broke out. As he held her, he rapidly told her in hushed, urgent

185

tones what had happened to Honey in Hong Kong. *"Merde,"* Disa sighed playfully into his ear. "That's so like Honey."

"This is different," he said. "Henri Bouscaral has kidnapped her, just as he did Kolina."

"But you don't know that for certain," she whispered solemnly. "Henri may be kinky as hell, but he's never given any indication that he'd go that far. You're just letting your imagination run away with you because you're upset that she hasn't let you know her change of plans."

"Dammit, Disa, that's not it at all. Honey doesn't even have her passport with her. If she'd *planned* on disappearing, wouldn't that be the first thing she'd take?"

Disa studied him seriously. "Maybe . . . but then again, with her money she could get a false ID anywhere in the world."

Dirk fumed silently, looking over her head out a window at the mountain's rocky gorges falling away with dizzying precipitousness from the tracks. The train was slowing down with each passing second as the grade of the mountain pass grew steeper. The steady, gentle rocking motion of the car kept pushing him into Disa, and he was increasingly conscious of her full, womanly figure. She was dressed all in bright yellow, in tight ski pants and a parka of a stretchy fabric that emphasized her voluptuous curves. He was jammed so tightly among the other standing passengers that he could not even pull away to admire the very figure that was turning him on. He could feel distinctly the firm mound between her thighs, and with each sway of the car, his long-dormant bird began to reawaken as it rubbed back and forth across her groin.

Smiling vaguely, Disa was watching his face as if she too were aware of their bodies so closely mashed. "I'm so glad to see you again," she murmured. "All these years

186

I've known Honey so intimately, and I barely know you."

"Is that my fault?"

"No one's fault, *mon cher,* never anyone's fault. We've just never had the opportunity."

"I can't remember being around you without Honey present," he said softly, and purposefully bumped his fluttering bird into her.

She laughed quietly, and as the car suddenly jarred, she placed her hands on his hips to steady herself. "When Honey's near me, I am terribly nearsighted. She's always had that effect on me. Ever since I first met her at school. I chased her shamelessly till I caught her."

"But not for long, eh?"

"Long enough," she replied coyly, "to know she and I are perfectly matched sexually. We still are."

Embarrassed by her confession, he glanced around at the people so closely packed near them. None of them were paying any attention, but were absorbed either in the passing scenery of rugged beauty or in their own conversations. He returned his focus to Disa, and his bird hopped up a full notch, straining at the front of his jeans. He leaned down to her ear. "I bet you and I would be perfectly matched too."

"Like sister, like brother?" she teased. "Doubtful, Dirk. Honey is the most erotic creature I've ever encountered. I can climax just by watching her beautiful face."

"Me too," he admitted quietly.

"Is it true you and she have never done the fabulous act?"

"Did she tell you that?"

"Many times," Disa purred. "I never really believed her, though. After all, I know from experience how sexual she is. And you, with all your beautiful models you photograph and have affairs with—Honey's told me all about them. So I just can't understand why you two have never made love, when it's so obvious that you love each other so very, very much."

"Believe me, it's not by *my* choice."

Disa raised her head in apparent astonishment. "You mean Honey draws that line?"

He nodded. "Silly, isn't it? After all, what's a little incest when you're in love?"

She laughed again and as if by accident, one of her hands dropped between them, grazing the front of his jeans, bumping the head of his straining cock. "My, my, my ... if you were my brother, I'd have tested your prowess long, long ago ..." Her exploring hand returned to his fly. "You seem to be so hot all the time."

"Runs in the family." For an agonizing moment he humped into her hand, then whispered heatedly, "Take it out. Set it free."

Apprehensively she glanced around at the crowd, half protesting, "My fiancé is right over there."

"Which one?"

"The balding one with the sunglasses."

Dirk located her new boyfriend and was pleased to note that in addition to his thinning hairline, the guy was short and much older than she. "Does he make you happy?"

"Sometimes," she murmured, and deftly unzipped his jeans. In a flash, Dirk's freed bird was in the palm of her hand. "Hmmmmm, Dirk, you feel so good. So strong. So virile."

Wordlessly he pressed closer in breathless excitement. The proximity of so many unaware people only increased his fervor. He pumped surreptitiously, wanting more. "Stay with me tonight," he urged in a harsh whisper.

"Damn, I can't," she sighed, and stroked the length of his hard dick, her long fingernails raking it agonizingly.

"Why not?"

188

"We leave for Tokyo tonight."

"Ditch the guy," he panted into her light golden hair.

She laughed throatily. "But in the morning you'll leave to find Honey, and I'll be all alone again."

"Come with me. Surely you, of all people, would know where Bouscaral might be."

"I remember once, our last year in school, Honey disappeared for over a month," she recalled sadly as she continued to stroke him. "Everyone was worried to death for her. Then she just popped up again. She'd been living with a gondolier in Venice the whole time."

Almost angrily he pushed his hand down into the tight space between them and grabbed her hand, squeezing it tightly over his raging dick. "Dammit, Disa," he muttered, "Bouscaral's already holding one girl against her will. That I know for a fact. And when Honey went to help her, she too disappeared. Doesn't that indicate something to you?"

She shrugged her full breasts into his chest. "Don't squirt on me," she whispered. "Such a sticky mess to clean up."

In reply he let go of her hand and fumbled for the zipper of her slacks. She shook her head madly at him, but he persisted until he had successfullly opened her slacks. Grinning at her alarm, he jammed a greedy hand between her legs and felt the damp hairs and the already parted lips. "Dirk," she warned him with gritted teeth, and tried to wiggle free.

But they were jammed too tightly amidst the other passengers. She was trapped, and knew it. "Damn you, Dirk," she hissed. "Someone will see."

"So what?" He poked a finger far inside her, and wiggled it back and forth.

"You are impossible," she said quietly, not letting go of his rigid dick.

"No, I'm easy," he joked, relishing her confusion and the lust he was raising in her liquid eyes. They were darting around, looking over the heads peering out the windows, but he could tell that she was as turned on as he was. His finger searched for and found her firm clit. Working it furiously, he bent his knees, leaning back into the person directly behind him. With his free hand he jerked his prick out of her hand and positioned its bludgeoning head at the very entrance to her pussy. Her eyes grew large at his daring, and she shook her head again fiercely. Ignoring her warnings, he bent his knees further, grateful that she was long-legged and tall. It made the task that much easier.

Slowly he eased his dipstick into her, loving her tightness and the wet, clamping warmth. Like a knife blade returning to its sheath, his stiff dick slid into her and he threw his arms around her shoulders, pulling her upper body into his. Her eyes rolled back into her head, briefly, then returned to lock with his. She moaned as Dirk gently rocked her back and forth.

He slipped his hands behind her back and down inside the waistband of her slacks, grabbing two handfuls of her soft ass. The rocking and swaying of the railroad car as it lumbered up the steep slope made it possible for him to just stand, knees slightly bent, and still maintain the secret fucking. With the steadiness of the train's chugging engine, he climbed his own peak of pleasure. Adroitly he plunged a finger up her asshole. Her eyes closed in obvious abandonment, her tanned cheeks turning apple red. Her luscious mouth parted, her pink tongue licking her lips.

Just as the train reached the very top of White Pass and poised to rush down the other side, Dirk froze on the edge of his own precipice, his prick twitching deep within her steamy tunnel. With a gasp loud enough to cause more than one head to turn and stare questioningly at the clutching couple, he shot his load deep into her. Again and again he detonated, each fusillade seeming larger in quantity and longer in duration than the preceding one. His knees buckled under the barrage, and if it hadn't been for the people pressed so compactly around him, he would have slipped entirely to the floor of the car, unable to support even his own weight. At the same time, Disa came too, squeezing his bird in the wild contractions of her creaming cunt.

With a screech of metal on metal and hissing air brakes, the train lurched to an unexpected stop, throwing forward all of the passengers, like a collapsing house of cards. "All out, all out," the conductor shouted. "We have a small fire in the engine room."

Instantly people were pushing and shoving to be out of the car, and Dirk, still inside Disa, found himself being pressed toward the front of the car. Hurriedly he extracted his drained bird and struggled to button up his fly in the jumble of exiting people. Disa, shaking and flushed, fumbled with her slacks, casting a guilty eye toward her timber baron. Dirk just managed to make himself presentable as he was ejected through the open door and out onto the gravel roadbed.

Disa tumbled after him and they stared at the black smoke pouring from the old-fashioned steam locomotive. They looked at each other and broke into gales of laughter. Her balding lumber magnate approached with curiosity, and still laughing, she introduced him to Dirk. The two men shook hands with wary respect, and as the trio chatted casually beside the stalled train, the sweep of mountains surrounding them with a naturally beautiful backdrop, Dirk noted that the timberman kept looking across at the front of his jeans. Not wanting to give anything away by checking his fly, Dirk waited until the all-clear signal had been given and people started clambering back into the cars before he glanced down at his jeans. To his embarrassment, he noticed that the tail of his shirt was sticking out of his fly like a limp dick, caught in the buttons of his jeans.

The rest of the journey to Whitehorse and back was uneventful. Dirk enjoyed the talkative company of Disa's new boyfriend, and basked in the bewitching presence of Disa. The rugged scenery was breathtaking, the steak dinner they shared back in Skagway that evening was delicious, the many drinks consumed providing an easy high. Throughout, he kept questioning her on her knowledge of Bouscaral and persisted in his request that she join him to search for Honey. She laughed him off, repeating her assertion that Honey was a big girl and could take care of herself. When it came time to retire for the evening, Dirk pulled her into his arms and kissed her tenderly. Flustered, she returned it briefly before rejoining her beau, linking an arm through his and waving a sad adieu.

Feeling all the more lonely and frustrated, Dirk returned to his hotel room and tried to fall asleep. But it was impossible. His doubts concerning Honey's and Kolina's safety nagged at his mind. Close to three in the morning, the phone rang. It was a long-distance collect call from the desk clerk at the Shangri-La Hotel. A cablegram had been received for him. Eagerly he listened to its cryptic, unsigned message, thanked the clerk for tracking him down, and hung up, lost in confusion, trying to decipher the cable. It had read simply, "Where Mom met Dad."

He knew for certain it was from Honey, but for the life of him he couldn't remember where the hell their parents had met. Tossing, turning, he stewed for hours, cursing himself for being so forgetful, and Honey for picking the one area in which his memory was weakest. Finally, before dawn, he checked out of the hotel and went to catch a connecting flight for San Francisco. The only place he knew he could get the necessary information was at the family home in Hillsborough. He was positive that he remembered seeing an old scrapbook of his parent's early days together. The clue to Honey's whereabouts had to be buried within its pages. It just had to be. It was his only hope.

15.

HONEY

On Menorca, one of the Balearic Islands in the Mediterranean, off the coast of Spain, she sat tensely under a large blue and white striped beach umbrella on the edge of the secluded cove, counting the minutes until Kolina's return from the village of Ciudadela. Every moment the beautiful girl was out of her sight, Honey was worried about Kolina's safety and could not relax. She had seen Bouscaral's mercurial changes of mood; sometimes they bordered on madness, even violence. He had the girl guarded at every moment with a growing possessiveness and jealousy that sent chills up Honey's spine. Other than the twice-daily French lessons, Kolina was constantly under Henri's thumb, and Honey was convinced that the longer the girl was held captive, the more her life was in danger.

But Honey had yet to come up with a certain escape plan. Every scheme she thought up she eventually rejected as being too risky. The single most significant factor working against her was Bouscaral himself. He never informed her of their destinations until they had already landed in his private jet; he never let on how long they were to stay in one spot, which periods varied widely, from overnight up to a week; he never let anyone not in his employ anywhere near his entourage; he whisked them in and out of countries, usually in the dead of night, without any of them having to go through customs or come face to face with any authorities or police. His seemingly unlimited bank account blanketed them all with a protective layer of isolation. The latest locale was a huge, Spanish-designed villa in which he had ensconced them all.

Only once had she been able to attempt to notify the outside world, and that had been by means of a hastily written message, accompanied by a hundred-dollar bill, that she had left in a ladies' room in the airport in Curaçao, asking the finder to send a cable to Dirk in care of the hotel in Honk Kong. But she had no idea whether the message had even been found, let alone sent. And that uncertainty only heightened her sense of desperation. For the life of her, she could not think of a way to get Kolina and herself out of their traveling prison.

"Claudine!" called the girl's voice from the other end of the beach.

With immense relief, Honey spotted the hauntingly beautiful girl running barefoot through the sand toward her. She was dressed in a gauzy, almost see-through dress of pure white; her windswept, light golden hair was the color of the sand, and the blue-green sea beyond her silhouetted her striking figure with a shimmering backdrop. Honey stood, adjusting her beach robe, which protected her fair skin from the hot sun.

"Claudine," the girl said breathlessly, and glanced over her shoulder at the fast-approaching guard. "I saw your brother! In town. But the guards did too, and they recognized him! I'm frightened for him, Claudine."

Honey was thrown into confusion—he *had* received her cable! Hope and fear mounted together. "Dirk? Here? Did he see you?"

"Yes, yes. And he tried to speak, but the guards shoved him away. The head one is going to tell Henri, I just know," Kolina cried. "Oh, Claudine, I'm scared for him. He looked so angry. I'm afraid he'll do something silly and get in trouble."

"Yes, most likely," Honey said, her mind racing. "But you must not let on. Now collect yourself at once. Here comes Tweedledum."

On cue, the younger of the tough-looking guards approached, eyeing them suspiciously. "Inside," he ordered Kolina curtly. "Now!"

The girl ducked her light blonde head and, with a side-long glance of concern at Honey, slipped away toward the stucco villa partially hidden in the lush foliage. Honey, pretending anger, stared after Kolina and turned to the guard, muttering, "That child will never learn. She wants to go swimming instead of having her lesson this afternoon. I must protest to Monsieur Bouscaral." Gathering the long skirts of her beach robe, she too marched toward the villa.

Once inside the luxuriously furnished villa, Honey ran lightly on tiptoes to the stained-glass door of Henri's library. Through it she could see the outlines of both Henri and the head guard, whom she and Kolina had nicknamed Tweedledee. Faint voices filtered out to her, and her fears grew. The guard was reporting the presence of the pesky Yank who had tried to speak to the girl both in New York and in Hong Kong. Henri spun away, sputtering angrily in French, "He is onto us. We must eliminate him. Find out where he's staying and see to it tonight."

Honey did not need to hear any more. She backed away from the door and ran to her room on the second floor. With a cold lump of concern blocking her throat, she watched from her window the exodus of the two guards, pulling away toward the village in the dark sedan. They were going to track down Dirk, and that night— she couldn't even finish the horrible thought. She must warn him. But how?

Her French lesson with Kolina that afternoon in the massive library was subdued, with an undercurrent of tension. Henri was present the entire time, watching them both carefully from behind the huge carved oak desk. Honey struggled to keep her tone as professional as before, but several times her voice cracked and Henri shot her strange, suspicious looks. Kolina, also, was behaving abnormally, her demeanor strained and worried. At one point, Henri demanded to know what was wrong with her today, but Kolina—bless her quick mind—responded that she was bored, bored, bored and that she missed her sister terribly.

After the lesson, Honey returned to her room to await anxiously the return of the guards. When she heard the sedan pulling into the drive, she slipped downstairs, hoping to overhear their report to Henri, but the three men took a long walk on the deserted beach. Honey watched from the wide, covered veranda, desperate to know of their impending plans. Later that day, as the sun was sinking into the darkening sea, she was surprised to receive an invitation to join Henri and Kolina for dinner. The rarity of the occasion only increased her wariness. Throughout the many courses of the huge meal, she spoke only when spoken to and in general remembered her subserviant position. The *caldareta*—a thick stew of chunky lobster meat—was delicious, as were the many wines and the dessert of fresh kumquats drowning in heavy cream laced with Cointreau, but Honey barely tasted the rich fare. All she could think of was Dirk and the fate that awaited him. Complaining of a severe headache, she withdrew early to her room.

She slipped into her most revealing negligee, a sheer gown of icy blue, and waited until she could hear the guards going into their room down the hall. Throwing a plain robe over her shoulders, she padded over and knocked on their door. Tweedledum answered, his youngish face registering complete astonishment. Honey brushed past him into the room. Tweedledee, the head guard, clad only in a towel around his waist, eyed her from the open bathroom door, his muscular, hairy body like a hard exclamation point. She smiled invitingly. "Pardon me, but I am greatly concerned," she began in French, all aflutter. "Kolina tells me there is a man in the village who has followed her around the world. I think she's in danger."

The head guard replied in his usual surly manner, "Do not concern yourself with our business."

"But I am concerned," she protested. "What does Monsieur Bouscaral intend to do about this man?"

The head guard laughed derisively. "Go back to your books."

She turned pleadingly to the younger, who was eyeing the rise and fall of her unfettered breasts under her robe. "Please, I want to help. Where is he staying? Perhaps I I could go tell him he's upsetting my charge and to please leave."

"You want to help us?" the young thug asked with a leer.

"Yes, yes . . . anything."

"Show us your tits," he ordered.

Protectively she crossed her arms over her breasts. "I do not understand," she murmured, as if shocked. "How can that help?"

The head guard wiped his wet hands on the towel around his waist, pulling it up high to reveal a muscular thigh. "You think you're better than us, no?"

"Of course not," she said defensively.

"Then how come you never talk to us," the second guard said with a sneer. "Or let us be friendly?"

"I . . . I didn't think you wanted to be friends," she replied.

The head guard, his squashed face full of expectations, walked slowly to her, rubbing his hard, hairy stomach. "We want to be friendly, see?" Chortling, he grabbed his cock.

The younger guard laughed uproariously and began tearing off his clothes, throwing them around the room. "Yes, yes, we want to be your friends."

She edged back toward the door. "Friends trust each other. Prove you trust me and I'll be your friend. Tell me where the man who is after Kolina is staying."

The head guard continued to rub the growing lump under his towel. "You prove first. Take off your robe."

She eyed them for a long moment, weighing her options, then slowly slipped off the robe. She stood before them, her luscious body displayed under the sheer nightgown. The eyes of the guards bulged with surprise. *"Mon Dieu,"* the older one muttered.

The younger guard, who was down to his white briefs, shook his head disbelievingly. "All this time, and we never knew you had tits like that," he pouted. "You've been hiding them from us."

"And you both are *still* hiding what you've got from me," she teased. "Come on, boys, don't be shy. I'll show you mine if you show me yours."

Like marionettes controlled by the same strings, the head man dropped his towel, the younger ripped off his shorts. Deliberately she studied their fast-growing equipment, a faint smile of recognition on her lips. Then, with studied nonchalance, she tugged her negligee over her head and tossed it aside. Their eyes were glued to her hairless pussy, and slowly she ran her hands over her full breasts, which jutted out like snow-covered peaks.

"How come you're bald down there?" the younger asked, licking his lips.

"I like the feel of it," she said coyly, and thrust her shaven pudendum at them. "Want to pet my pussy?"

As one they pounced on her, their hands grabbing at her clean-shaven mound of Venus. "Easy, boys," she urged. "There's plenty for all."

Their hard pricks, thick and stubby, poked into her thighs as they continued stroking her bounteous treasures. In spite of the circumstances, she felt a rising heat within her. Other than the one session with Kolina in the Tahiti sauna, she had been totally celibate for days and days. Grasping one of their hot dongs in each hand, she began pumping as they stood on either side of her. Each had a finger in her snatch, one jabbing her button of lust, the other delving deep into her cunt.

A wet mouth fell forward onto each of her breasts, and they jabbed and sucked as if there were no tomorrow. She caught a glimpse of herself in the dresser mirror across the room—Honey sandwich, her alabaster body clamped between two hairy apes. Their attentions to her long-denied body were creating an insatiable desire deep within her. Her legs began to tremble, and joy juice began to flow readily. She gasped and tried to maneuver them across to one of the beds. They clung to her by mouth and fingers as she inched forward, not missing a stroke on their blunt, hard tools. With a cry, she threw herself forward onto the bed, bringing both down with her.

In a tangle of arms and legs, she thrashed, trying to find

a comfortable position. They were still sucking her tits and fingering her apertures, thrusting their penises into her hands with driving hips. She longed for one of them inside her and rolled on her back, opening her milky thighs wide. At once the head guard positioned himself between her legs, aiming his thick shaft and plunging it into her. At the familiar but never dull sensation, she groaned with satisfaction—then choked as the younger guard stuffed his hot dick into her open mouth and pumped like a rabbit.

Soon this younger guard pulled out of her mouth and scooted down, pushing her and the older guard over on their sides, freeing her soft white ass. She felt the young guard's hot cock, slick with her own saliva, poke at her anus. She forced those muscles to relax and let him ease into her. Squeezed between the two hairy guards, one in her cunt, the other in her ass, she rocked back and forth with them, relishing the feeling of being completely filled again. They grunted and sweated on her, seesawing her between them. She was just getting into the swing of things, settling down for a long, satisfying ride, when the older guard popped a puny climax, followed at once, as if on direct orders, by the younger guard in her asshole. Not even bothering to bring her to climax, they yanked their stubby dicks out of her, jumped off the bed, and headed for the bathroom, congratulating each other on a fine fuck.

Shaking with her own unreleased tensions, she followed and found them sharing a large shower stall, with several jets of water streaming from all sides. Over their protests that they were going to be late, she slipped in between them. They ignored her and she finally lay down on the wet tiles, putting her open legs up on one of the walls and positioning herself so that one of the hard jets of warm water was aimed directly at her clit. Bouncing her hips at the sensational feeling, she quickly brought herself to a rousing climax, her squeals of pleasure echoing off the tile walls. The two guards busily soaping their bodies, stared down, mouths ajar, at this hot French teacher who did not need a man to get off. Then, with a smirk, Honey bounced out of the shower without even a goodbye.

In her own room, she hurriedly toweled off and dressed in her darkest clothes. Locking her door from the inside, she clambored out the open window and carefully crawled along the wide ledge until she gained the safety of the upper veranda. Once there, she stood and ran down the exterior stairs to the garage. Crawling into the back seat of the dark sedan, she threw a lap robe over herself and waited. Not long afterwards, she could hear the two guards approaching, then climbing in, the auto starting and heading for the village. Holding herself as still as possible, she listened to the two thugs congratulating themselves on finally "fucking the shit out of that stuck-up piece of ass." The younger one made a disturbing comment, however, saying he thought the schoolteacher was a hell of a lot like that hot bitch who had blown them in the Jockey Club's first-aid room.

As soon as the car had parked and the two guards exited, Honey waited for several moments, then carefully crawled out. The sedan was parked deep in the shadows, in an alley next to a Moorish-looking hotel. In the distance a band was playing raggedly. At the alley entrance she spied the two guards strolling around the corner. Taking a penknife from her purse, she quickly jammed it into a rear tire, and as soon as the air started escaping, she ran toward the brightly lit street and slowed, checking their whereabouts. The pair were entering the hotel by the main entrance. She hesitated, wondering how she could get to Dirk before they did. Stepping out onto the sidewalk, she pulled up abruptly—the guards were leaving the hotel. With a dash, she made the shadows of the alley.

They passed by her so close she could have spit on them. As they moved on, one pulled out of his jacket a nasty looking snub-nosed revolver, flipping it open and examining the cylinders before packing it away.

Honey started after them, sticking close to the buildings. The band music drew closer, sounding more spirited. There were quite a few stroller's about, well-dressed tourists and locals out for their evening promenade. She fell in behind one group who all spoke in Scottish brogues. The guards were half a block ahead, skirting a large plaza-like park, in the center of which a small military band was blasting forth. A large crowd had gathered and she could see the guards lingering by a tree, focusing their attention on one section of the audience. She scanned the crowd in that area and saw him at once. Dirk's sandy blonde head towered over the others nearby. Her heart jumped into her throat. The Scottish tour disbanded, some moving into the park to listen, others continuing on up the street. She inched closer to the martial music, trying to think of a way to warn him. The music was so loud, with a heavy emphasis on brass and drums, that she was positive a gunshot would barely be heard.

Keeping a steady eye on the guards lounging against the tree trunk, she rummaged in her purse and found a scarf, which she tied around her head and under her chin. With that minimal disguise, she began moving in a heavy manner, changing her walk as much as she could, head down, as if weary from long hours working in a factory. Closer and closer she moved toward Dirk, fighting the desire to run to him. She glanced up to locate him, and cursed under her breath. He had moved off by himself and was standing at the rear fringes, surveying the crowd, his tall frame a perfect target.

She was fifty feet away when she detected movement from the guard with the gun. He had taken off his jacket, bunched it around the pistol, and laid it across his arm, propped on the tree trunk. He was aiming directly at Dirk! She shouted, "Dirk! Duck, dammit!"

He whirled in surprise toward her voice just as the pistol cracked. The bullet must have just missed his head by inches, for he immediately dropped to the grass. But he was searching for her. She started running toward the other end of the park, shouting over her shoulder, "Soon!"

She ducked into the crowd, and it was several precious moments before she emerged on the far side. It took her still more time to locate a taxi. Urging the old cabbie to drive as fast as he could, she collapsed into the back seat, her heart still pounding like the bass drum in the park. Outside the entrance to the isolated villa, she paid the driver handsomely and darted through the thick foliage to the beach. Once there, she skirted around to the front of the villa and noiselessly made her way up the outside stairs. The squeal of tires on gravel announced the hasty return of the guards. They'd been faster changing the tire than she had hoped. Scrambling along the ledge on her hands and knees, she climbed in through the open window and stripped off her clothes, climbing into bed just as the door was thrown open.

The overhead light flashed on, and there was Henri, in his bathrobe, flanked by the suspicious guards. She feigned sleepiness and asked groggily, "What is it, Monsieur Bouscaral?"

He cast a glance at her open window and at her clothes strewn about on the floor. "Get up. At once!"

"What is it?" she asked, and hauled herself out of bed, covering her nudity with a large corner of the sheet.

Henri whirled to the older guard, demanding, "Are you sure it was she? Positively?"

The head guard shrugged in confusion, looking to his companion for confirmation. The younger one was equally at a loss and muttered, "The taxi on the road back. It could have been—"

Henri glared at her. "Why are you breathing so hard, as though you've been running?"

"I'm frightened, sir , . . what is this all about?"

Her acting must have been better than she thought, for he waved his hand in agitation. "Get packed. We're leaving at once." With that he pushed the two guards out of her room, grumbling at them for having failed their duties. Relieved, she sank to the bed and tried to recover her equilibrium. Only one thing was certain in her mind, but it was enough. Dirk was safe. That was all that mattered.

16.

HONEY

Rented in Iquitos by Bouscaral, the splendid, 159-foot private yacht chugged slowly down the moonlit Peruvian Amazon. At the aft deck rail, all by herself, Honey watched the moon's reflection in the inky black water. Along the riverbanks the dense jungle pressed close; twisting vines overhung the sluggish waters. Occasionally, lights from the passing yacht would flash on the glowing eyes of animals hidden in the thick foliage, and she recalled some of the captain's list of wildlife in the area, which included monkeys, tapirs, ocelots, and caimans.

Under different circumstances, Honey would have treasured the experience, luxuriously cruising the headwaters of the world's longest river, surrounded by some of the most primitive and fastest disappearing jungle on earth. However, on this night she felt imprisoned in a floating cell, the infamous Henri Bouscaral her jailor.

Honey's nerves were strained to their limit. Only her

strong willpower and self-discipline had kept her from cracking thus far. Though the night air was heavy with the scent of tropical flora, all she was aware of was an over-whelming desire to protect the vulnerable Kolina.

Without warning, the bright moon suddenly blackened and the skies released a torrent of rain. Drenched instantly, Honey ran through the warm rain to her cabin on the upper deck. No sooner had she slipped out of her clothes to dry off when a piercing scream shattered the night's stillness. It was Kolina, she was positive.

Hastily, Honey pulled on a robe over her bare form and dashed down the covered exterior corridor toward the continuing and rising shrieks of fear. Without bothering to knock, she burst into Bouscaral's cabin suite and froze in shock at the bizarre scene that greeted her.

A naked, tumescent Bouscaral stood at the foot of the large bed, on which lay a deliciously nude Kolina. Between the girl's supple thighs knelt a wizened, grizzled, and equally naked native man, as brown as a berry and as stringy as catgut. Proudly and with great determination he was attempting to enter Kolina's cunt.

But this was not what Honey found so strange. Her gaze was fixed in riveted fascination upon the elderly Indian's groin—from which sprouted two erect and quivering penises!

Honey shook her head, blinked, rubbed her eyes, and looked again. No, the strain of the past days had not sent her over the edge; the old man did, indeed, possess twin cocks, equal in size though somewhat smaller than average, each as dark as mahogany, with a leek-like head. At once Honey knew that this was the sole reason for Bouscaral's hurried flight to this remote part of the world; he must have heard about this amazing old man through the underground grapevine of seekers of the unusual.

The proud possessor of this anatomical oddity was

grinning toothlessly, completely unaware of Honey's un-invited presence as he thrust his duplicate dicks at the poor girl's passionless portal.

For her part, Kolina was too disoriented by the double assault to take note of Honey's arrival. But not Bouscaral. He glanced up, first startled, then enraged. "Get out!" he barked.

Thinking quickly, Honey stepped forward with a se-ductive smile. "Oh, Monsieur Bouscaral," she pleaded in a throaty voice, "since Kolina is so frightened, please let me take her place, I beg of you. The very thought of being pierced by this gentleman's odd couple reduces me to a quivering mass of arousal."

He stared at her as if she had just volunteered to fling herself overboard for a skinny-dip in a school of piranha. "You *want* to fuck this old man?" he asked in obvious disbelief.

"Oh, absolutely," she purred as she inched forward to stroke first one, then the other of the delighted native's dual appendages. "What is the American saying? 'Double your pleasure, double your fun'?"

While Bouscaral wavered, considering her proposal, Honey seized the moment—and the two stiff cocks—yanking the elderly native off the bed. Throwing off her robe, she flung herself upon him like a she-wolf in heat, wrestling the horny old man to the carpet, throwing him flat on his back. Squatting over his bony hips, she took a prick in each and sat, thrusting the two organs deep into her. Gasping in sheer delight, she began to rock up and down, her heavy, full breasts swaying and bouncing over the scrawny chest of the startled but appreciative old geezer.

Though neither one of the twin dicks was large by itself, her pussy was stretched to its limits by the two together. Through half-lidded eyes, she could see that Kolina had ceased her caterwauling and had risen up on one elbow, her cries forgotten as she watched Honey's amazing performance. Bouscaral's mouth hung open in amazement. The old man wheezed and whimpered happily while Honey rode up and down on the matched pair in wild abandon.

Beneath her, the old man reached up his bony fingers and pinched her dusky-rose nipples. His toothless, withered face leered up at her like that of a deliriously happy child as she impaled herself repeatedly on his unusual organs.

Honey felt her own climax approaching, and at the last moment she raised herself off the double helping of meat and turned herself sideways to reach behind and beneath her. Grabbing one stiff pecker, she rammed it up her anus, while, with the other hand, she jammed the other one into her dripping honeypot. The double entry did the deed. Moaning and quivering, she rode the two-headed oddity to an extremely satisfactory climax, while the old geezer, giggling inanely, let loose with his own double-barreled blast.

Weakly, Honey rolled off the old man and collapsed on the rug, her whole luscious frame shaking with sensual vibrations. She cast a glance at Bouscaral, who gaped as if seeing her with new eyes. Kolina, however, pouted, obviously disapproving of the entire episode, and bounced off the bed, grabbing her nightgown and fleeing from the stateroom. Honey wanted to run after her, but Henri appeared to have other plans. For the first time since she had been in his employ, he revealed his drawn sword to her. Long and sleek, it rose from between his legs like a lethal weapon.

Honey rose to her feet and, stepping over the recumbent form of the elderly native, swept up her robe. Pulling it on, she smiled sweetly. *"Merci,* Monsieur Bouscaral," she murmured. "Forgive me for intruding upon your play-time." She started for the door, the very epitome of decorum.

"Wait," Henri barked, and kicked a lazy foot out at the old man. The ancient debauchee scrambled up and, grinning thankfully at Honey, hobbled out the door, clucking happily in his native tongue. Bouscaral waited until the door was closed before patting the bed beside him. "Come here, Mademoiselle Fortel," he said quietly.

She hesitated. There was something out of the ordinary in his manner. The sharp planes of his decadently handsome face were filmed with a light layer of sweat, and the way he smoothed the edges of his trim black mustache gave her pause. His streamlined organ had not drooped a centimeter, and pointed at her like a knife.

Pretending embarrassment, she cinched the robe's sash tighter. "Monsieur Bouscaral," she began formally, "I think it is not wise for us to ... to become involved on a personal level while I am working for you. It has been my experience that—"

"Fuck your experience," he said. "You have deceived me."

Genuine alarm flooded her system, and a warning bell of caution sounded in her ears. "Deceived?" she repeated innocently. "I do not know what you mean, Monsieur Bouscaral."

He smiled wickedly. "All this time you have worked for me, I had no idea you were so sexual. Why have you hidden it for so long?"

She bowed her head, blushing effectively. "I did not want you to find me a poor influence on Kolina."

"*Au contraire*," he replied, one of his jet-black eyebrows arching upward. "She likes you so much, she might have loosened up a bit by seeing your example."

"She is very young, Monsieur."

"Nonsense. She's a nymphet. Been screwing since she was twelve." He paused, looking down at his hard root. "Did she tell you how she threw herself on me when we first met? She begged me to screw her. And after I did, she pleaded with me to take her away from her school. Did she tell you that?"

"A schoolgirl crush, perhaps? Very understandable. You are so generous and handsome. A fantasy come true for any girl."

He eyed her appreciatively. "You have good taste."

"Alas," she sighed, "what has it gotten me? Very, very little."

"What do you want that you do not have?"

She managed a small smile, wistful, longing. "So very much."

"Perhaps I could help. If you are nice to me." The implications of his statement hung heavy in the air.

She held his gaze. "As long as you have the girl, you do not need me," she said.

"A man can have an appetite for many dishes."

"True, I suppose. But I would not feel right with the girl around."

"You want me to get rid of Kolina, is that it?"

"I do not want you to do anything you do not want."

Bouscaral scowled, and his slim, sleek cock began to twitch like a divining rod. Honey decided not to press her luck too far. With a slight tilt of her head, she offered demurely, "Now if you will excuse me, I will retire to my cabin for the night."

"Dammit," he grumbled, grabbing his hard organ in both hands as if strangling a poisonous snake. "I want to fuck you. *Now!*"

Raising her head stiffly, she replied, "I am flattered, to be sure. But I will not play second fiddle to the girl.

Bonne nuit." She turned and left the room, closing the door firmly behind her.

Going to Kolina's cabin, she tapped lightly on the door. "It's Claudine," she said softly.

"Go away," came the girl's sullen reply.

"Please, I need to talk with you. It's important."

It took a while, but finally the lovely blonde girl threw open the door. She was nude and pale, and she immediately returned to her bed and crawled under the covers. Honey closed the door and crossed to sit on the edge of the bed. "Please, Kolina," she began, "why are you angry at me?" A small smile touched at the corners of her lips. "Were you jealous?"

"Don't be absurd!"

"Then why were you carrying on like that in there?"

Kolina's lower lip began to tremble. "The old man frightened me."

Honey reached out with a gentle hand and brushed back a lock of the girl's white-blonde hair. "Poor baby . . ."

"Henri used to be so much fun," Kolina muttered, then broke down completely, weeping into the covers. "I used to love him so desperately."

Honey pulled her into her arms, patting her back, kissing her tear-streaked face.

Sobbing, Kolina clutched her French teacher, crying, "Oh, Claudine, I love you so. Promise me you'll not leave me."

"I promise I will not leave you," Honey reassured her. "Not until we are out of Henri's sphere of influence and you are happily on your own again."

That only made the girl weep harder, gushing great quantities of tears on Honey's shoulder. "Oh, we'll never be free. Never!" she cried.

Honey took the girl's shoulders firmly and pushed her away to arm's length. "I will not let you even talk like that, understand? We will escape, be assured of that. You must trust me. You do, don't you?"

"Yes, yes," the girl whimpered.

"I swear this all will be over soon."

Tenderly she kissed the girl's sweet lips, sealing her vow, and prepared to stand. But Kolina, clinging to her desperately, would not let her rise. "Don't go, Claudine. Please. Stay the night. Please?"

The invitation was so tempting, Honey felt her resolve wavering. The girl's bare breasts poked fetchingly above the covers, round as two peas in a pod. Honey bent forward and kissed each one directly on the tip of its tempting pink nipple. "I cannot tonight," she breathed into them.

"But why?"

"Because tonight I must persuade Henri to set you free."

"But how?"

Honey managed to stand, smiling oddly. "That, my darling, is my secret. Now you sleep, my pet." She kissed her again on the lips. "Sweet dreams." Before the dear girl could protest any further, Honey slipped out of the cabin.

The tropical rainstorm had ceased as abruptly as it had begun. Once again the night skies were clear and the moon shone brigthly, casting a pale glow on the dense vegetation lining the banks, and on the slowly moving surface of the broad river. The engines of the huge yacht were silent, and yet the luxurious craft moved steadily, drifting in the center of the Amazon, rollowing its natural flow toward the Atlantic, over a thousand miles away. From the jungle, exotic cries of parrots and other strange birds called into the darkness, adding a lonesome eeriness to the unfolding scene.

On the upper deck, Honey marshalled her strength for the task ahead of her. Squaring her shoulders, she moved from the rail toward Bouscaral's cabin.

He answered her knock wearing a robe of antique maroon velvet, and stared coldly down his sharp nose. "What do you want?"

"You," she said simply.

"You are too late," he said, and started to close the door.

She caught it with a hand and pushed past it into the spacious cabin. "I think not," she replied coyly, and started undoing the belt of her robe. Slowly she parted her robe, revealing her awesome breasts. "I apologize sincerely for my previous behavior. May not a woman change her mind?" Like a goddess unveiling, she dropped the robe to the carpet and stood mutely. He drank in her statuesque figure like a man long denied. Not taking his eyes from her magnificent breasts, he closed the door and moved to her. Abruptly he grabbed her in his arms and crushed his mouth to hers, his hard prong underneath the velvet colliding with her belly like a soft fist.

She did not struggle or protest, but merely allowed him to continue his kiss without offering any encouragement or exchange of feelings. Her passivity increased his fervor. "You beautiful cunt," he gasped into her neck. "Suck me."

Silently she slipped to her knees and opened his velvet robe. His erect member bounced out at her face, its hard sleekness a direct extension of his cold, brittle personality. Taking it in both hands, she caressed its length, as if admiring its beauty. It twitched expectantly in her hands and a drop of seminal fluid oozed from the slit in the blood-red cap. With the tip of her tongue she licked the drop away, tasting its sticky saltiness, then teased the small opening.

He tore the velvet dressing robe from his thin frame, tossing it in a corner. Twining his fingers in her thick hair, he jerked her head forward over the end of his prick, ramming it deep down her throat. Fighting the gagging reflex, she relaxed those muscles, allowing his full length to enter fully. She coated his slender prick with a thick covering of saliva, running her tongue again and again along the hard bulges. With increasing urgency he pumped into her mouth, jamming it in and out, his loosely sacked balls bouncing into her chin. She folded her tongue around his prick, creating a warm, slippery nest. The more she sucked, the hotter she became, and her fingers sought her own nest.

He whipped his cock out of her mouth and rasped, "On your hands and knees."

Obediently she fell onto her hands and he walked behind her, pulled her full hips towards him, and sank his dagger to the limit in her wet pussy. He fell onto her back, and clutching her around the waist with both arms, he began to plunge in and out with alarming speed. Trying to keep upright under his weight, she braced herself on her arms and wiggled her butt into his lap, adding a new twist to his frenetic screwing. It did not take long for her to understand Kolina's fascination with him. Bouscaral was a champion.

His hands clutched at her heavy, swinging breasts and his deeply buried prick battered into the walls of her canal, adding immeasurably to her pleasure. Reluctantly she had to hand it to the Prince of Kink—he surely knew how to fuck.

Abruptly his cock vanished from its burial place; he had pulled out and now was ordering her to lie on her side. She did as requested and he lay down facing her, taking her top leg below the knee and flinging it high up in the air, holding it there, forcing her ever wider. Immediately

216

he plunged into her love channel again, and set about his hurried but skillful plundering. With growing heat, she began to meet his every move, her dislike of the man fast disappearing under his expert ministrations.

Bouscaral took her in a variety of positions. To each she responded with the same enthusiasm, her own sexual gymnastics increasing his ardor. Like a man possessed, he attempted to top her, to get the best of her. But she refused to give in. An inhuman growling rose from her lips, her breathing became labored, and still she demanded more.

When at last his energy began to flag and his movements slowed, she prodded him on, raking his back with her long nails. Wrapping her long legs around his trim waist, she bucked, twisted, and kicked, screams of unfulfilled lust raging from her lips.

On into the night they fucked and fought, each refusing to come before the other. Finally, with a concerted effort, Honey threw him over on his back and sat on his exhausted pecker. Placing her hands flat on his hairless chest, she arched her back and cried, "Fuck me, you fool. Fuck me!"

Inspired by her pleas, he threw himself into one last round of energetic pumping and promptly, with a cry of anguish, he came furiously, far up inside her. A grin of victory flashed across her aroused face, and she lowered her heavy breasts to his heaving chest, climaxing with a great shout of triumph.

After a moment she climbed off him and he rose and staggered to the bar in his room. "I've never had a woman outlast me," he grumbled as he poured himself a snifter of Courvoisier. Swirling the amber contents, he sank into an easy chair and proceeded to toss the brandy down in one gulp.

"But did I not please you?" she persisted pleasantly.

"What is pleasure?" he asked boyishly. "One person's pleasure is another person's pain."

"Not necessarily," she purred and slipped out of bed, padding to his chair. Kneeling before him, she looked up at him in total humility, her deep blue eyes filled with worshipful longing. "You are the very best I've ever had. I would do anything—anything—to be allowed to be only your property for as long as you desire me."

He contemplated her with a brightening expression, his black eyes sparkling with aroused interest. "You would do as I say?"

"Willingly," she said softly and took one of his hands, kissing the palm. "On one condition. You get rid of that little girl forever."

He shrugged helplessly. "I'm hooked on her. If I don't get my daily fix of her, I'm certain I will go mad. The more she rejects me, the more I want her. It used to be the other way around, you know."

"If you keep her, you can't have me."

He stared down, his face tense. "You force me to choose between you?"

"I'm not forcing you to do anything," Honey said. "But I know one thing for certain. If she stays, I go. I will not compete with her for your attention."

His shoulders rose and fell as he sighed, "I will hate to lose your fine talent, but I have no recourse. Kolina is the very core of my life.

"Your services are no longer required," he said, almost apologetically. "Things were better before you showed up. I will see that you are dropped off at our next destination. Now, please, leave me alone."

She hesitated, wanting to plead, to change his mind. But it was as though she had already left and he was alone. Feeling she had failed in her mission, she moved heavily from his cabin and into the bright moonlight.

17.

HONEY

Bouscaral's Learjet landed in the dead of night on an airstrip deep in the Pacific, but Honey was not told where. Emerging from the rear passenger compartment, she blinked at the mist-shrouded, desolate airport, and with a rapidly sinking heart she recognized where Bouscaral was going to dump her—on the isolated archipelago of the Galapagos Islands, straddling the Equator, six hundred miles off Ecuador.

Before she could even protest to Bouscaral, who refused to come near her, the guards whisked her into a jeep, and a convoy of several vehicles roared across tiny Baltra Island to the westernmost shore. There she was hustled into the second of three native boats Bouscaral had rented. Once used for fishing, the boats were now available for the more lucrative transportation of tourists to any one of the nineteen islands and forty-two islets. As the large craft putted away from the rocky, barren coast, she caught a glimpse of Kolina in the first boat up ahead and felt a sharp pang of remorse. Ever since her wild sexual encounter with the Prince of Kink, he had kept Honey far away from the sweetly beautiful girl, not even allowing a single French lesson.

As the sun crept higher into the sky, Honey stood in the bow of the boat, the wind whipping her hair, the fine spray of salt water misting her face. She scanned the slate-gray ocean dotted with absurdly tiny and rocky volcanic islands, trying to discern why Bouscaral had come to this impossible remote section of the world. What thrill could be found within these primitive piles of rock? Surely he must have chosen the locale not for any available sexual kicks, but only because he wanted to dump her quietly, raising no suspicions or inquiries by authorities.

She was all too aware how easily he would be able to achieve this goal. Any of the miniscule outer islands were totally unpopulated, reachable only by hired fishing boat. Bouscaral's accompanying entourage was so large, including four women, who would notice one missing on the return voyage? Money closes many eyes, as she knew all too well.

By the time the three fishing boats anchored in a small inlet of one of the smaller islets, the sun was high overhead, blasting down waves of intense heat. A crew had arrived earlier to set up a large tent compound on the only flat space on the entire rough-hewn rocks. Upon landing, she joined the scramble for the protection of large awnings to escape the searing heat of the sun. She chose the one under which Kolina had scurried, but she was forcibly removed. One guard firmly latched on to each of her arms, marching her to a small tent up against the cliffs, the farthest away from the master's tent. She was shoved inside the sweltering interior and Tweedledee sat not far away under an outcropping of rock, keeping the front of her tent in constant view.

The blazing sun had diminished in intensity when Honey later emerged from her tent. Clad in a coral string bikini which barely covered her mons veneris and her protruding nipples, she pranced down to the water's edge.

To the young guard watching her through sleepy, bored eyes, she was a bolt of exotic lightning. She was a vision of white marble skin and sensuous curves, her legs as long as a thoroughbred's, her rounded hips provocatively alluring, her flat stomach emphasizing the sudden, awesome sweep of her proud breasts. He got a hard-on just watching her ripe, pear-shaped ass sway into the water as she waded out. She surface-dove, submerging completely and refusing to break for air until she had swum her usual one hundred strokes. When she finally surfaced, she slicked back her hair and surveyed the beach encampment from a distance halfway to the first anchored fishing boat.

Tweedledee stood at the water's edge, a look of relief on his face—as if he had been concerned by the length of time she had been out of sight underwater. She waved to indicate that she was fine and swam the length of the cove and back again. All the while she was taking mental pictures of the topography, hoping the information would come in handy later. Until Bouscaral made his move, she could only wait.

Both guards watched her exit from the water, as did every other male in the camp. She searched for Kolina but did not see her among the gaping faces. Inside her tent she changed into a filmy beach gown and sat in the shade of the tent awning, watching the many prehistoric-looking iguanas resting in the crevices of the island's volcanic rock.

When she was called for dinner, the sun had dipped far behind the cove's cliffs. The temperature had dropped considerably and there was a bonfire, around which were clustered the serving and maintenance staff. As she sat on a camp stool off to one side, eating the spicy, native stew of fish and octopus, drinking a dry sauterne, she eyed Kolina with Bouscaral at a table for two some distance away.

Dinner was not even concluded before the elegantly attired Bouscaral went into his tent, to come out a short time later dressed in a tropical bush jacket, fatigue pants, pith helmet, and high leather hiking boots. Then the crew began rounding up an odd assortment of gear—large nets, torches, and rifles. Some sort of night hunting party was being formed, but Honey could not imagine what their quarry might be.

It was not until a bowl of fruit was brought around by the elderly cook that Honey learned the real purpose of Bouscaral's visit. "The female iguanas," the old woman whispered. "That's why the master came here."

"The iguanas?" Honey echoed, mystified.

"The female ones," the elderly Frenchwoman explained, as if to a child. "The natives swear eating them increases one's potency."

In disbelief, Honey stared at the old woman. "You mean they kill these harmless creatures just for that?"

"*Oui,* absurd, no?" cackled the old servant. Still chuckling to herself and shaking her head, she hobbled away, leaving Honey sitting in amazement.

Killing iguanas to test an old wives' tale! How absurd could Bouscaral get? But at least his planned festivities did not include Kolina; the girl was still dressed as if for dinner at Maxim's. That eased Honey's concerns and she returned to her own tent in a state of hope, in spite of the native guard outside.

Through the mosquito netting she observed the final departure of the hunt contingent. Almost all the men had joined, leaving only two for guards—one for her, one for Kolina. The women servants had withdrawn to their tent and Honey could hear them drinking, playing cards, and laughing. She waited until the sky grew dark.

Wearing boots, jeans, and a T-shirt, she took a sharp knife she'd stolen from the cook's utensils, slit the rear wall of her tent, and eased out. Hidden in the shadows of the cliff, she made her way to the section she'd observed earlier. Carefully she began her ascent, inching up the rock facing. Upon reaching the top, she slid behind a rock and stood to scan the horizon. Then she walked gingerly along the edge of the cliff above the camp spread out below, until she had circled around to Kolina's side. Finding the point she had planned to use, she began descending the steep incline.

In back of Kolina's tent she knelt and using the same knife, cut open a deep slash in the canvas. Kolina gasped in surprise as Honey slipped in to join her. A finger to her lips, Honey doused the kerosene lantern and drew the girl into her arms, kissing her passionately. Like an ice cube in the afternoon sun, the girl melted into her, pressing her full breasts against Honey's, as her hands explored Honey's ass. With reluctance, Honey had to take the girl's arms away. "Kolina," she whispered, "we do not have time, not even to talk. I must leave at once."

"Leave?" the magical blonde cried softly. "Where to? How? Why?"

"Hush, please," Honey urged. "I have every reason to believe Henri will leave me here when all of you go."

"No ... he wouldn't," the girl protested halfheartedly. "Would he?"

"I can't take that risk. That's why I've come to say

goodbye. I've spotted a light on a nearby island. I'll make for that. It's a lovely night for a long swim."

"We're over five miles from the nearest island," Kolina cried, and threw her arms around Honey's neck. "You'll never make it!"

"It's surprising what one can do when faced with no other choices."

Tearfully the girl's beautiful face rose in the half-light of the outside bonfire. "How about one of the dinghies? We'll take one of those."

"The dinghies are well watched. Besides, what's this 'we' business?" Honey asked. "You are in no immediate danger. Once I get free, I will be able to rescue you more effectively."

"You won't know where we are," Kolina wept. "You'll never be able to locate us! Henri will see to that."

Honey kissed the girl's cheek. "I promise that I will seek you out and get you away from him."

The girl pulled back, her voice firm as she said, "I'm coming with you, and that's final. I will not spend another night with that horrid man."

"Kolina, my pet," Honey began, "I love your offer, but it is too risky. One of us has to get out of this in order to help the other."

"If anything should happen to you, I would never forgive myself," Kolina said with a quavering voice. "So don't argue. We haven't the time." Abruptly she began disrobing, her womanly figure appearing briefly before being covered by an outfit similar to Honey's.

Before Honey could voice too many arguments against the girl's plan, Kolina was dressed. Together they crawled out of the tent through the back opening, and silently made their way up the steep incline behind the camp. At the top, Honey pointed to the faint light twinkling so far away across the black water. "It's a good distance," she said softly. "Still game to try?"

"More than ever," Kolina uttered. "We'll be there before anyone finds out we're missing.

Honey took her by the hand and started walking her across the rough, craggy rocks. "Unfortunately our closest point of departure is on the same side of the island where Henri and his men are picnicking."

"You mean eating those ugly lizards? Ugh! Honestly, Honey, what will that horrible man think of next?"

As quickly as possible, the pair made their way in the near darkness toward the yellowish light of flickering torches down by the water. Skirting the hunting party, Honey hurried Kolina through the giant boulders to the lapping water of the cove. They began pulling off their clothes and boots, stuffing them all out of sight in a chasm in the ledge. Naked, Honey pulled Kolina close, smothering her face in kisses and copping a quick feel of the silky skin and smooth curve of her buttocks before releasing her. Giving Kolina a thumbs-up gesture for luck, Honey walked out hand in hand with the girl into the water, where they struck out for the tiny speck of light on the horizon.

The sea was warm, inviting, the waves minimal and almost free from tugging tides or undertow. "Slow and easy," Honey whispered between strokes.

Farther and farther into the blackness they swam, away from the flickering circle of light and the boisterous group of iguana killers.

Above, beneath, all around them was velvet darkness. If it hadn't been for the far pinpoint of light, which never seemed to grow any nearer than it had been when they commenced their flight, Honey would never have known which way she was heading.

After several hours, Honey began to feel an undeniable tide tugging at her legs, sweeping her along. After a few moments she concluded that the tide was carrying them directly toward the island from which the light beckoned them. Kolina's spirits perked up when Honey relayed the good news.

Suddenly the sky above them was rent by a blinding flash. "A flare!" Honey cried out in alarm. "They've discovered we're gone!" Almost at once the rumble of engines could be heard across the water.

"They're out in the boats!" Kolina gasped. "He'll know we set off in this direction. It's the closest point of land."

The sound of engines drew steadily nearer, and flares periodically burst above them. From behind them, slashing searchlights pierced the night as the boats closed in.

Pushing her screaming muscles harder, Honey set a quicker pace, pleading with Kolina not to give up. The pursuing flotilla was so close she could hear the crews calling to each other across the water. Kolina began whimpering, and Honey felt the cold hand of fate clutching her own throat.

Then, a miracle! Out of the blackness ahead, an unlighted craft materialized, astonishingly close and unexpectedly large. They were so close to it, they could hear the water lapping on the wooden hull, the decks creaking in the constant rise and fall of the sea. Honey hailed it as loudly as she dared, and almost simultaneously a rope ladder clattered down the side of the now clearly visible fishing boat. With a cry of relief, Kolina floundered for it and grabbed hold of the ropes. Honey had to push the girl's sweet ass up the steep steps, and had difficulty hauling herself up, her arms and legs were so worn out. Strong, calloused male hands grabbed her arms and lifted her aboard.

Their rescuers were a crew of four young, rugged Ecuadorian fishermen who were struck dumb by the naked but weary mermaids they had been so lucky to land. Half drunk on brownish wine that they quickly shared with the girls, they had been just drifting about, curious about the approaching boats. Now they responded to Honey's pleas in Spanish to get the boat under way without lights. Hopping eagerly to their duties, the young brown fishermen soon had the craft moving rapidly away into the protective darkness. Wrapped in a smelly but welcome blanket, sipping the warming, fiery homemade wine, Honey stood in the unlit pilothouse and watched the searchlights of the trio of boats fade far behind. By her side, Kolina, also blanketed, jumped up and down excitedly at their apparently successful escape, her zestful energies fast returning.

By the time Honey was assured that Bouscaral's boats no longer presented a threat, all four of the squat, strongly built young crew were pressed into the pilothouse, gaping admiringly and jabbering jubilantly at their good luck, one playing merrily on an ancient concertina. Kolina was soon drunk on strong wine and liberation. She threw off her blanket, launching into an impromptu dance of such playfully funny and teasing erotic sensuality that Honey had to warn her to cover up or face having to service the four long-at-sea men. Laughingly the girl took to the suggestion with the fervor of one free at last to make her own choices. She grabbed one of the young sailors and soon had him stripped; his hard brown body testified to his difficult and strenuous lifestyle. His rigid harpoon was so appealing that Honey could not resist the temptation. She tossed off her blanket and set to work thanking her rescuers properly, tugging the remaining three outside, where she had no difficulty getting them out of their clothes and into her.

The resulting party on the poopdeck was a lustful scene

227

of rousing good times. Spread-eagled flat on top of the largest of the three, she took his long staff straight up the butt while, on top of her, kneeling between both pairs of legs, the second pumped ecstatically into the most beautiful hairless pussy he had ever even dreamed existed. The third knelt beside his lucky buddies, up close to her head, and with very little neck strain, she was able to suck on his mast. It did not take the randy sailors long to fire their weapons, and even less time to grow stiff again.

With the wheel lashed so the boat made a large, lazy circle, Kolina and her first mate were soon added to the quivering quartet outside. New combinations and contortions were tried, with satisfying results. The action was fast and furious, athletic and adventuresome. As the sailors came again and again in every possible orifice of the obliging young sea nymphs, their periods of recovery grew longer. During these rest periods they contented themselves to sprawl on the deck, fondling their never-empty weapons, watching the two ladies go down on each other, Honey on top, her head jerking up and down as if bobbing for apples. The two luscious female bodies meshed perfectly, their lustrous skin catching the lantern light, creating an arousing collage of arms and thighs, breasts and hips, asses and wide-open quiffs.

When Honey came up for air, she was pleased to see that the young crew was so ready to go again that they were doing each other unabashedly. The homoerotic activity of their slim brown bodies reminded her of paintings an ancient Greek vases. They were having such a good time that she hated to interrupt, but she was so tired that all she wanted to do was come once more and fall asleep for days. Her good-natured pleas quickly brought two stalwart, ready-to-perform crewmen to her side, the other two leaping upon Kolina.

With one in her pussy and one in her ass, her own

finger urging her lust trigger to hurry up and fire, Honey threw every last ounce of energy into her swansong. Her gyrations and enthusiasm were so heated that the sailors were, in short order, exploding their submerged torpedoes deep into her nethermost regions. The warm bath set off her own buttons and, with a deep cry of complete satisfaction, she eased into a tidal wave that hurled her along its seemingly never-ending crest. Miles and miles she rode, balanced on the very lip of curling white water, squealing with joyous release. She did not remember ever coming down, for she drifted into a deep, contented sleep before reaching the end of the longest climax of her life.

18.

DIRK

At Lanai, the Wildon winter home on Kauai's lush northeast coastline, he sat in a large wicker peacock chair on the cool veranda, sipping a piña colada, watching with intense interest Barbro's erotic harem dance. Framed by a backdrop of shimmering golden sands, sparkling blue-green ocean, and vivid tropical flowers, she swayed and rolled her hips in time to taped Middle Eastern music—violins, drums, ouds, bouzoukis wailing spiritedly into the late afternoon. Wearing only a filmy sarong draped low over her wide hips, her large breasts swinging free with the sensual beat, Barbro spun gracefully, arms raised over her head, her hands speaking their own language with a tinkling of small finger cymbals. Behind one ear, in her light blonde hair, she had tucked a large pink hibiscus that matched the delicate hue of her nipples' aureoles.

The music slowed, and her artistic dance evolved into an expressive collection of hip undulations. Barefoot, she sidled closer to him, her eyes locked on his in total communication between performer and audience. Her creamy stomach rolled and dipped, expanded and rippled, her arms liquidly shaping the fragrant air. Dirk felt like a pasha dallying away an otherwise tediously frustrating afternoon with his favorite concubine.

On a whim he had stopped off in Cartagena, Colombia on his return flight from Spain and picked up this delectable creature, wanting her to come with him to Hawaii to await Honey's promised arrival with Kolina. Barbro, more than eager to accompany him, had promptly quit her job to be free to join in the maddening vigil on the spectacular shoreline of the Garden Island. Though the scenery could not have been more inviting or the company more appealing and satisfying, the days seemed endless and Dirk struggled with mounting frustration and increasing anxiety. He felt impotent, helpless, useless in whatever plan Honey had up her sleeve.

The attempt on his life in Menorca was proof positive that he and his sister were playing with fire, dealing with a desperate and driven Bouscaral, who would stop at nothing to keep what he felt was rightfully his. More than anything, Dirk wished he had never involved his sister in his quest to free the girl with the magical face. It was not knowing what was happening to Honey and Kolina, not even knowing where they were that caused him greatest fear and concern. If it had not been for the quieting, steadying influence of Barbro—a magical presence in her own right—he was positive he would have gone berserk hanging around, waiting on razor blades for Honey to show up or send word.

Timing the swing of her tantalizing hips to the rising rhythm of the music, Barbro plucked the pink hibiscus from her hair and incorporated it in her magnetically riveting dance. With one hand she held it in the deep valley

232

between her large breasts, where it bloomed like a third nipple. Slipping to the deck of the veranda, she knelt, leaning back, shimmeying her hips until her blonde head touched the floor. Her transparent sarong barely covered her taut thighs and emphasized the bushy mound between her legs. Her stomach fluttered, rising and falling like a storm-tossed sea, adding to the erotic allure of her talented offering.

Dirk held the tall, ice-filled glass in his lap, cooling down his persistent boner, which it seemed he had possessed ever since arriving back in his favorite retreat with this sensuous, giving woman. He wore only ragged cut off jeans—his usual beach attire—and his lean frame was burned rosy pink from the golden afternoon spent snorkeling and lying in the hot sun. His whole body tingled with heat, and the cool drink in his lap did little to dissuade his insistent bird.

Her undulating belly, as she rose again in a glissando, beckoned to him provocatively. She tugged open the knot of her patterned sarong and, with her back to him, took the ends of the sheer scarf and opened her arms wide, the colorful material creating a swath of dancing butterflies across her broad tempting ass. She swung to face him, her trunk swaying like the tall palms encircling the beach house, her breasts like large pale coconuts. She thrust her pelvis at him as the pounding beat drove her to a more frantic pace. Her bare pussy flashed like rose petals fringed by soft blonde grass, a tropical garden of earthly delights ready to be deflowered.

He was so concentrating on her performing pussy that he was startled to glance up and note the tears filling her eyes, seeping from under her long lashes. Her fluid steps faltered and her dance ground to a halt. With barely controlled emotion she stood panting before him, her full, ripe breasts pumping like bellows. Imploringly she searched his eyes, then spun, dropping her veil completely as she ran inside the open French doors.

He rose to follow, spilling his drink, not caring, only wanting to comfort and hold her. He found her in his bedroom, her voluptuous nude body flung face down across the king-sized waterbed, weeping profusely into her arms. He stretched out beside her, turning her over, into him, taking her exquisite face in his hands, kissing her tenderly, murmuring, "Please don't cry. It'll all work out. You'll see . . ."

"We don't even know for certain they're alive," she wailed.

"No, we don't," he replied gravely. "All we can do is hang on and pray."

"Dammit," she cried, "I've been doing just that for weeks and weeks." She clung to him like a life raft in the open sea. "I'm sorry," she groaned, trying to stifle her sobs. "It just gets worse, doesn't it? The time gets heavier. The tension becomes unbearable. I can't even find joy in my dancing anymore, always remembering why we're here. And that we can't *do* anything to help them."

He kissed her pert nose, which, above all of her astounding physical attributes, reminded him of her young sister's. Her soft, pliant breasts mashed into his bare chest and he fought the desire that rose like an express elevator inside his chest. She wrapped her long arms around him, her breath quickening, and returned his kisses with increasing passion. His bird of paradise poked insistently into her creamy belly, struggling to be free of the confining cutoffs. Deftly her hands slid down his front and she unbuttoned his shorts. At once his stiff bird fluttered out and into her warm palm. Almost absently she began pumping on it, and his fingers sought out the moist folds of her pussy. Probing deeply, he brought a gasp from her and she opened her thighs wider, granting him freer access to her buried treasures.

He was just about to ease into her when a female voice called out from the living room, "Hello, hello, anyone home?"

"Honey!" he croaked in surprise and bounded from the waterbed, leaving Barbro riding the resulting waves by herself. He trotted into the large green and white main room full of white wicker furniture, and pulled up in joyous disbelief.

Coming to him with open arms, his sister, dressed in baggy white sailors fatigues, glanced at his free-flying bird and stopped short, a smile tweaking her mouth. "My, my, my," she teased. "Caught you in the act, eh?"

Behind her, Kolina, also attired in the strange naval attire, whirled to look out the open front doors, a becoming blush coloring her magical face. Embarrassed, he stuffed his fast-dwindling pecker back into his cutoff's and rushed to embrace Honey, sweeping her into his arms. "How'd you get away? What happened? Was there any trouble?" he asked in quick succession, his heart overflowing with love and relief.

"Kolina!" squealed Barbro behind him, as she dashed into the room, tugging on his short bathrobe. "My darling sister, you're free!" The two sisters ran into each other's arms, shouts of joy and tears of unmitigated happiness flowing freely.

The unexpected reunion of the two sets of siblings was a confusing jumble of hurried explanations and expressions of love and devotion. Even Dirk found himself teary-eyed, overwhelmed to be in the warm circle of his dear sister's love once more. Gradually the incredible story of their escape from Galapagos and their subsequent rescue by the Ecuadorian fishermen surfaced to the point of

235

comprehension. Honey and Kolina had been picked up off the fishing boat by an obliging U.S. Navy supply ship —hence their sailors' garb—and brought to within helicopter distance of Kauai. They had landed on the beach only moments before, and now danced excitedly around the living room, congratulating themselves on their luck and thankfully praising the powers that be for their miraculous escape. Again and again he kissed his sister, not wanting to let her out of his arms.

When the three women finally retired to the bathroom to shower and change into more appropriate attire, Dirk broke out a special bottle of chilled Lafitte Rothschild champagne, vintage 1928, that he had been saving for just this occasion. Four glasses were poured and ready as the trio of lovelies returned, dressed in brightly flowered, flowing Hawaiian gowns. Ceremoniously he handed them each a full tulip glass and raised his in a toast. "To happy reunions and happy endings," he intoned solemnly, and sipped, his eyes wandering from happy face to happy face. He felt blessed to be surrounded by such unbelievably beautiful ladies; each was as lovely as the next, and each glowed with a special energy befitting the moment. But the magical Kolina was the one who caught and held his eye. Almost shyly he studied her exquisite beauty, mesmerized all the more by her intoxicating loveliness.

The bottle of champagne was finished quickly and he popped the cork on another. The high-spirited chatterings and exclamations continued, joined by the Rolling Stones blaring out of the top-of-the-line stereo system. Still more vintage champagne was consumed, along with some sensational home-grown Hawaiian grass, which flourished in a bushy plot beside the secluded, slate-roofed house, and line after line of Dirk's top-grade coke.

By the time the sun sank behind the palms, the quartet were as high as kites on a windy March day and they had joined forces to prepare a giant feast of celebration. The freezer was raided for pheasant and squab, the vegetable garden provided greens and yams, the fruit trees were stripped of bananas and mangoes, nectarines and papayas. As Dirk concocted a huge fruit salad, Honey baked the birds and vegetables in the microwave oven, and the two sisters created a fresh strawberry pie topped with mounds of whipped cream.

The candlelit feast turned out to be as delectable as the company, and they stuffed themselves, laughing, chattering, singing, and drinking more bottles of Rothschild's champagne. Dirk brought out one of his cameras and began recording the joyous event for posterity. The women's flushed, relaxed, and breathtakingly lovely faces were a photographer's fantasy come true, not to mention their alluring bodies, so modestly draped in Honey's colorful gowns. He longed for them to disrobe so he could really get down to his true forte of nude shots, but he did not press it, knowing that all good things work out according to their own timing. Besides, he was getting off on the trio's interreactions, the sisterly way in which all three related to each other, full of love and respect and good-natured kidding, as though they had grown up together. Barbro could not stop touching her younger sister as she hung on her every word and often burst into tears of unadulterated joy.

As night deepened, stars forming a bright canopy overhead, they trailed outside in the balmy air full of sweet tropical fragrances of gardenia and jasmine. The gentle waves on the beach at their doorstep whispered good tidings and Honey was the first to doff her gown, running like a flash of pale moonlight into the water, laughingly calling the others to join her. Dirk watched in stupefied delight as the Swedish sisters eagerly stripped off their long dresses and, giggling, bounced to the waves, their high, proud breasts jiggling like Jell-O. He did not need a second invitation and immediately dropped his shorts, blissfully unaware that his bird of paradise had taken wing and was jutting out from his groin. Only when he dove into the warm water did he notice the drag of his hard rudder. Groaning at the unexpected tug, he flopped over on his back.

Laughing hysterically at the sight of his stiff periscope, the ladies splashed and frolicked in the waves, their luscious bodies glistening and sparkling in the dim light reflected from the beach house. He floated near Kolina, and playfully she made a grab for his partially submerged bird. Her fingertips just grazed it before she shrieked with uncontrollable laughter and swam away. He dove under the surface and came up, latching on to her smooth legs, wrestling her to him.

The touch of her fair skin on his sent him into a state of righteous enjoyment. Willingly she allowed him to explore her body beneath the water. His hands were all over her, not able to get enough as she was constantly wiggling free. He clamped his arms around her waist and dragged her close, digging his stiff peter into her thigh. She chortled and wrapped her legs around his hips, her mouth seeking his. For a delicious long moment they kissed, her tongue raking the inside of his mouth. He grabbed two handfuls of her ass and ground his hips against hers. The head of his panting bird poked like a homing pigeon into her open nest, and she writhed on his lap.

"I can't thank you enough," she whispered into his ear. "If it hadn't been for you, I would never have met Honey. Or be free of that horrid man."

"My pleasure," he murmured heatedly, and pushed more of his hot member into her. His long-held desire to do exactly what he was now doing overpowered him with its strength. He let his legs drift to the sandy bottom, and standing, trembling, holding her tightly, he sank his shaft deep into her watery vagina. She was as tight as he had imagined, and obviously savored the sensation, for she began bouncing up and down, moaning sweet endearments into his neck.

The surrounding warm water was like an extension of her womb, and he felt as though he had crawled completely inside her. With her magically beautiful face pressed close to his, her surprisingly large breasts floating between them, brushing and pushing into his chest with their own rhythm, he relished the total sensuality of the moment. He fought to prolong it as long as possible, but his buried bird had a mind of its own. Rapidly it approached its moment of truth, and he bit into the soft flesh of her neck in exquisite agony. "Kolina, Kolina," he groaned, and pumped faster and faster, rising toward the ultimate goal with incredible speed.

He came with such force that it blew him off his feet, and they fell into the waves, going completely under as he detonated into her wet warmth. Sputtering, gasping for air, they surfaced, still locked together, and he felt her contractions pushing her own climax. Eyes wide with bliss, she flung her arms over her blonde head and floated on her back, still joined to him, her love channel filling now with her own fluids, her breasts rising from the water like emerging islands.

Realizing at last that they were not alone, Dirk glanced sheepishly over at the other pair to see if they had noticed the nocturnal activity in the moonlit water. He need not have worried. Honey was so wrapped up in the warm caresses of Barbro that she was enveloped in her own pleasures, completely unaware of everything except the tasty dish in her arms. The sea around them was frothy with their rapid underwater movements. Soon he could hear the unmistakable grunts and groans of a mutual climax and he felt at peace, knowing that his sister was getting hers too.

The deliciously weary foursome eventually drifted out of the water, across the sand, and up onto the wide veranda to dry themselves and sip more champagne. The night was still, except for the lapping waves that had brought so much enjoyment to all of them. Seeing the three women sprawled so gracefully nude on the wicker fan chairs, Dirk grabbed his camera and began snapping pictures of their wonderfully vibrant bodies. Each one personified perfection in her own way: Honey with her alabaster skin, amazingly full breasts, and a pussy devoid of hair; Barbro with her tightly packed dancer's form, her wide hips, and enticing, firm thighs; and Kolina with her angelic face and voluptuous woman's body. Individually each would have been a masterpiece; together they were a surfeit of splendors, and it took considerable concentration on his part to keep his mind on the lens settings for the extremely low available light. He completed a roll of film and urged them softly into the house, where he would have more light. Without a murmur of protest they followed his lead into his bedroom and draped themselves fetchingly on his waterbed.

Coiled together like three muses, the two genuine blondes and the bogus brunette were a single meshing of languid, relaxed bodies. He slipped a new roll of film into his Nikon F3 and began to snap some extremely hot shots as the fair trio entertained their exclusive photographer, their exaggerated poses and emphasized eroticism growing increasingly more realistic.

Suddenly a harsh voice broke into their sanctuary. *"Bon soir."*

The ladies screamed as one, and Dirk whirled in astonishment just as Henri Bouscaral marched into the room. "What the fuck?" Dirk growled, and flung himself up off the waterbed. He could hear footsteps approaching from the living room, and fully expected to see Bouscaral's two henchmen appear in the doorway.

Instead, a vision of silver-headed loveliness materialized—a mature, exquisitely dressed, and bejeweled woman with a regal, aristocratic bearing. She smiled graciously at the confused tangle of nude flesh on the bed. "Good evening, all. Please forgive our unannounced intrusion upon your festivities. I came as soon as I could."

"Madame Bouscaral!" Honey breathed in astonishment, and sat bolt upright, making no attempt to cover her nakedness.

"Berengere-Marie!" squealed Kolina and darted up, dashing across the room to throw her arms around the older woman.

In amazement, Dirk stared at the lovely duo, who were embracing like long-lost mother and daughter. Each was so spectacularly beautiful, he had forgotten totally about his own nudity. Suddenly he remembered and grabbed a towel from the floor, wrapping it around his middle. "Would someone introduce us properly?" he asked no one in particular, unable to take his eyes off the older woman.

Honey bubbled with laughter. "Marquise Berengere-Marie Bouscaral, may I present my brother, Dirk Wildon. Dirk, this is the mother of Yves and Henri."

"Well, I'll be damned. Hello there," he managed to murmur, and cast a glance at the Frenchman. Henri stood frozen like a statue off to one side, his face an obvious mask of embarrassment and chagrin as he eyed Kolina. Dirk noted that the young woman was deliberately ignoring the man. But it was the older woman who attracted Dirk's eye, and at once he felt a surge of lustful desire rush through him.

The Marquise was smiling tantalizingly at him. "*Enchanté,* Dirk. And Honey, it is such a pleasure to see you

again. Even under these rather awkward circumstances."
She turned to Barbro. "You must be Kolina's sister. She's
told me so much about you, I feel we've already met."

As Barbro effusively greeted the mature beauty, Honey
gathered three sarongs from the closet and tossed one to
each of the sisters, pulling on the third herself. With a
sad sense of loss, Dirk watched their ripe bodies disappear
beneath the brightly patterned material. Even Henri
seemed disappointed to be deprived of the sight of the
beautiful figures. He slumped against the wall and stared
at the floor.

His mother turned to him with a small frown. "Henri,"
she began with a trace of vexation, "it is time to follow
through on your promise."

"Mama," he mumbled without looking at her, "must I?"

"But of course," she insisted. "Now stand straight like
a man and speak up."

With the aggrieved sigh of a put-upon child, Henri
pulled himself upright and sheepishly addressed Kolina.
"Forgive me, Kolina. I am truly sorry for what I put you
through. I got carried away with my love for you." Unable to hold her disapproving gaze, he quickly glanced to
Honey. "And you too, Mademoiselle. I regret everything."

"And me?" Dirk asked sharply, remembering the whizzing bullet in Menorca. "Am I included in this?"

"*Oui, Monsieur,*" the Frenchman said contritely.
"Please forgive my actions, and those of my overly zealous
men. Believe me, I meant only to frighten you away."

"Well, you nearly damned well got me—"

"Dirk," Honey interrupted. "Henri has expressed his
regret and I, for one, believe him and accept his apology.
I am certain we owe the Marquise a huge debt of gratitude for bringing about his abrupt change of heart."

The Marquise beamed broadly, her strikingly handsome face a beacon of internal light. She reached out and placed a graceful hand on Dirk's arm.

His skin prickled at her soft touch, and all resistance melted away as she spoke intimately. "And you, Dirk? Do you forgive my son? I promise I will do anything I can to make up for his ill-mannered behavior."

He felt lost in her mesmerizing gray eyes. He fumbled for words, feeling the unmistakable reawakening in his groin. "Yes, of course, I forgive him—providing he does not revert to his former behavior."

"You have my fervent word," she said softly. *"Merci,* Dirk. I am indebted to you forever."

"And I am at *your* service, Madame."

"Voila," Honey chimed merrily. "Let's open another bottle of champagne and properly celebrate our coming together!"

19.

HONEY

Under the old wooden beams of the loggia, she relaxed in a comfortably cushioned garden chair, sipping cold champagne with a plump strawberry floating in it as she watched the two beautiful Svensen sisters trailing down the brick paths of her herb and flower garden. English countryside flowers bloomed in profusion, masses of lavender and pink rose bushes scented the spring air, and beyond the two lovely blondes admiring her garden, a huge horse-chestnut tree framed the distant green expanse of the uninterrupted meadow. In all ways it was a terrific view, and she felt suddenly at peace, contented to be home at last.

"Oh, Honey," Kolina cooed as she approached, "everything is so beautiful here. How lucky you are."

Honey refilled the girl's glass, commenting, "Gardens and surrounding countryside are the main reasons for

245

having a rural house in England. More champagne, Barbro?"

Nodding eagerly, Kolina's older and equally lovely sister came up to them and sank into one of the other garden chairs. "I can see why you insisted we accompany you home. It's charming here, absolutely beautiful."

Honey trilled an appreciative laugh. "Would you believe that when I bought the place it was nothing more than two decrepit Victorian cowsheds?"

"No!" the sisters exclaimed in unison.

"All it took was time, money, and two talented designers from London working round the clock with a crew of twenty for over a year," Honey laughed, her eyes sweeping proudly over the nearby low brick house built from the former ruins. "It's the very first home I've had that's totally mine. Dirk and I share the family home in Hillsboro and the retreat at Kauai, but this is mine alone, and I escape here as often as I can."

"And Dirk?" Kolina asked shyly. "Does he come to visit often?"

"Oh, heavens no," Honey said with mock anger. "In fact, the scamp's never been here. He's wrapped up all the time with his photography in New York or gallivanting around the world."

"Do you think he'll show up now?" Barbro asked in the same longing tone her sister had used when speaking of him.

"Maybe. Maybe not," Honey hedged. "Depends on how soon he burns out his latest infatuation."

"The Marquise?" Kolina queried somewhat petulantly. "Honestly, she's sixty-five if she's a day."

"But what a breathtaking sixty-five," Honey offered. "May we three be so lucky at that age."

Kolina tossed her white blonde head spiritedly. "The Marquise Berengere-Marie Bouscaral is just as guilty as her son Henri," she said with a sharp edge to her voice. "After all, she was supporting him lavishly all the while. If it hadn't been for the family money, he wouldn't have been able to afford all those . . . perversions."

Barbro touched her sister's arm. "Now, Kolina, we should all be grateful to the Marquise. She's cut him off without a penny and forced him to return to the family chateau as her personal secretary."

"I bet he won't stay there," Kolina snapped. "He'll go crazy with boredom."

Honey plucked the strawberry out of her goblet and nibbled on its champagne-soaked sweetness. "He won't have much choice, Kolina. The Marquise has put a definite end to his kinky lifestyle. She reclaimed all her foreign property and canceled his credit, which has reduced him to a pauper. He's fortunate to have a roof over his head."

Barbro started to giggle, a girlish, joyous sound that lightened the spring air like the song of a meadowlark. "Serves him right. If the Marquise hadn't flown straight to Galapagos and taken him in tow, who knows what he would have done to find you again."

Kolina pouted into her champagne. "I think he got off too lightly. He belongs behind bars somewhere."

Honey could not help but laugh, the girl was so adorable even in her childish anger. "But I think he is. The Marquise was so appalled by what I wired her of her son's activities, she's vowed that he won't step out of the chateau without her permission."

'It was so smart of you, Honey," Barbro said, "to wire the Marquise straight from that U.S. Navy boat the way you did."

"It was a long shot," Honey admitted. "But I figured she would be the only one in the world who had enough power over him to put an end to his kinky endeavors."

"And stop him she did," Barbro stated with another laugh. "I'll never forget the look on his face when she forced him to apologize. I thought he was going to die on the spot."

The memory evoked laughter even from Kolina. "And poor Dirk," she sighed. "He was so confused by it all."

"He came around pretty fast," Barbro smirked.

"That's Dirk for you," Honey offered gaily. "Can't keep a good man down for long."

Kolina snorted, not at all amused. "The way he moved on the Marquise, though, coming on to her like a schoolboy with a mad crush. Honestly, I thought it was all a bit much."

Honey eyed her over the rim of her goblet. "We've all had our crazy infatuations, haven't we?"

Kolina sat up primly, as if rejecting the notion that she had ever gone off the deep end in any of her relationships. "Dirk barely said goodbye to us, he was in such a hurry to accompany the Marquise on her return flight to France. I thought it was a bit rude, to tell you the truth."

"Now, Kolina," cautioned her older sister gently. "Both he and Honey risked a great deal to help us. Especially you. So I think you'd better remember that and stop feeling so damned sorry for yourself that he found someone else to make him mad with desire."

"But she's so *old*," Kolina repeated, eliciting another round of laughter from the other two. "Well, it's true," she said firmly.

"The same could be said for the difference in age between you and Henri," Barbo offered. "But you chased him for a year before he took you off with him."

"Well, that's different," Kolina asserted. "Young women are naturally attracted to older men. But young men to older women . . . ugh."

Honey tried not to laugh too hard at the girl's limited

point of view. "Kolina, you are a precious child, but you have a lot to learn about life. It offers a wide variety of experiences You'll be very grateful for that when you're the Marquise's age. Now I think lunch must be ready. Is anyone besides me famished?"

In the spacious, rustic dining room, the trio of beauties ate ravenously of saddle of lamb and broccoli hollandaise, and polished off a bottle of 1959 Louis Latour Corton-Charlemagne.

They were so full and pleasantly high on the delicious wine, not to mention all the champagne they had been consuming all morning, that Honey suggested a nap in her spacious yellow and white bedroom. Sprawled on the king-sized bed in just their filmy slips, they dozed off intertwined like young sisters, listening to the chirping of songbirds outside.

Honey awoke sometime later with a consuming heat inflaming her loins, and was pleasantly surprised to see between her legs Kolina's white-blonde head bobbing and dipping. For a long while Honey just lay there, pretending still to be asleep, enjoying the attentions of the gorgeous young woman's extraordinary tongue. Soon Honey could not contain her joy. Abruptly she sat up, stripping off her slip, startling the secret licker. Kolina raised her head and gazed in open admiration at Honey's snow-white expanse of delectably full breasts. The rosy nipples were already alert. At once Kolina scooted up and kissed one of the stiff little appendages, flicking its tip with her tongue, kneading and molding the other breast with her eager, feverish hands.

Honey squirmed with pleasure and rubbed the girl's strong young back, eventually hiking up Kolina's slip and pulling it over her head. Kolina's large breasts rubbed playfully against the satiny skin of Honey's belly. Honey squeezed a hand between them and inched it toward

Kolina's pussy. Kolina raised her hips, allowing freer access, and Honey took advantage of the offering, inserting an exploring finger into the moist, heated quim. Wildly, Kolina drove up and down on the extended finger, moaning softly into Honey's ear, kissing her creamy neck and fair cheeks. Honey concentrated her deeply imbedded digit on the firm clitoris buried in the fleshy folds and with the same hand managed to get a thumb into her own pussy.

"Unfair," Barbro groaned groggily, awakening to discover the surreptitious activity beside her. She rolled over against Honey and murmured, "Got room for one more?"

"Be my guest," Honey purred huskily, and waved a trembling hand toward the nightstand. "Top drawer, if you please . . ."

Barbro rolled across the bed, opened the drawer, and extracted Honey's ancient ivory dildo. "Oh, how lovely," she squealed. "A petrified prick. And with two heads!" She scooted up on her haunches and tugged off her slip. Her heavy breasts rolled out like banks of white fog. Grabbing the old instrument of pleasure, she knelt between Honey's legs and pushed her sister's hips up off their hostess's pelvis. Licking one bulbous head of the double-ended dildo, Barbro then stuck it into Honey's flaming funnel as far as she could.

Honey groaned with delight and pulled Kolina up by the hips until the young woman sat straddling her face. Reveling in the satisfying plunge of the dildo, Honey drank in the sight of the delicately hued vagina so spread before her. The pale lips looked like the petals of a tropical flower liberally sprinkled with dew. The sparse fringe of soft blonde hair ringed the pulsating opening like parentheses, and Honey raised her head to delve into the tempting valley with her tongue. The dewy meat was as sweet and delectable as it looked.

With rising ecstasy, Honey lapped at the tender opening and thrust against the ersatz penis in her own pussy. The Svensen sisters were a pair of sensational lovers and she could easily understand why Dirk had been so taken by them both. Each had her own special gifts and techniques, and each of their bodies, though similar, contained enough uniqueness to satisfy even the most discriminating of tastes. Kolina was an energetic free spirit and reminded Honey of herself at that same age, willing and eager to explore anything and everything sexual. On the other hand, Barbro's enthusiasm was more refined, her passion more controlled. As a trained dancer, she would marshal her strength for a long performance. Together the duo formed an irresistible combination, and Honey surrendered to the overwhelming tug of emotions and sensations that swept through her mind and body.

The threesome were so absorbed by their mutual attractiveness and sensuality that they did not hear him enter the room. Silently Dirk dropped his suitcase and stood at the foot of the big bed, gasping with envious admiration at the trio of writhing bodies so erotically displayed. Barbro's wide hips thrust wildly up and down, riding one end of the old dildo as she drove the other end deeply into Honey's gaping cunt. Kolina also had her beautiful backside to him, her sweet buns brushing against Honey's full tits as she writhed on the tongue of his tantalizing sister. Though the Svensen sisters were about as magical as two women could be, it was Honey's sensational body that attracted and held his yearning eyes. She was a delicious piece, and he found himself with a bird so stiff he opened his pants to let it fly. Stroking it with one hand, he struggled out of his clothes, not missing a beat, his eyes not straying from the horny trio.

He was completely nude by the time he was noticed. "Dirk!" Honey panted in surprise, looking through Kolina's legs. With a squeal of delight, both Barbro and Kolina flew to him, smothering him with welcoming kisses and hugs. Kolina gamely latched onto his hard dick and tugged him onto the bed. "You naughty boy, you. Didn't you get enough from that Marquise?"

He chuckled knowingly, but refused to divulge a single detail of his whirlwind fling with the magical Marquise. Instantly, Kolina pressed him flat on the bed, her mouth to his. She squatted on his pleased bird with a childlike enthusiasm and was bouncing away before Barbro had a chance to climb back onto the bed. "We missed you," Kolina's sister murmured, grabbing his balls and giving them a friendly squeeze.

"I missed you too," he rasped, and winked at his sister, who was still recovering from the unexpected interruption.

She smirked and stretched her luscious body, pointing her proud breasts toward the ceiling. "I knew I'd get you here eventually if I had these two beauties hanging around."

"Which two?" he teased, thrusting his bird into the sweet, moist nest over him. "Those on your chest or these others?" Laughingly he tweaked a tit of each of the Svensen sisters.

Her heart overflowing with love, she watched her dear brother banging away into the same pussy which, only moments before, she had been sampling. He looked marvelously rested and relaxed, and she was dying to ask him about his recent mad affair, but realized it was neither the time nor the place. Instead she leaned over and kissed him tenderly. "Welcome to England, you old tramp. Going to stay a spell?"

"With such household comforts around, why leave?"

Barbro tugged Honey down beside her. "Ignore him, darling. He's as busy as a spring bee."

Willingly, Honey fell into her open arms and their tongues dueled heatedly. Soon, Barbro and Honey were riding tandem the old dildo, lost in their own erotic endeavors, completely oblivious to the activity next to them. Side by side the Wildon siblings screwed the Svensen sisters, and all had a flourishingly fine time.

Before the afternoon was over, Honey and Dirk switched partners, and proceeded to expand the girls' repertoire of tricks and learned a few new pleasures themselves. Honey had no reservations about fucking in the presence of her younger brother; in fact, the close proximity only added to her excitement. She did, however, draw the line at making it with him, even though he pestered her persistently after he had enjoyed the Svensen sisters. "Dirk," she warned in her big-sister voice as he placed a hand on her snatch. "Get your fucking hand out of there."

"Aw, come on, sis," he pleaded. "We used to mess around a lot."

"Years ago," she sighed. "Too many years ago. We can't go back there again." Firmly she took his hand away and placed it on Kolina's exhausted quim.

"Why not?" he growled good-naturedly. "We're both enlightened, liberated adults."

"Not that liberated, thank you," she said breezily, and bounced off the bed. "I'm going to take a shower. Enjoy your desserts, baby brother. But I'm not one of them." She swung her hips exaggeratedly as she exited. His laughter followed her into the bathroom.

She was under the flowing water when he stuck his head over the glass door. "Honey, I need your help."

"What is it?" she asked.

He opened the shower door, his boyish face serious. "Promise me you'll help."

She eyed him gravely. "You know I'd do anything for you. Just name it."

"I . . . I saw this girl in Paris . . ." he began.

"*Almost* anything," she said, and turned the shower on harder, so that the sound of rushing water drowned out the rest of his words.

DIANA'S DEBUT

Lytton Sinclair

She came, she saw, she conquered . . .

Travel is meant to be a broadening experience. And even the delicious Diana, who though a simple girl from a little town in Pennsylvania had seen and done a thing or two, found that travel can always teach you something. For it was in Rome that, despite an international incident of unforgettable violence and bad taste, she met so many warm-hearted people with fantastic bodies eager to communicate with a voluptuous down-home American girl; in Rome that she learned to let go of her small-town hangups about sex and *really* enjoy herself; in Rome that she discovered just what her mother's beloved minister (who was, in fact, her own first great love) meant when he told her, 'Diana, you have so much to give.'

DIANA'S DEBUT

They call Rome the city of Love – but it took Diana to prove it.

FUTURA PUBLICATIONS
FICTION
0 7088 4028 0

All Futura Books are available at your bookshop or
newsagent, or can be ordered from the following address:
Futura Books, Cash Sales Department,
P.O. Box 11, Falmouth, Cornwall TR10 9EN.

Please send cheque or postal order (no currency), and
allow 60p for postage and packing for the first book
plus 25p for the second book and 15p for each additional
book ordered up to a maximum charge of £1.90 in U.K.

B.F.P.O. customers please allow 60p for
the first book, 25p for the second book plus 15p per
copy for the next 7 books, thereafter 9p per book

Overseas customers, including Eire, please allow £1.25
for postage and packing for the first book, 75p for the
second book and 28p for each subsequent title ordered.